CHIEF

Governor Trilogy
Book 3

Lesli Richardson

Dear Coppu,
Thanks for reading.
Lesl. Richardson /
[signature]

Chief
Governor Trilogy Book 3

Copyright © 2018 by Lesli Richardson

First Print Publication: September 2018

www.LesliRichardson.com

DEDICATION

To Hubby, for everything he does. To Sir—He knows why.

To my bestie & PA, Trish, who believed in Carter when I introduced him to her.

And massive thanks to Sadie Haller for the pep talks!

AUTHOR'S NOTE

Florida politics are messy, nasty, sexy, brutal, funny, insane, impossibly complex, and a lot of fun to write about. (Mostly because they're messy, nasty, sexy, brutal, funny, insane, and impossibly complex.)

Since the focus of this trilogy isn't the politics so much as it is the people, I've taken certain liberties and simplified a few things here and there.

The kinky shit, however, is absolutely realistic.

Also, in this world, Covid-19 isn't a thing, so it's not mentioned.

Events in this book reference events from *Governor* (Governor Trilogy 1) and *Lieutenant* (Governor Trilogy 3). Eddie's story is mentioned in *Yes, Governor* (Governor Trilogy 4) and is told is *Pet* (Governor Trilogy 5). The books in this trilogy are best read in order.

CHAPTER ONE

Now — Election Night

They say behind every good man is a good woman. That's sometimes true.

In this case, behind one particularly good man is a real fucking bastard.

That would be *me*.

A bastard extraordinaire, as Owen dubbed me so many years ago. But he also knows he'd never be where he is without me. We both know that. All I did was watch him, figure out what he wanted, needed, and loved…and then gave it to him.

With a few strings attached, of course.

I wouldn't be a bastard if I didn't do that.

I grew up the youngest of seven boys in a house that valued stereotypical masculinity above all. My dad was Airborne. My mother was an Army brat. I wanted to go to college, but if I'd broken from family tradition and failed to enlist after that, I would have faced life-long shit from my family.

So I enlisted. Unlike my brothers, who took ROTC in college, I go in straight out of high school to get it over with. Earned me a Purple Heart for my efforts, which got me a medical discharge, a disability pension, the adoration of my family…

…and led to me meeting Owen at the start of our second year

of college at USF in Tampa, where we were randomly assigned as roommates in the dorm.

In retrospect, I'm good with that trade-off.

The main obstacle in my path to winning Owen's heart was Susannah Joleen Evans. Which, all things considered, wasn't nearly as difficult to overcome as I'd thought it'd be.

There's a reason Owen and Susa call me the bastard extraordinaire—it's because I *am* a bastard.

They're absolutely right.

Unfortunately, I learned the hard way early on that being a bastard was the only way to survive. It would also be the only way to get what I really wanted.

I wanted Owen.

* * *

The three of us have a tradition now on election nights. We rent space for that night's party at the same downtown Tampa hotel we've always used, and we reserve a suite there for us for after the party. Once the results are in, and the party ends, and we can finally peel ourselves away from the supporters and campaign staff and press to retreat to the safety of our suite, I'm usually reflective.

Tonight, the night of Owen's re-election, is no different.

It's hard to remember the man I was twenty years ago when I first crossed paths with Owen at the beginning of our second year of college at USF in Tampa.

By the time I met Owen, nearly every last bit of good has been burned from my soul. What little good is left is scorched, seared, and I show it to no one.

That's what it feels like, anyway.

The perfect emotional makeup to be an attorney, it would seem. Cold, calculating, exposing no weakness.

During my first year of school, I keep to myself, study my ass off, and while I'm pleasant to my immediate fellow dorm occupants, I enforce a polite distance. I keep what little vulnerability I have left locked down tight.

I pretend my nightmares are about what happened that day in the desert, and sometimes they are.

Mostly, they're not.

I hated the roommate I was given my first year. Sure, I could have *not* turned him in to the RA for underage drinking in our room.

But by turning the kid in and getting rid of him, it meant I had a room entirely to myself.

I wasn't going to complain about *that*.

Hey, wasn't like I didn't warn the kid I'd do it, either.

Don't give me a hard time about it. He and his friends were breaking the law and putting both my freedom and my scholarship in jeopardy.

Fuck that shit.

My plan for my second year of college is to do the same thing—observe my roommate, evaluate them for weaknesses, and then obliterate them. They'd never see me coming.

Until Owen enters my life and that plan disintegrates.

I know I'm in love with Owen from the moment I first set eyes on him. I thought Owen was fucking gorgeous when I first walked in to my newly assigned dorm room and realized he was my roommate. He was hot and had no clue that he was, which made him even hotter. Polite, fumbling, innocent, apologetic, a bundle of nerves and submissive, chaotic, low-key needy energy that drew me right to him.

I thought he was charmingly adorable when I realized he couldn't fold clothes or make a rack worth a damn, and the harder he tried, the more flustered he grew.

I thought he was heartbreakingly endearing when I learned more about him, his childhood. The bitch who'd given birth to him and who also emotionally tortured him for his entire life.

I recognized his fragility, wanted to tuck him close to my side, protect him from the world, and never let him out of my sight.

I wanted my arm around his shoulders, my collar around his neck, my ropes around his body, and his mouth around my cock.

I wanted to do whatever it took to win this man over and make him happy. Make him *mine*.

As I get to know him, it's almost as if the charred shell I'd withdrawn inside of to protect myself has suddenly shattered, leaving me vulnerable for the first time in years.

Wanting to be vulnerable to Owen, and not even knowing how.

It makes me immediately shift my plans from wanting to learn everything about him so I could weaponize it against him, to wanting to know everything about him so I could make him *mine*.

I…*needed* him.

It also scares the fuck out of me.

Unfortunately, I recognize that, from the moment Owen sets eyes on Susa just a few days later, he's in love with *her*. That nearly makes me hate my future wife on sight. The *last* thing I want to do is share Owen with Susa Evans.

Until I realize who she is and what she can do for Owen.

And once I finally admit she has the power to make him happy in ways I never can.

It also means my life quickly distills down to one point—I need Susa to get Owen. Which I suspect won't be too hard, because it doesn't take me long to suss out that Susa's attracted to *me*. This works to my advantage, meaning far less effort required on my behalf.

Am I proud of that?

Not particularly. Not that I give a fuck, either.

Soon after Owen and I meet Susa and go over to her house that first night to help rid her of her ex-boyfriend, Owen makes a very apt joke about him being a well-trained pet.

He isn't wrong.

His narcissistic mother has trained him in many ways, both subtle and blatant—ways that Owen doesn't fully understand, at the time.

That also works to my benefit.

It means I will have a much easier time training him as *my* pet. But to do that, it means I also have to train Susa, and convince her to want Owen as her pet as much as he wants to *be* her pet.

To get her to want to *keep* Owen as her pet as much as she wants to be *my* pet.

Because, ironically, Susa is in love with me.

I suppose a good man, upon discovering a girl nearly ten years younger than him is in love with him—a girl who's also the object of his best friend's affections—would have walked away from the situation.

I am not a good man, and have never claimed to be one.

I am a bastard.

In this case, it works in my favor.

Not only do I *not* discourage Susa's affection, I nurture and groom it. Shamelessly.

Also in secret, because—ironically—I don't want to hurt Owen. It's easy to convince Susa to keep things quiet, too, and why. Because she cares about Owen. Is attracted to him, even.

But it's *me* she lusts after. Once I realize who she is, who her father is, then yes, I *absolutely* have to have her.

We *need* her if I'm ever going to get Owen elected governor. More accurately, we need her father and his pull over movers and shakers in the GOP if we're ever going to gain traction to make a successful third-party run.

While I did my time in the Army and not the Marines, the motto *Improvise, Adapt, Overcome* applied there, too. Especially in-country.

I apply it to this situation.

Hooah.

Thus a heavenly third-party union is forged in the tropical fires of Hell that are Florida politics. I wouldn't subject Owen to allegiance to one party or the other. Fuck both of them. Both have strengths, and both have even more weaknesses.

Fatal flaws. Flaws I refuse to inflict upon Owen's political career. I'd rather lose honestly as a third-party candidate than bend over and whore him out to the elephants or the jackasses.

Neither of them are good enough for him. We'd build something from the ground up, something better.

Something we could look back on and be proud of.

Something that was *ours*.

And we have, even if Benchley Evans publicly "jokes" that our status as Independents somehow contributed to his heart attack.

No, asshole, that would be too much booze, a shitty diet, and smoking cigars for over forty years that did it to you.

Your daughter achieving what she has in her career should be considered the crown jewel in your life's accomplishments, not something to fucking joke about with a wink and a nod to your buddies that indicates you all think she did this *because* of you, not in *spite* of you.

More accurately, *to* spite you.

I think all these things, but I hide them behind smiles and well-placed *yes, sirs* and *no, sirs* when talking to the man.

I'm a bastard, but I'm not stupid.

If I piss him off too much, he'll do anything he can to hurt Owen, even if it means Susa's political career becomes collateral damage in the process.

I know this, because Benchley is as much of a bastard as I am.

Fortunately, I have more than a little leverage against the man to keep him in line.

Leverage Susa and Owen know nothing about.

And, hopefully, never will.

* * *

This has been a long and interesting journey, these past twenty years. Tonight, as I stand here in this hotel suite and watch Susa and Owen at the window, where they're staring down at the downtown Tampa skyline following our public victory celebration downstairs, I can't help but smile.

My pets say I have different smiles, and this one is probably the one they've labeled "*that* smirk."

I watch Owen hold his arm out and Susa tucks herself against his side, his other hand coming to rest on her tummy as he drops a tender kiss to the top of her head.

My sweet pets. I love watching them together. The re-elected governor and lieutenant governor of the great state of Florida.

Hopefully, in four years, Susa will take Owen's place as governor.

And they're both *mine*.

Thankfully, I decided to go for broke and claim both these beautiful souls. Because if I hadn't, had I run Susa off like I'd originally wanted to all those years ago, she wouldn't be here to give Owen that gift which I could not, and finally help heal that last lingering wound within his soul.

She will make him a father.

The one thing I always wished I could be and never can. Not now.

Not after the last person I trusted before meeting Owen and Susa turned me into the fucking bastard extraordinaire I am today.

CHAPTER TWO

Then

Most major decisions I make in my life have come about in one of two ways—carefully and thoughtfully, after weighing all the options and available facts, or snap judgments, which are usually reserved for life-or-death kinds of scenarios. Or, barring it appears to be a life-or-death decision at the time, snap judgments I've made frequently end up being life-shattering or life-altering decisions, when looked upon in retrospect.

Throwing myself over my three guys that day in the desert was a snap judgment.

Going home with Elsa the first time was a snap judgment.

Kissing Susa Evans in her kitchen that first night we were over at her house—a snap judgment.

I've already spent our evening with Susa finding myself drawn to her in an uncomfortably keen way. Not because I'm in love with her, but because I can see how smitten Owen is with her already, even though we *just* met her earlier that morning.

From personal experience, I know how dangerous this instantaneous infatuation can be. Case in point, I'm already trying to plan how to make Owen mine.

Another case in point—I survived the flip side of this scenario.

Barely.

Some parts of me didn't survive, and it's why I'm now the bastard extraordinaire.

Owen's immediate feelings for Susa will also be a problem, I know, because we share a fucking class with her three mornings a week. Unless she drops the class, we'll be seeing her Mondays, Wednesdays, and Fridays.

I need to handle this situation, *now*, before it spins out of my control.

Except the more I talk with Susa that evening, I can see how damn *hungry* she is—for success, for power, for her own identity separate that of her father's reputation and name.

Hungry to obtain the very same office I know Owen wants.

All things I can respect her for. Very much so.

She's worked damned hard already, has a brilliant mind, and even keener political insight.

It isn't just idle talk on my part when I sound her out and discuss the possibility of a third-party run with her, the possibility of getting Owen elected first, with her as lieutenant, so she could run on his coattails.

Best-case scenario? They could make an awesome team together. Combined with my bastardly instinct behind them…they could be unstoppable.

They could *both* get what they want.

And so could I.

I had honestly thought I would approach this evening the way I'd started out approaching the school year with Owen—to observe, evaluate, and then obliterate Susa, to eliminate her as a potential threat to my plans. Use our time tonight with her to hopefully learn what I'd need to strike a lethal blow to whatever fledgling love for her was taking root inside Owen's soul.

Unfortunately, plans change. Maybe fortunately, in this case.

Ironically, as with my boy, I quickly realize my plan regarding

Susa needs rapid revision, a tactical response.

Owen wants her, but will never take steps on his own to claim her. Just like he really wants to hold office, but will never achieve it if left to his own devices. Besides not having an ounce of self-confidence, he doesn't have the cut-throat DNA to make it through the grueling slog of a campaign.

I will need someone like Susa to help Owen's career.

More accurately, I'll need someone with Susa's connections.

Meaning her father.

Plus, as convinced as I am that I can win Owen over, I know it would only be one part of the overall issue I'd have by doing so. It would make me happy—and I'd definitely kill myself to make Owen happy—but it would cause both of us problems in the process.

Meaning alienating my family.

Meaning sacrificing his dream career.

Meaning the fact that I know how much Owen wants kids.

At the close of the evening, when Owen excuses himself to the bathroom and leaves the living room, all of these things flash through my mind in the time it takes me to formulate the snap judgment to stand and silently approach Susa from behind.

I think that's when I make the decision to claim Susa, and thereby guarantee I will win Owen's heart. Walking away from Owen isn't possible for me. Not when the more I learn about him, the more I *have* to have him. I want to teach him about unconditional acceptance. I want to give him the stability and positive reinforcement he craves.

I want to hold him and breathe him in while he helps keep my nightmares at bay.

I want to show him the true face of love.

I'd be lying if I said I didn't want to be the man standing in the shadows behind Owen when he gets elected as our state's governor.

Selfish?

Absofuckinglutely. I'll own that. Every bit of it.

Unapologetically.

I *am* a bastard, after all.

I want him to be *mine*, and I know I'll do nearly anything to have him. Including making sacrifices of my own to make his dreams come true and make him happy.

Step one stands directly in front of me.

When she turns and realizes I'm standing right behind her, the way her blue eyes widen hardens my cock. Not because she's beautiful—which she is—but because of the fear I see sweep through her gaze before it flashes over to something else I can also recognize and appreciate.

Hunger.

Need.

Desire.

Her lips part as I stare down at her.

"You *really* want to be governor?" I ask.

She nods, but it's the way her pupils flare a little at that, her sharp intake of breath.

She doesn't just want it—she *needs* it.

She *needs* that future to nourish her soul every bit as badly as I need Owen to nourish mine.

"I do," she whispers.

"I want Owen to be governor. He wants it, but he'd never go for it on his own." I let the pause hang in the space between us and make it more than obvious I'm checking her out. "I don't want to hurt him."

I really don't. Except there are many kinds of pain. And I *have* to see if she's truly on the same wavelength I am, or if in this way she's still a child and this is nothing more than a game to her.

If it is just a game to her? I'll easily scare her off. No problem.

If not?

Game on.

"Me, either," she says.

"I mean, there's a *lot* of stuff you don't know about him, or me." Which is an understatement I don't have time to explain right now. "We do this, *together*, but we do this *my* way, and you don't argue with me or deviate from the plan. *I'm* in charge. That means keeping this a secret from him, for now. You fuck the plan, or you lie to me, and we're *done*. No second chances. Understand?"

I know I have her, that she is *already* mine, when she answers. "Yes, Sir."

I wonder what she thinks of my smile, if she thinks it's sexy, or if she mistakes it for sexual desire.

In truth?

It's victory.

Because with those two words, she's *literally* given me *everything* I need—every last key to open every single lock within her soul.

I now own her.

No, that's not a metaphor, either.

Damn, this will be easier than I thought.

And a *lot* more fun.

My cock's aching, *throbbing* from the thought of what delicious hell I'll put her through to make her earn both my trust and the right to be with *my* boy. Things I won't be able to do with Owen yet, and maybe not for weeks, or even months—if ever—but things she'll be eager and begging for from me within the next few days, or sooner.

In fact, I already have her in my arms, one hand possessively cupping the back of her neck, when it finally registers I am kissing her.

That's when I know I've made my decision.

That it is the correct one is reaffirmed when she not only doesn't resist when I slant my lips over hers, but she eagerly kisses me back.

And that she tries to chase when I pull away.

I stop her with a finger to her lips.

"My *very* good girl. We're going to do great things, the *three* of us."

* * *

I quickly come to discover Susa's demons aren't quite as dark as mine, but they're pretty damn close.

Her darkness, however, was born, not made.

I envy her that.

I envy her natural dark paths, the shadows and shade that organically took root and flourished within her soul.

I envy the joy she takes mapping every bypass and detour, every tunnel and bridge.

I envy that she can look at all the things I do to her, relish them, and beg for more with an unapologetic, wild-eyed hunger in her gaze that nearly brings me to my knees before her.

Not because I want to be there, but because old habits die hard.

A tiny part of me hates her, and always will, because she'll forever own a slice of Owen's heart and soul that will likely remain locked to me. I use that hatred to show her no mercy during our "play." Every time I think surely I've crossed a line that will make her safeword, end this insanity between us, and allow me the opening to take Owen and run with him, she grabs my hand and drags me deeper, darker.

I savor the fear she begs for, and happily give her more, my demons' wings unfurling with everything I do to her.

I crave her tears and take great pleasure in them. Unlike when Owen cries and I want to do nothing more than soothe his aching soul and make him smile and feel safe.

I *get* the fucking irony, believe me.

Fortunately—and more importantly—so does she.

The longer this continues between me and Susa, I also hate that there is part of me which will always envy Owen the freedom he feels when submitting to her.

Because it's a freedom I will never again feel.

I hate even more that, because of that same longing, there is now and always will be a part of my soul vulnerable to and owned by her.

And that terrifies me even more than the thought of losing Owen.

* * *

A muffled giggle tickles my ear in the darkness.

I blow out a breath I didn't even realize I'd been holding, and I can't tell if it's relief or resignation filling me now.

I thought for sure *this*, if nothing else, would be her breaking point. *The* night I scare her off. That tonight would be *the* night she safewords, calls me an asshole, and Owen and I can finally part ways with her.

Not that I want to run her off, not really. I want to force her to keep actively choosing to be with us to the point she never leaves. Barring that, I need to be certain she can handle me at full throttle. I won't put Owen through the heartbreak of her leaving after a year or so because she has a change of heart.

I don't want to put myself through that, either.

Because while I know we really do need her to get Owen all the way to Tallahassee, there's still part of me who never wants to share Owen with her.

Owen, I'm sure, would be horrified, and rightly so, if he ever saw…*this*.

This side of me.

Hell, this side of *her*.

I am not *going to be able to fucking move tomorrow.*

I already know that tomorrow morning's PT with Owen will be

a slow, ambling walk.

I don't know what else I can do, short of *literally* crossing a line I gave her my word I wouldn't cross, to scare her off.

Since she's not going away, she's not scared off, it means I'm going to end up marrying her.

That scares *me*. For a variety of reasons.

Because what *won't* she let me do to her? What if I can't pull the emergency brake one day? She's not Eddie, and she's not a hardened combat vet.

Then again, I'm not the man I was, either. Not physically, anyway.

The way I'm feeling right now is ample proof of *that*.

I wearily drag myself into a seated position and lean over to switch on the desk lamp I'd brought in to her spare bedroom earlier. It's on the floor, because there really isn't any furniture in this room. It's storage. I'd thought about getting a room at a hotel to do this, but didn't want to risk someone calling the cops on us if they saw or heard something. Then I'd have to explain to Senator Benchley Evans that I'm not only fucking his daughter, but that she enjoys a disturbing level of consensual non-consent play that would make even the hardiest and most jaded kinkster extremely uncomfortable.

And she wants *more*.

I used vet wrap to hold her panties in her mouth as a gag. I'd considered duct tape, but it would have stuck in her hair and made it hard to explain to Owen how she got any marks on her face. But the vet wrap sticks to itself, and also makes a great blindfold. I'd basically wrapped it all around her head and mummified her, just leaving a gap around her nose free. It also meant I could easily rip it with my fingers, if I needed to free her quickly.

Tonight, I'd taken her down in her front hallway, before she'd even gotten all the way in the front door. No time to run, no time to fight back, and I'd blindfolded her before she could see it was me.

I'd parked the Snot Box in her garage so she didn't even realize I was there. As far as she knew, I'd decided to stay home at the dorm tonight to sleep while she took Owen out for dinner and a movie before she dropped him off at our dorm.

I left a note for Owen that one of my buddies from the Army had been admitted to Haley, and I went over to visit him, which would buy me most of the night. I didn't want to text him both because I didn't want a time-stamp on when I left, and I didn't want him tipping off Susa that I had gone out.

Before she realized what was going on, I had her stripped, bound, gagged with her own panties, wrapped in a blanket, carried her out to the garage, and roughly dumped her into the back hatch of the Snot Box. I did all this without saying a single word to her. I even took a shower before I came over and used a different soap than I'd ever used in hopes of throwing her off a little and getting her to safeword because she doesn't know it's me and she's genuinely freaked out.

Then I drove around for about twenty minutes, because I wanted to disorient her. I returned to her subdivision from a different street so she wouldn't recognize the turns, backed into the garage, and hauled her out of the back hatch.

The whole time she sobbed, cried, begged, sounded terrorized.

But she never safeworded.

Meaning no matter how scared she is, she's still assuming it's me.

Meanwhile, that whole time, I spent it with a grin on my face and a cock that could cut through concrete.

I actually carry her through the living room first and make a few turns to disorient her even further. As much as she's been crying, I doubt she can smell anything right now to know she's in her own home. Taking her into the spare bedroom and dumping her onto a sheet I've spread out on the floor will likely confuse her even more.

It'll be fucking hell on me and my body later, but I've worked on this plan in my head for a week.

I drop my voice, disguise it. "Got a party planned for Daddy's little princess," I growl. "Found several guys who are going to breed that cunt and ass of yours until you can't walk."

I'll admit pain from the exertion of the takedown and carrying her to and from the car has softened my cock a little by the time I finally got her in the bedroom and unwrapped her. I was already hurting, but the way she starts to struggle and scream again fires me up. Obviously I don't have the stamina or loads of cum a gangbang's participants would.

But they do make strap-ons with swappable dicks, and I've been shopping online.

The first one's all me—with a condom, thank you very much—up her ass. I even give her the courtesy of finger-fucking her ass with two lubed fingers, but the fucking I give her is hard, brutal, and has her crying again.

By the time I've fucked her pussy with the fourth and last—and largest—fake dong, I'm nearly ready to drop from exhaustion. I'm also pretty sure she's come at least five or six times just from the fucking and things I'm saying to her.

When I finally flop over on my side and am ready to admit defeat...

That's when she giggles.

Fuck.

I get as far as turning on the lamp and using a pair of bandage scissors to free her wrists. Then I flop over again and let her finish freeing herself. "You can rip the vet wrap that's on your head. You don't have to cut it."

A minute later, she's like a squirming, happy puppy, snuggled tightly against me and playfully flicking her fingers at the strap-on I'm still wearing, like she didn't just spend the last hour begging for her freedom and for my mercy.

17

And now I've got fucking rug burn on one knee, because in the dark, I got off the sheet somehow.

Goddammit. Hopefully Owen won't notice it.

She looks like she could run a goddamned marathon.

Hell, at this rate I know I'm going to *need* Owen's help to keep her satisfied. She's going to fuck me to death.

"Hand me my phone, please, pet." I point.

She grabs it and passes it over. I check the time—10:37. I sigh and set a timer to wake me at midnight. "Help me up, please."

Jumping up, she offers me her hands and helps me to my feet.

She giggles again and flicks the dildo.

"Watch it," I warn. "They don't go soft."

Susa bounces up on her toes to brush a kiss across my lips. "That was *amazing*, Sir."

After I unbuckle the harness and drop it on the sheet with the other dongs, I pull her in for a kiss. "Please have all that cleaned up and safely stowed somewhere Owen won't stumble across it by tomorrow evening."

Her eyes twinkle in the dim light. "Yes, Sir."

"You didn't even think about safewording, did you?"

Her grin widens. "No, Sir."

"Why not?"

She shrugs. "You used tape on my wrists and not on my head. If you'd been a bad guy, you wouldn't have cared. Plus, a bad guy would have just raped me here." She nuzzles her nose against mine. "And I doubt someone would break in to my house and park in my garage just to take me somewhere else. Plus, my door has this weird little creak it makes when it's nearly all the way up. I keep meaning to have them come out and check it. I heard it both times."

Goddammit.

She's brilliant, and smart, and fucking ballsy.

And she's *mine*.

This creates a weird mix of feelings within me, both good and…ambivalent.

All I need to do now is convince myself this is the right thing to do for Owen, and for me.

Because once I marry her, it's for life. But I have to be sure she's got Owen's best interests at heart and can do right by *my* boy.

CHAPTER THREE

Now

I join my pets at the hotel window and drape my arms around their shoulders. We won't have much time to savor tonight's victory because we still have work to do in our state.

A *lot* of work.

Maybe it only reinforces my bastard rep, but I take great comfort knowing that there's no way Owen will ever leave us now. Not willingly, and not if he's still breathing.

The new life within Susa is all the guarantee I need of that. It brings me comfort on a number of levels, soothes my soul.

My dreams can finally come true via my boy's love for us both. *His* dreams can come true, too.

Now all we have to do is spend the next four years working toward getting Susa elected, and the hat trick is complete.

Doctors say our son appears healthy and is developing normally, according to schedule despite the ordeal he and Susa endured. Susa's face still looks a little more gaunt than I'd like to see, and she's still about ten pounds under her weight at the time of the plane crash, but doctors have assured me she's doing well.

A very large part of me wishes Owen and I had begged her to pull out of the campaign, coerced a promise from her in the hospital, pleaded with her to return to private life so we could just...*be*.

Be a family.

Be *happy*.

I am not a crier, especially in front of others, but I unabashedly wept tears of joy when I was reunited with her, put eyes and hands on her, confirmed without a doubt it absolutely was her and not a cruel mistake.

Until I saw her lying on that stretcher, part of me was still convinced, despite seeing a crappy picture sent by the ship's crew, that it wouldn't be her.

Don't get me wrong—no matter my plans, my scheming, my bastardly ways, I do deeply love this woman. I wouldn't have married her if I didn't love her. I wouldn't have done that to her or Owen.

Except there are many kinds of love. Mine has deepened and grown for her in unexpected ways since that afternoon in Las Vegas. She's my pet, and I take that responsibility seriously. She's my friend, and I never wanted to betray that friendship. She's my wife, my partner in crime, my sounding board, my political muse.

All these complicated pieces fit together perfectly within my heart in ways I never anticipated. I don't want to contemplate what would have happened to me if it hadn't been her that was rescued.

I honestly don't know if I would have had the strength to keep going. She has become a vital part of my soul, moving through my body with every beat of my heart, in different ways than Owen has, but every bit as important to me.

And now, she's going to be the mother of our child.

Over our years together, Susa's helped make me a better man, and I recognize this. Owen will always come first in our lives, but she's a close second, in my heart and soul.

It also means I give my all to making her dreams come true, and one such dream is for her to become governor. I promised her this at the beginning, and I might be many things, but I am no longer a man who ever goes back on his promises, as long as there is breath in my body and the ability for me to keep going.

I never want to be *that* man again, the man I was before the full-on bastard extraordinaire.

The man who could walk away and not look back.

I don't recognize that man anymore, over twenty-five years later. Maybe Sarge can remember him, because he formed a lot of who I was then.

Even the bastard has his limits.

So now we start Owen's second term in office, even while casting a careful eye to setting up everything for Susa's election bid. We'll make no coy equivocations about whether or not she'll run in four years—we paint her as the heir-apparent from day one of Owen's second term.

Tomorrow morning, we'll start our day by delivering a journalistic ratfuck to one Kevin Markos. Give him some payback for that bullshit interview four years ago after the school shooting, where he outrageously accused Owen of it being a publicity stunt.

All week I've been squirreling on the guy regarding an interview time for tomorrow, changing it on him several times, finally granting him a walk-and-talk first thing in the morning, at the hotel, letting him have first chance at interviewing Owen before we sit down with any other networks.

What the fucker doesn't know yet is I've already scheduled a sit-down at WFLA, the Tampa NBC affiliate. It'll happen first thing, immediately after Owen talks with Kevin Markos. We're talking to WFLA's local political reporter and doing both our *Today* and MSNBC network interviews from their studio.

Only I'm part of the interview, because we're going to give them the scoop that Susa's pregnant.

I'm hoping we hear Markos' howls all the way across Tampa when that news breaks.

Hey, you do *not* fucking piss me off.

The fastest way to fucking piss me off is to fuck with or piss off my boy or my girl.

Especially my boy. My girl is a political animal who is more than capable of standing up for herself with the press, but she likes it when I get protective.

Someone messing with Owen, however, will bring out my inner grizzly bear, even if it takes me years to finally gain my revenge.

Soon enough, the world will know about our son.

If we're really lucky, Kevin Markos will be out of a job.

Well, probably not, but a guy can dream, can't he?

"We need to get some sleep," I tell them. "Tomorrow's going to be a long-ass day."

Owen sighs and meets my gaze before he kisses me, then Susa. "Yes, Sir. I know."

I rub his head, loving the way he sighs, the tension flowing from him. "Such a good boy," I coo.

Although what I'd love to do is fuck both their brains out tonight, Owen and I are extremely careful with Susa. The doctors gave her permission to continue normal sexual activities unless she exhibits symptoms of premature contractions.

I'm still…cautious.

I won't spank her or do any kind of play like that with her, don't make her kneel, despite her feeling up to doing it and begging me to allow her to kneel. One compromise I did make was she is allowed to sit on the bed, or couch, or a chair, and do modified versions of the poses, but I flipped Owen into equals mode to help me gang up on her and demand she allow us to be overprotective dads-to-be.

I even played the guilt card—hello, *still* a bastard—and reminded her that we thought she was *dead*. The least she could do was allow us to set reasonable limits that put our minds at ease.

She finally caved, even though she pouted like crazy over me not doing impact play with her.

I know she's secretly pleased that we're both fussing over her behind closed doors, babying her. As much as she loves and misses the darker side of the sadist, I see the way she smiles when I make her sit down and relax, or I refuse to let her do something and I do it for her when Owen's not with us.

Which, unfortunately, because of the campaign, he's frequently not with us.

My absence at his side on the campaign trail is easily explained—*duh*, my wife had a near-death experience. I try to miss as few events as possible, sometimes sending Dray with him, or having Dray and Gregory stay with Susa so she's not alone, if I go with Owen.

That, I *know*, is driving her crazy—that we will *not* leave her alone unless she's in a bathroom or safe in her office. At first it was me and her parents, then her parents, after I resumed working full-time at the office.

Once she finally convinced her parents to stop coming over every day, I personally paid from my own pockets for off-duty FHP officers from her security detail to come in and stay with her when Dray couldn't work from our townhouse, drive her to doctor appointments when I couldn't be there, and never leave her alone.

She *haaaates* that.

Yet she's tolerating it, because when I told her I was doing it and she argued with me, Owen broke down sobbing and *begged* her to give in and let me do it.

Thankfully, my pet is even more of a softy about our boy than I am, in some ways.

Yes, I rewarded him well for that later, even though it wasn't planned, on his part.

She only took two weeks off from work, and even then she was working remotely from the townhouse. For the first few weeks, she would only come in to the office during the mornings and work from home in the afternoons because she was just too exhausted to stay longer.

Finally, we strip and go to bed, Susa cuddled between us. There aren't many nights where Owen can spend the entire night with us now, but this is one of them and I'll savor it.

Before her ordeal, Susa and I would always put him in the middle on these rare nights, so he felt both of us.

Now, Owen wants her in the middle, protected by us both, even though nothing will threaten our wife tonight.

I don't argue, and neither does Susa. I know she wouldn't ask to be in the middle for herself, though, even if she wants to be there.

When my alarm goes off far too early the next morning, I fumble for my phone on the nightstand, managing to locate it on the third try. "Motherfucker."

Owen laughs in the darkness on Susa's far side. "God, I miss that."

"Miss what?" I ask.

"Your morning grumpiness." I hear the sheets rustle and Susa mutters something unintelligible, then Owen's hand finds my hip in the darkness and gently squeezes.

My cock throbs. *Ooooh, yes.* My boy and I will definitely be showering together this morning, without a doubt. We usually get more time together than he does with Susa, because I normally head to the mansion early every morning for our workout, either on machines there, or a jog around the neighborhood surrounding the mansion while tailed by the security detail.

Then I always take my shower there, with Owen, not that the public knows that part.

As his chief of staff I can get away with stuff like that, and no one's batting an eye about it. They assume I'm dedicated to my job.

Since the very beginning, when Owen officially became my

submissive, our post-workout shower routine has been an integral part of our day. I pin him to the wall and he asks me for an orgasm.

And then I give him one.

He's not allowed to masturbate without permission, even this many years later.

He's our good boy and obeys us.

Because he loves us, and he trusts us, and he knows we'll always take care of him. All he has to do is ask.

I switch on the lamp and give Owen's hand a squeeze before I sit up. When I look, Susa's pulled the sheet over her head and rolled to face Owen. She's still mumbling, and Owen's wearing an adorable smile as he stares at the Susa-shaped lump under the covers.

I pull the sheet down and lean in to kiss her tummy. "Good morning, Petey." Then I kiss her. "Good morning, pet."

And my boy. This morning he grabs my head and *kisses* me. Fortunately, we'll have a shower and time before the walk-and-talk downstairs with Markos for our lips to not be swollen any longer.

The last chance we'll have to really *kiss* like this—versus a quick kiss that's a mere brush of lips over lips—until tonight. And then after tonight, our opportunities will be limited mostly to weekend nights at the townhouse, when we can make it look logical that Owen would stop by.

I savor my boy's *kisses*, these sweet moments outside of time, the feel of his fingers pressing against the back of my head, the rasp of morning stubble against each other's cheeks.

Kissing.

He's a damn good kisser, and always has been. His *kisses* like this have always been able to harden my cock every bit as much as the darker, secret play Susa and I shared in those early days together.

His tongue traces my teeth, plays with my tongue, thoroughly explores my mouth as he reacquaints himself with territory denied to him too frequently these past few months.

I don't rush him. He's always good about minding the time, and he needs this from me today.

Besides, I'm damn sure enjoying it.

When I feel Susa's fingers wrap around my cock, I don't even stop that, although I had planned on putting that load inside Owen's ass in the shower.

There are few things I can deny my pet now, even though, before, she would have been thoroughly spanked for trying to make us late.

Owen swallows my needy groan and intensifies this *kiss*. I can feel the warm silk of Susa's hair against the hollow of my throat as she strokes me, and then Owen's gasp makes me realize I'm not the only one she's taken control of like this.

Okay, fuck it. No shower sex today. This is better.

Much better.

She sighs as we settle into a rhythm fucking her hands, now doing all the work for her. I reach between her legs to play with her and give her relief and realize Owen's hand is already there.

I go lower, sliding one finger inside her pussy and my cock jerks in her hand at her sweet moan.

And still, Owen and I *kiss*.

I don't even bother holding back, wanting Owen to have more of her undivided attention this morning. I slide my other arm under his head and take control of the *kiss*, nibbling and biting his lips as I come and spill all over her hand and her stomach. With Susa sweetly squirming between us, I know it won't take long for him to come, either.

I pull my finger from her pussy, swipe it through the mess I've made, and draw my lips back from his just enough to slide my finger in there.

He eagerly sucks it, swirling his tongue around my digit and completely cleaning it. I do it again and again, his green gaze looking sweetly subspacey as he finally groans with his own climax.

"Take care of pet," I order, releasing him.

He immediately dives between her legs, and then I kiss her as he makes her moan and arch and squirm for us.

She's gorgeous, and she's ours.

Just like with Owen, I know she's not going anywhere, either. All those years ago, she fell as hard for the bastard as I fell for Owen, and as hard as Owen fell for her.

After she's come and she's finally patted Owen on the head to stop, he returns to us, kissing her, and then me.

I run my fingers through his blond hair. There's some grey there now, just like there is in mine, but it makes him look even more handsome. I still see the boy I fell for in the dorm room, the lovable, lonely man who stole my heart.

He turns his face to kiss my palm. "Okay, so that's a nice way to start the day." He smiles as Susa giggles.

Her giggle hasn't changed, even though, like us, there are more lines in her face, a little grey in her brown hair, which she's stopped coloring, for now.

I can still see the girl ancient beyond her years, the girl whose shadows seduced mine.

The girl whose father probably still wants to kill me, even though he's learned to tolerate me around her.

"Good morning, Sir," she says, kissing me. Then she turns to Owen and gives him a longer kiss, wanting to do right by our boy. "Good morning, boy."

His eyes always light up with her. They do for me, too, but it's different, and long ago I learned not to begrudge that.

The important thing is we're together, and we love each other.

And in a few short months, we're going to be parents.

The one dream I thought I'd never be able to make come true for our sweet boy, and the one thing I know will finish healing the last thin spots in his soul after the childhood he survived.

Although, I guess in some small, secret way I should give private thanks to Elandra Marriott Solemar being a raging, narcissistic thundercunt. Because if she hadn't, I might not have been able to so easily win our boy's heart.

CHAPTER FOUR

Then

I have spent the past weeks I've known Owen studying him, studying how he interacts with me and with Susa, learning everything I can about him. Gently testing cause and effect variables in ways that might make me a bastard but which won't cause him harm or distress.

I need to know these things about him.

All of that pays off when, four weeks into the semester, that Thursday morning Owen is summoned—and literally that's how I'd label it—to Orlando for a Saturday night dinner at his mother's house.

He.

Freaks.

Out.

I'm not even exaggerating.

Owen's terrified. All I want to do is pull him into my arms and hold him, promise to take care of him, and give him anything within my power to if he'll just walk away from her and never look back and give himself to me.

These are all things I cannot say to him. Not yet.

While I know Susa is deeply in love with me, Owen doesn't

even know I'm bi yet, much less that I'm in love with him.

But finally getting to meet Owen's mother means I'll be able to study the dynamic they have in person. I mean, I'm positive she'll be on her best behavior tonight, in front of a houseful of guests, but every narcissist has their tells, and Owen's been beyond her direct reach for over a month.

She's more than likely to strike at him, meaning Susa and I can finally begin the deprogramming process in earnest.

That Owen lets me set rules for him for the evening, and lets me drive us over in his car, just emphasizes how emotionally wrecked he is right now.

Susa and I are his safe oasis, his unconditional acceptance.

Love.

Things he didn't get from his mother. Things I suspect she's incapable of giving.

Hopefully, having me with him will only help highlight to him how sweet and easy being with me and Susa feels compared to… *this*.

The first time I meet Owen's mother, the bastard extraordinaire wants to tell her to go fuck herself and spirit Owen out of there within five minutes of our arrival. That's because upon our initial introduction, she gives me a blatantly obvious glare while looking me up and down before deciding I will do as a guest in her home that evening and then dismissing us both.

Boy do I want to tell her to go fuck herself.

I behave myself, though.

Barely.

Instead, I do play dirty and turn on the charm, calling upon my own past to roll the narcissist's game right back at her, kissing her hand instead of merely shaking it. That initial greeting buys us a little bit of peace so I can figure out how to get Owen settled. Fortunately, we're a bit over-dressed.

"If you want, you can leave your blazers in Owen's room, on

his bed. Owen, will you please show your friend around and introduce him?" Elandra turns without waiting for a response.

Perfect.

"First barrier—passed," Owen mutters before leading me through the house.

His room has less personality than our dorm room did before we started moving in, but I totally get now what he meant by having more room. The room he had to himself is larger than our dorm room and has an en suite bathroom. There's a queen-sized bed, two large dressers that would be about six of the one we each have, an armoire, entertainment center, and a walk-in closet nearly as large as our shared bathroom.

"Wow." I shrug off my blazer and hand it to him. He neatly lays them on his bed.

"I know." He shrugs. "This is what I meant," he whispers. "More room."

I've seen the stuff he's got in the storage unit. "You really did totally move out." He apparently left nothing behind but furniture.

"Yeah. She can use this room as a guest room now, if she needs to. I have literally nothing here."

I start to say something about how he's *definitely* staying with me between semesters, but then I bite the words back.

We're still a long way from that, even though it's my goal.

Okay, screw that, my goal is to have him in my bed—and not just to soothe me back to sleep after a nightmare—*long* before the end of the semester, but it's not the current reality and I don't want to spook him.

I'm glad I came tonight. If for no other reason than to see *this*. A glimpse into his psyche.

Meeting the monster in person.

The house feels too perfect, borderline sterile. Like a perfectly staged house for sale instead of a home. No surprise, considering she sells real estate.

What's conspicuously absent, however, are any visible pictures of Owen, even though there are plenty of portraits of Elandra and Austin together, Elandra in younger years, and even a few of Austin.

Literally, the *only* picture I find of Owen is one taken most likely at his high school graduation because of the cap and gown he wears. In it, the couple flanks Owen, and the woman's too-wide smile is no doubt intended to make her look like Mother of the Year.

The house screams narcissist.

Owen's step-father, Austin, is a weaselly little man who obviously enjoys being pushed around by his wife.

Ah. Now I can see Elandra's "type." She married one and trained another.

It's a valuable insight I tuck away for later.

As the evening progresses, while Elandra's obviously trying to evaluate me, it turns out that there are more than enough of her husband's co-workers at the dinner they're hosting to ensure she's on her best behavior.

For now.

I'm careful that, during the entire evening, I keep an eye on Owen and I casually intervene and redirect Elandra's attention from him to me if I think she's pushing his buttons a little too hard. Usually by using flattery and asking well-placed questions about Florida politics and what she does for a living. Questions that make her look good as a host, and reflect well on her by my obvious knowledge of what we're talking about.

Thank you, Susa, and thank you, eidetic memory.

When people find out I'm a decorated combat vet, it makes Elandra puff up a little. Now I'm a value-added accessory to her main narcissistic supply's presence at her little soirée. That means I'm promoted in status from being merely tolerated in her home to that of a welcomed guest, and I practically have to peel her off of me from that point on.

But, because I'm more than a bit of a bastard, I also let a few exchanges briefly play out between Owen and his mother, just to see what happens.

Because I *need* to see what happens.

Not because the sadist in me likes watching Owen cruelly twist in the wind at the end of his mother's sharp and well-honed tongue, or blush under her cold glares, but because I want to see *his* reactions. How he responds to her, and the things he tries to do to keep her from acting like that in the first place.

The dance they're doing around each other.

The painful comments she slings at him disguised as "just kidding" sorts of jabs. Camouflaged. Verbal harpoons her guests can see striking their target and sinking into Owen's flesh, but they don't recognize them as such and even laugh at their impact.

Perhaps in a different family, such as the one I grew up in, those kinds of comments absolutely would be harmless, funny, even, in a far different context.

But not tonight.

She's trying to get her overdue pound of flesh out of Owen in any way she can, and it disgusts and angers me.

That's why I let her go on for a little while. I want Owen to have a new baseline from *this* moment forward. Tonight will be a study in stark contrasts—choosing the hell he has here, or the welcoming, gentle haven he has with me and Susa.

I want to be the one to pick him up and dust him off, to comfort him on the flip side of this endurance test.

Bastard. Extraordinaire.

Yes, I admit it. I own that title, and I proudly wear it.

Owen spontaneously offers to fetch her—and me—food, drinks, always seems to be watching her for any subtle cues for him to come to her, listening for her even as he talks with others.

She's like the flame my sweet little moth is pulled inexorably toward, even though he knows she's going to singe the fuck out of him every damn time without her giving a shit what she does to him.

These are all things I *need* to know if I want to make sure I properly train Susa in the correct care and feeding of our self-proclaimed pet.

Oh, I know he didn't mean it the way I mean it, but absolutely, that's what's going to happen.

I want Owen.

I want him the way I've never wanted anyone or anything before in my life.

He's gorgeous, he's smart, he's funny, and he's submissive.

Even better, he doesn't realize he's any of those things—not the way Susa and I see him—and that makes him even more attractive.

I don't care that he's not gay, or even bi. That's completely irrelevant. By the time I'm done with the first stage of training him, *he* won't care, either.

Ask me how I know.

Go on, ask.

Let's just say I've been on the other side of things and discovered that, with the proper motivation, you can train someone to love and beg for almost anything.

Even things they hate.

Case in point—Owen's *here* tonight, instead of telling his mother to go fuck herself.

I want to take care of him. I want to show him what real, true love is.

I want to give him affection and attention and positive reinforcement.

I want to show him how to *win*.

I'm dead serious when I say I want to get him elected governor. I know he can do it, if Susa and I can get through to him.

I damn sure know Susa can win. But the best way to help her win is making sure Owen wins first.

No one left behind.

This means I start looking at multiple options.

It also means talking to Susa about the three of us taking a trip to Vegas.

And not simply because Owen's father lives there.

* * *

Owen didn't get his beautiful green eyes from Elandra, that's for sure. Her icy blue gaze attempts to skewer me several times when I've unobtrusively slipped into a conversation next to Owen. Owen's so used to my presence in his life that, without thinking, he automatically opens his stance to include me.

Defers to me.

Elandra's eyes flash fire when she realizes that, but someone else remarks how admirable it is that I'm a veteran and now working on my law degree, and it tamps down her rage somewhat because we're back to I've made her look good.

She might hate me on the back end of this evening, but she'll also be forced to admit that I made a great impression, even if I denied her more than a little satisfaction in drawing all the emotional blood from *my* boy that she wanted.

Because that's how I think of Owen—*Mine.*

He just doesn't know it yet.

Maybe it's better that way, for now. I want to make sure by the time I openly lay claim to my boy that he can't free himself from me.

That he won't *want* to free himself from me.

When I claim him, I want him to willingly choose me and the safety and trust I guarantee him. I want him to understand there are benefits to this nontraditional union I'll offer.

Even if he hates me more than a little for backing him into that corner, I want him to be able to see I'm right.

Stacking the deck?

Damn right. I'm no idiot.

Susa wasn't part of my initial plans, until I realized how hard she's fallen for me. And how hard Owen has fallen for her. And, of course, what she can do for Owen. That means I have to play the pivot and will bring them together. Exactly how, I'm not yet sure. But Owen's twenty-first birthday is rapidly approaching.

Alcohol is a great equalizer. Despite my early proclamations about not being a heavy drinker, this is one time I'm thinking I'll make an exception, because I need the fastest way to drop Owen's defenses. It'll hopefully allow me the chance to finally delve into Owen's hidden darkness and see the animal we all conceal within us.

But is my pet a tame house-cat, or is there a dark tiger lurking there, just waiting for the right person to coax him out?

That's what I can't wait to find out.

Either way, he's mine. Or soon will be.

First, I have to get him through this visit with his mother without him having a nervous breakdown.

CHAPTER FIVE

At one point, I even go so far as to take a seat on the sofa before dinner. Once dinner's served I don't rise, waiting for Owen to look for me as he has been every thirty seconds or so since we arrived. I motion him over.

That's when I hold my hands out, waggling my fingers. "Sorry."

He helps me to my feet as he's done before, and I make a point of wincing and needing to hold on to him for a moment, as if I'm not steady on my feet.

Elandra sees this but makes no comment.

Meanwhile, two other people who are close by reach out to help steady me, and I graciously smile and thank them.

"I get really stiff if I sit too long in one position," I explain. "I'm in a bad pain cycle right now. They tell me that will likely get better over time. Not as bad as I used to be. At least I don't need my cane today."

Although I had seriously considered bringing it, but didn't want to deal with maintaining that level of commitment to faking it tonight. I need my focus on Owen.

Plus, I would've been too tempted to whack Elandra with it.

No, seriously.

We survive dinner and have finished the dessert portion of the evening when Elandra is chatting with someone and hooks an arm through Owen's, holding on to him as she talks.

He cannot easily escape her.

I'm standing across the room, listening to some old guy who's a partner at Austin's firm drone on about his glory days in Vietnam, which were apparently filled with beloved bouts of drunken debauchery, before he was wounded and shipped home. He's also on at least his third glass of wine of the evening and looking a little unsteady on his feet.

I watch as Owen's gaze drops to the floor and his entire demeanor changes, tense and wary. Shoulders hunched.

He looks terrified to move.

Like he's prey and a predator is about to strike.

I've had more than enough, and I can tell Owen has, too. I've also seen all I need to see, have more than enough data to put to good use. We've done more than be social tonight. I know the narcissist will try to fault Owen for leaving early, but I'll draw her ire onto me.

I'd left my phone in the pocket of my blazer on purpose. I pat my pants pockets and interrupt Grandpa Blazing Guns. "I'm sorry, do you have the time?"

The guy's wearing a watch that's probably easily worth what I made in five or six months in the Army. The kind of watch I one day want to be able to effortlessly afford.

"It's almost eight."

"Ah, thank you. I'm so sorry, I should have taken my medicine an hour ago. Please excuse me."

"Not a problem son." He pats me on the arm as I limp past him, aiming for the spare bedroom, where our blazers are as we left them on the bed.

I make sure to emphasize my limp even more than I have been, and to move slow and stiffly, so everyone can see the gimpy guy.

I remain inside the spare bedroom just long enough to make it look like I've checked my pockets before I return to the living room, slowly threading my way around people to appear at Owen's side.

I lean in but make sure everyone can hear me. "I'm sorry to interrupt, Mrs. Solemar, but I think I left my meds out in Owen's car, and I'm overdue to take them. Owen, if you'll give me your keys, I'll go get them."

I've made sure to stand with my foot close to Owen's, and I'm willing him to look me in the eyes.

It's almost like it takes him a moment to realize I'm there and talking to him. He makes eye contact with me as his mother releases his arm so he can retrieve his car keys. He looks close to panic and I feel him tap my foot with his.

He hands over the keys and I offer him a smile and a subtle tip of my head. "Thanks." I focus on his mother again. "I'm so sorry to interrupt."

"Oh, not at all, Carter."

Yeah, what's she going to do? Bitch out a wounded vet who needs his meds?

Riiiight.

Despite how I want to grab Owen and get the fuck out of there, I keep my gait slow and pained, limping, taking my time. I make it look good, pausing at his car and sitting in the passenger seat with a pained grunt, in case anyone's watching me from the house. I make a show of searching for something, including hauling myself out of the car and looking in the backseat, spending several minutes making this charade look real.

When I finally return to the house, I immediately head directly for Owen.

I don't know if he realizes I'm keeping his keys, for now.

"Man, I am *really* sorry. I think I left my meds sitting on the counter back in our room. I can't find them. I could have sworn I'd put them in my pocket."

Owen's a quick study, for sure. "Oh, we really need to get you back, then. How overdue are you?"

"An hour." Everyone's already heard the story about how I was injured, so no one's going to question me about that, or be so gauche as to ask me specifically what my meds are for.

Hopefully.

If they do, I'll simply glare at them.

"Yikes," Owen says.

I turn to Elandra. "Ma'am, I am *so* sorry about this. I feel like such an idiot." I glance at Owen. "I mean, I could drive home and take them and come back to get you, if you'd rather? I'll pay for the gas—"

"Don't be silly," Elandra says. "It's quite all right, Carter." I'm sure there's a flare of panic in her that perhaps someone went in to the bedroom and swiped the pills from my blazer pocket, but she doesn't say it, and neither do I. The way she speaks just a touch faster than she was before betrays her.

The last thing she needs is for anyone to think someone stole a wounded vet's medication while in her home.

"But I feel so bad about this. I know Owen was looking forward to tonight. He was so excited when he received your text the other morning."

The narcissist is slick, but very predictable. Now she's annoyed at me and not Owen.

Which is exactly what I wanted.

"We're just very glad you were able to come with him this evening, Carter," she says. Her smile looks right, but the arctic chill in her eyes tells the true tale. I'm not her favorite person right now, but she doesn't think I did this deliberately. She also knows she can't complain about it for fear of looking bad in the eyes of her friends, or without someone wondering if I *did* bring my medication, but now it's disappeared.

That would be more horrifying to her than someone spotting a cockroach in the middle of the dinner table.

"I truly appreciate your hospitality, Mrs. Solemar. I had a wonderful evening. It was great to get out of the dorm tonight. We're usually busy studying and don't get out that often. Especially with as badly as I'm usually hurting. Owen's so nice, he hangs out with me, brings me food from the dining hall, runs errands for me—he really takes care of me." I don't want her to think Owen has a life—or fun—away from her.

"You're welcome back any time, Carter. It was a pleasure to meet you."

Oh, I've got a hot news flash for her—from this point forward, she's never seeing her son outside of my presence.

Not if I have anything to say about it.

Frankly, she's never setting *eyes* on her son in person again, if I have anything to say about it.

I make a mental note to step up my contact with Gerard Taylor.

Owen's father.

I friended him on Facebook a couple of weeks ago and was open about why I was approaching him on the sly—that I'm Owen's friend and roommate, that I'm older than Owen, that I could tell Owen was troubled regarding his relationship with his mother, and because I want to help Owen.

Fortunately, the man doesn't strike me as an asshole, so we'll see what happens there. I haven't told Owen any of this yet. His father has agreed to keep it quiet, for now, knowing what a shit Elandra can be. The secrecy works to my advantage and gives me time to plan.

We say our good-byes and Owen retrieves our blazers. Now it's after dark, and I hold Owen's arm as we make our way outside and down the front walk.

Admittedly, being able to hold on to Owen was another reason I left my cane at home.

I'm a bastard—so sue me.

"You okay?" I softly ask once we're about a house away.

"Yeah. Thank you." He doesn't sound okay. He sounds anything *but* okay.

"It's all right." It's not, but it's as all right as I can make it for him tonight.

He leads me over to the passenger side and opens the door for me, helping me in. I lean over and start the car for him as he rounds the front and slides behind the wheel.

"Stop just outside the development," I order with more than a little command and control tone.

Dom tone.

I've never used it on him quite like this before, and hope he doesn't rebel.

He doesn't. "Yes, sir." His quiet tone rips at my soul. My poor boy is miserable right now, and I feel helpless.

I hate feeling like this. I want to *do*, to *fix*.

Until he's officially mine, though, all I can do is be a friend.

He doesn't start crying until after we've swapped places and I'm behind the wheel. Tonight I settle for patting him on the thigh and letting him cry it out. It's stress, it's a lifetime of toxic patterns, it's fear—and right now, it's probably mostly relief.

He's out, he's free, and he's relatively unscathed, for tonight.

We're almost to Lakeland on I-4 before he speaks. "Thank you."

"Little bro, I've got your six. You don't even need to ask. This is a given. *This* is what family does for each other."

I know it's playing dirty, but I want him to see me like that. I want that familiarity. I want his defenses completely down around me.

I need to see him without filters and protective walls.

I can give him everything he needs, but first and foremost, he needs to *trust* me. That's the only way this will work. He can love me or hate me, that I don't care about.

I need him to *trust* me. The rest will fall into place.

I stop for gas in Plant City. When I finish filling the tank, I find him staring out the windshield at the darkness.

"Penny for your thoughts," I say.

"I can't believe we got out of there so easily. I honestly think she liked you."

"Well, we'll have to come up with another excuse for the next time, to get us out of there early," I fib.

That makes him turn. "Next time?"

"Yeah. Next time she summons you. You don't think I'm letting you go back there alone, do you?"

Right now, he doesn't need to know that I'm not ever letting him go back there.

He stares at me, those beautiful green eyes looking dark and wounded in this light, just a hair too bright, the tears threatening to reappear.

"Thank you," he whispers.

"Hey, no man left behind. I mean that." I grin. "Maybe next time we *will* let Susa come with us. Would've been a hoot watching her playing with some of those snooty stuffed shirts who thought they were big-shots."

He finally laughs. "I was thinking that, too."

"I'm going to need your mom's number, though."

"Why?"

"Because I want to text her another apology."

"Um, why?"

I shrug. "We set it up so that she feels socially obligated to invite your roommate to future events." In reality, I want to stroke her ego and pull her attention from Owen. I don't need her forcing my hand too soon.

"Sonofabitch, I think that would actually work on her."

"Of course it will. Narcissists love to think they're so

unpredictable, when the truth is, you can practically set a clock by them."

It's after ten when we return to the dorm. While Owen's in the bathroom, I text Susa.

Home. Awake?

She must have been waiting for my text, because she replies almost immediately.

Yes, Sir.

I tap out my reply. I have a plan, but I need her to go along with it.

She's a cunt, worse than I thought, but I know what we need to do now. I'll give you details tmrw night. You still going to Tllhsee on Owen's bd wknd?

I need Owen hooked deep in her heart for this to work. I know she's attracted to him, even if she wants me more.

My plan leaves no one behind. Now, having met his mother, I see the clearest way though that wilderness so we all can get what we want and need.

Yes, Sir. Why?

I want the house for the wknd. I have a plan, but need privacy and 2 nights w/him.

I see the bubble as she's typing her reply.

Then you can use the house.

I smile to myself.

:) Good girl. Tnk you. Sleep tight. See you tmrw.

The use of the emoji was calculated. Just as I've been carefully testing around the edges of Owen's psyche, so I have with Susa, too. It's a little easier to do with her, though, considering the circumstances, so I do it far more blatantly.

Yes, Sir.

I smile to myself. *Bingo.*

A few minutes later, after Owen's returned from the bathroom and settled in bed, he's so exhausted from stress that I hear him fall asleep almost immediately.

That leaves me lying there in my bed and replaying the evening in my head. Owen's not a complicated guy. He likes to serve, he likes to take care of people, and he's starved for positive reinforcement and love.

He's starved for basic human touch. He's got skin hunger.

I plan to give him all of what he needs, and more.

Much more.

In my own way, of course.

I wouldn't be a bastard if I didn't add that caveat.

CHAPTER SIX

Now

I finally get Owen out of bed—which, admittedly isn't a place I want to leave, either—and we head for the shower. Susa's going to shower in the other bathroom, one of the benefits of getting a suite.

Owen eyes me as he soaps up the washcloth. "I want it understood, *Sir*, that I'm *not* happy about this."

He doesn't need to clarify what he means. I also know from the way he emphasized *Sir* that it's only my relationship with him that's making him obey me on this one.

He doesn't dare say no to me about a direct order, because he's my very good boy and always has been.

"But think about how epic it'll be when he realizes how we ratfucked him!" I counter. "If we simply cut him out of interviews today, he'll attribute it to our rightful grudge against him and his network. Not only do we ratfuck him, but we get his hopes up that we've moved on from four years ago." I grin. "This way, he'll know without a doubt how we feel, and I'm going to be wearing a smile worthy of the Cheshire cat later when we have the sit-down with him."

He blows out a long breath and grumbles as I turn so he can scrub my back. This is another cherished ritual we have from the early days, a way to connect with each other even when we don't have time to "play."

"Yes, Sir."

"If you're a good boy for me today," I only partly tease, "I'll let you fuck my ass tonight. But *only* if you don't gripe about Kevin Markos all day."

I'm not expecting it when his arm wraps around my upper body and pulls me tightly against his taller frame. Owen is six-four to my five-ten.

Pleasure ripples through me at the feel of his breath in my ear. "You *sure* you want to do that, *Sir?*"

I bask in the feeling for a moment before I spin and easily pin him against the shower wall with my left forearm across his throat. But the triumphant gaze he pins me with tells the truth—he knows he had me for the briefest of moments. My boy is definitely *not* a Top, but every once in a while he enjoys it when I let him get frisky with me like that.

He reaches up, an ingrained response now, and his fingers close around my arm.

I lean in and suck on his lower lip, nipping it. "Kinda ballsy boy this morning, aren't you? Don't think I won't send you out for your sit-downs with a vibrating butt plug up your ass and the controller in *my* pocket."

His nostrils flare as his eyes widen.

He knows I'll do it, too.

Part of him dreads that thought.

Part of him *craves* it.

I smile as I take pity on him and start stroking his cock without making him beg for it this morning. "*Buuut*, I guess, since you were such a *good* boy and got re-elected last night, I can let the snark slide a little, *Governor.*"

He's already rocking his hips in time with my motions. I honestly didn't think he'd have a second one in him so quickly this morning, but I'm glad of it. It means he'll be more settled, relaxed when he's being interviewed today. A little of our routine added to a day always helps him out. I don't drag it out, either, because we don't have the time and we've already taken too much. It'll never be enough with either of them, but it is all that we can steal for ourselves today.

By the time we finally finish our showers, including shaving each other, Susa's already done, has her hair blown out and styled, is dressed, and is putting on makeup.

Owen's halfway dressed, slacks and a belt but still shirtless, when he drops to his knees in front of her, wraps his arms around her, and presses his face to her tummy.

I can't help it—I snap a picture with my personal phone.

Dammit, something that's *ours*.

Her gaze catches mine as she smiles and strokes his hair, rubbing his scalp in that way he loves.

I walk over and stand behind him, wrapping my arms around her, too. "I promised him fun tonight if he doesn't gripe about Kevin Markos all day. But he needs to finish getting dressed."

Her face lights up. "Ah, the good boy earned a reward." She pats the top of his head and he finally, reluctantly stands. "You heard Sir. Get dressed. Now."

He smiles as brushes a kiss across her lips before he grabs his undershirt.

She drops me a wink. "Dray will be here in five." She holds up fingers and waggles them at me.

"Yes, dear."

She laughs and playfully swats me on the ass, and that makes *me* laugh.

Laughter.

It's so good to hear it again after those three bleak weeks just a few months ago.

We were lucky.

Damned lucky.

Don't think I don't know that.

It also makes a tiny part of me worry that we used up a lifetime's worth of luck. Then what will we do in the future when something bad sneaks up on us?

* * *

Kevin Markos must have mainlined a gallon of coffee to look as awake as he does right now. His too-blue eyes are likely contacts, and his blond hair is a shade lighter than Owen's and laying perfectly. Dray went first to confirm Markos was there and ready before we took the service elevator down, our security detail in tow.

Our campaign is actually paying for the extra troopers, yesterday and today, and related travel expenses. Just because Owen was re-elected doesn't mean we can get lazy and sloppy. The only way to get Susa elected is to not fuck up.

I let Owen go first and stand a couple of steps behind with Susa, holding her hand. Dray stands off to the side, ready to cut in with a time warning in three minutes if I haven't been able to get Owen moving in two.

"Governor Taylor, congratulations on your re-election victory last night," Markos says, his sound guy holding a boom right over their heads as the cameraman stays tight on them. "How does it feel to have secured such a decisive victory?"

Owen slips his hands in his pockets, looking deceptively casual, but I know it's more to hide the fact that he's clenching his fists. "I think it means the voters have once again spoken with a clear mandate. We're still waiting on final tallies, of course, but it's looking like we earned even more votes than the last time. I hope that means the voters want me to keep doing what we've been doing and working on the initiatives we started in our first term..."

When Susa pokes me in the ribs, I glance at her and immediately realize my smile had been sliding toward Joker-Poisons-Gotham territory.

I can't help it. Imagining how pissed off Markos is going to be when he realizes what we've done is just...

Fucking *sweet*.

At one time, the guy was a well-respected and level-headed anchor, leaning fiscally conservative and maybe a little more hawkish than I agree with on nat-sec, but socially a liberal, and a firm believer that "religion" has no place in government. At one time, he probably would have been called a Libertarian, even though he's supposedly GOP.

I would have even been tempted to tap him for comms at the state, if he hadn't completely shredded his integrity working for Full News Broadcasting. Well, that, and I know we can't afford him. But by working for that network, I know from private conversations with Benchley and others, the man has basically ruined any hope of him ever having a safety net. Some talent can go on to be a campaign advisor, or press secretary, or fill similar roles.

If Kevin Markos does leave FNB? He's already made himself a pariah among mainstream media companies and most politicians with an ounce of common sense.

And I *really* need to stop thinking right this minute about hoping he gets fired, because Susa's poking me again.

I can't help it. The thought of him getting shit-canned makes me smile.

Also makes it difficult for me to concentrate on what Owen's saying.

I catch Dray's eye and he holds up one finger—one-minute warning.

I release Susa's hand and step behind Owen as our security detail patiently waits. I lay a hand on his arm. "We need to go,

Governor."

I keep an arm around Owen as I start moving, bringing him with me as I hold my other hand out for Susa to take it, and now we're walking.

Markos and his crew scurry along with us, Markos trying to get in as many questions and responses as he can. To the asshole's credit, he actually asks intelligent, insightful questions that, had he asked *those* kinds of questions to Owen before the first election, I wouldn't hate the fucker *now*.

Make no mistake—while I resent what his implication was about me that day, it's the fact that Markos upset and pissed off *Owen* that makes me hold such a deep, unyielding grudge against him now.

By the time all four of us—including Dray—are safely in the back of a black Tahoe and on our way to the TV studio, I'm unable to contain my grin.

Susa starts poking at me with both hands. "You nearly had me laughing. Stop that."

My grin widens. "I can't help it. It's like two Christmases."

Owen sighs. "You realize he's going to be a fucking prick later, right? During the sit-down?"

I shrug. "Then it's obvious he's retaliating and we win again."

I'm still unable to contain my smile later as the three of us are under lights and being interviewed. They've put us on a casual set usually used for a syndicated daytime show they also produce. It's the anchor, Sheila Hooper, on the far right, then Owen to the left in a chair by himself, and then Susa at the end of the couch closest to Owen, and me, with my arm draped around her shoulders.

"Congratulations on your re-election victory last night, Governor Taylor, Lieutenant-Governor Evans."

"Thank you," Owen says. "It's a pleasure to be here." Now he's smiling, his mood greatly improved by this.

"I also wanted to thank you again for coming on our morning

broadcast."

"Well, Tampa is our hometown, really. We miss it, living up in Tallahassee. Don't get me wrong, we love the people there, it's a great city. But there's a reason we have our campaign headquarters here, and always have our election night parties here. This is our home."

Sheila knows to throw the next question to Susa. "You miraculously survived a very dramatic ordeal just a few months ago. How are you doing, Ms. Evans?"

My pet is a master with the media. "I'm feeling great, Sheila. I'm ready to spend the next four years in Tallahassee."

"Any plans past that you'd like to share with us?"

"Absolutely. It's not a secret—I'm going to run for governor at the end of Governor Taylor's term."

"You survived something even experts said is pretty miraculous. Did anything in particular help you hang on while you were waiting for rescue?"

"I had everything to live for, a family who loves me, a job to do. One I've worked my entire life to achieve."

Now, Sheila throws to me. I've avoided interviews for years, so this is a double coup, for her. "Carter Wilson, you're Governor Taylor's chief of staff, in addition to the husband of the state's lieutenant governor. How does that put extra pressure on you?"

"Not going to lie, it was…tough after her plane went down. The three of us have been close for twenty-plus years. We *are* a family. Owen's my brother in everything but name, and everyone we know will tell you that very same thing. It was every bit as hard on him as it was me. Even harder, because he had to stay here and run the state while I was overseas and alone. It's a miracle upon a miracle, though."

I had warned her I'd feed her an easy lead-in to the million-dollar scoop.

"How so, Mr. Wilson?"

I share a planned glance with Susa, who smiles as she nods at me. I refocus on Sheila. "Because we'd like to announce that Susa's expecting our first child in March, a boy."

The entire crew reacts, and whether it's because they know how fucking big this scoop is, or because they're genuinely happy for us after what happened, they start cheering. Sheila was Susa's first sit-down after I finally relented and let Susa speak to the media after her ordeal, so this is two scoops we've handed them during our administration.

Hey, WFLA has a huge viewing audience, one of the biggest markets not just in Florida but in the Southeast, and not only in Tampa. They have viewers all up and down the entire west coast of Florida, and east into Lakeland.

I'm not stupid. I want them on our side.

By the time we get out of there to make it to our next interview, Dray's grinning. "It's breaking on *WaPo*, *The New York Times*, *CNN*, and #susaspregnant is already trending on Twitter."

Susa and I high-five each other and Dray. I notice it takes Owen a second longer to reach in, too.

When he does, his expression looks a little…tight.

I reach around Susa, who's sitting between Owen and me, and squeeze Owen's shoulder, refusing to let go until he meets my gaze.

"Love you," I whisper.

And like that, the storm has broken. Owen takes a deep breath and *this* smile looks real. He accepts a nuzzle from Susa, and then she grabs his tie and pulls on it, makes him lean over even farther so I can kiss the top of his head.

"Love you, both," he whispers before sitting back with a sweet smile on his face.

He's happy, and that makes *me* happy.

Both my pets are happy.

Susa holds his hand, and I squeeze his shoulder again, keeping my arm there, with Susa bracketed between us.

CHAPTER SEVEN

Then

Now that I've met the monster masquerading as Owen's mother, have seen the enemy up close and personal, and witnessed her tactics first-hand, I know what I need to do with him. It also means I can step up my game with Susa, now that I'm sure I can win over Owen. I'd hesitated to take things farther with Susa before I knew that for sure. I didn't want to crush her heart by discarding her if Owen would never be mine. The trick now is balancing Susa and Owen so I get the timing right to bring the three of us together.

Susa's loyalty is nearly guaranteed at this point. That means it's time for me to work on Owen.

I have a plan for celebrating Owen's twenty-first birthday with him. It works out even better since Susa won't be around for it.

Much better.

Because my plan is to get him shit-faced, hopefully enough to loosen his tongue and start him talking, and then shamelessly explore his fantasies with him.

It will hopefully reveal if I am totally wasting my time, or if I can start turning up the heat on Owen.

The frog doesn't jump out of the pot when you heat the water gradually like that.

I can't tell you how many times I beat off in the shower thinking about Owen, especially in the morning after our PT sessions. I also won't deny there are mornings I keep us at a slower pace and shamelessly claim I'm in pain just so I can more easily talk with him. I mean, I'm always in pain, but there's tolerable pain and intolerable pain. So technically I wasn't exactly lying to him on all those mornings.

Although I do lie to him at other times, to hide what Susa and I are doing.

I'm not proud of that, but it's for the greater good and to prevent hurting him.

The first night he helped me out of a nightmare, it took everything in me not to lean over and kiss him then, and I've only fallen harder for him since that night.

He's hot, and gorgeously subby, and sweet, and smart as fuck.

Yet he has practically no self-confidence, thanks to his thundercunt of a mother. Now that I've met her, and Owen understands I'm not scared off by her, that hurdle's successfully been jumped. I know one of Owen's fears was that I would meet her, be charmed by her, and not believe a word he said about her and think he was a liar.

The thing is, I completely believed him when he told me about his mother and what she'd done to him over the years. Absolutely. I've known people just like he described.

Survived my own relationship with one.

Barely.

I can't tell Owen any of that yet, though. Not now, and maybe never. I don't like to think about Elsa, or what I survived under her. Unless Owen is committed to me, I don't want to bare myself like that to him. Even if I do decide to tell him some of it, there are parts of that tale I will never talk about.

Parts of it that need to die with me, and with Eddie.

Seeing Owen in the belly of the beast, how he reacted to his mother—how he deferred to her—gives me my best tactical advantage of how I can manipulate him.

Uh, *hello*, bastard.

He responds quite well to positive reinforcement. I learned that the day I met him.

I also want to see what buttons I might have to push when a little extra motivation is needed, as well as what triggers I need to avoid entirely so I don't trip an emotional IED and get my balls metaphorically blown off in the fallout.

Susa? That's easy, a no-brainer. I *know* what she wants. She's not coy at all when it comes to stating her case.

But I want Owen. He's my true endgame.

Susa's my ace-in-the-hole.

Except I have to get Owen *to* the hole before I can actually play it.

Thanks to Elandra and Austin, it looks like I'll easily be able to get what I want.

God help them if they try to fuck with my boy once he's well and truly *mine*. Because I *will* bring the wrath of the heavens down upon them.

Hell, I'll turn Susa loose on them. They'll never know what hit them.

Owen's special, malleable, willing, and open.

All I need to do is show him how good it can be and coax him into our arms—me and Susa.

First, though, I need to make sure I haven't been misreading his nonverbal cues all this time. Cues I'm sure he doesn't even realize he's throwing off.

The way he started getting doors for me and for Susa. The way he willingly takes care of both of us, without us even asking.

Despite us telling him he doesn't have to.

It makes him happy when we thank him, give him praise.

Hug him.

Snuggling with him on Susa's couch to watch TV, all three of us, it lights those gorgeous green eyes of his in a way I've never seen anyone glow before.

He loves and appreciates the simple things most people take for granted.

It makes me want to make him mine even more, mold his natural tendencies around me and Susa so he never wants to leave us, and then spend the rest of our lives together making each other happy.

Yeah, I'm a bastard, all right.

Ask me if I care what you think about me.

Using Susa's house for Owen's birthday weekend will logistically make everything so much easier on me. Not just for working with him, but hopefully allowing Owen to more readily open up to me without her around.

Having to share a bed with me.

Also might have been my idea for Susa to hold off on buying a bed for the guest room.

The potential to get Owen naked in the hot tub or pool doesn't escape me, either.

That Friday night, I treat it as a date. I take him out to a nice steakhouse and smile as he drinks his first rum and Coke— unbelievably, the first alcohol he's *ever* had. By the time we make it to the tap house later, he's adorably buzzed and happy, smiling in a way I usually only see him smile for Susa.

He's having fun, enjoying himself.

Yes, I played dirty and ordered several sampler flights for him. #sorrynotsorry

He's totally wasted by the time we return to Susa's. I help him undress and get into bed, and yes, it's soooo fucking tempting to go down on him right then and show him how good it could be between us.

But even this bastard has a limit. I refuse to take Owen's

consent from him. Even if he did consent right now, he's drunk and can't give informed consent.

Buuut...

That doesn't mean I can't sound him out, now that his defenses are down. I'd been looking at Doctor Who rings I found via an ad that popped up on Facebook. When we start talking, I set the laptop aside so I can give him my full attention. Besides, I'd love to put one of those rings on Owen's hand, except we're miles from that point.

Or...*are* we? I realize as we're talking that I have an easy way to direct the conversation exactly where I want it to go. "Well, we could talk about fantasies..."

And after finding out that, *hell* yeah, Owen *has* been actively fantasizing about Master and slave scenarios with Susa—with him as the slave—I grab my laptop again and pull up a couple of my favorite videos to show him.

The first is a FemDom scene, fairly tame, but Owen ends up shoving down his boxers, grabbing his cock, and stroking it.

I fight the urge to do a touchdown dance. When that clip ends, I switch it to a stricter male-male scene, and...*yeah.*

I've hit pay dirt.

"I bet you'd be a good boy for me, wouldn't you?" I ask, unable to decide if I want to stare at his eyes or stare at where he's stroking his gorgeous cock.

"Yes, sir."

I risk reaching over and stroking his blond hair. "I could teach you positions. Let you serve me. Teach Susa how to be a good Domme for you. Would you like that?"

He nods, unable to pull his gaze from the screen, where the scene continues playing. "Yes, sir."

I can't help it, but hey, I'm a bastard. I tightly grip his hair. "Then show me how much you'd like it, *boy. Come* for me. *Now.*"

After his cock explodes he promptly passes out, the sound of his soft snores making me chuckle.

Duuuude. He's fucking adorable. I can't help smiling as I press my lips to his forehead. "Happy birthday, boy," I whisper.

I get a wet washcloth from the master bathroom, and Owen doesn't even stir as I clean him up. It's tempting to lean in and suck his cock…

Too tempting.

A little taste, that's all.

I'm just *so* fucking lonely. I've tried to hold a wall in my heart against Susa, but it's slowly starting to crumble. I certainly haven't shown her all of me. I don't even know if she really wants *me*, or what she thinks I represent.

Someone *not* her daddy.

Besides…

She's not Owen, and *he* is the one who owns my heart. Hell, she could be gone at the end of the semester, for all I know.

I don't know her true loyalties. Not really.

Owen, however…

He's different. It's easier for me to map his heart and soul because in many ways, I know what he's feeling.

Except I know he's feeling it mostly for Susa.

I close my eyes and deeply inhale his scent as I slowly swirl my tongue around the head of his soft cock. Then I force myself to sit up and carefully tug the waistband of his boxers back into place.

I settle in bed next to him and pretend we just made love. I nuzzle my face in his hair and deeply inhale. Knowing I'm torturing myself, I grab my phone and tuck my head next to Owen's and snap a selfie of the two of us together.

The next day, I order the ring anyway. I don't care it's not a sure thing—I have hope.

For the first time in a long fucking time, I have genuine, deep hope.

Fuck me, I'm so screwed.

* * *

At least the night brings a breakthrough. From the next day on, I'm able to officially start training Owen as my willing submissive. Now it's only a matter of time before he's in my bed all the time, and in all ways. With Susa's help, Owen is quickly craving more, thriving on our attention and domination.

Until Susa accidentally triggers *me*.

It's less than a week after the new world order starts, on Friday night, and we're at Susa's.

She didn't mean to do it, I know she didn't. But if *I* can trigger that hard, god only knows how hard Owen could have triggered about that, or about something else we haven't even stumbled across yet.

We're sitting on the couch and Owen's standing in front of us. I'm paying attention to how Susa's working with him, and I'm carefully watching Owen for any sign he's about to freak out, so I can step in, if necessary. She orders him to finish stripping and he's nervous, I can see it.

"How do you feel right now, boy?" she asks.

"Nervous, Ma'am."

"Why?"

"Because I don't want to disappoint you, or Sir."

I hear Susa's sigh, likely part gentle exasperation, and part sadness that she's as gutted as I am about the emotional depths Owen's mother dragged him to. "Don't be stupid," she says, "you could never—"

"*Devotion*, boy. *Now*." I'm already standing and heading for the hallway, not even looking back once I see that Owen's dropped into the position. "*Susa*, a word. *Now*."

I don't wait. I hear her scrambling to follow me and once she's in her bedroom with me, I close the door and wheel on her. I struggle to keep my voice down.

"Don't you *ever* use that word with Owen in that way again.

Ever. Do I make myself clear?"

I harden my heart against her wide-eyed shock. "What? What'd I say?"

"You called him *stupid*." No, not directly, but I have no clue what triggers Owen might have. The last thing I need is Susa uttering one careless fucking word and sending Owen fearfully skittering away from us.

If it triggered *me* and it's been several goddamned years, I can only imagine what Owen's triggers might be.

"I-I'm sorry. I didn't even think—"

"That's right." I jab a finger at her as I let Sergeant Wilson take over. "You did *not* think. You have no *fucking* clue what a careless word might do to him. You promised to put Owen first, and that was *not* putting him first, *girl*. So let me make myself perfectly fucking clear—if I *ever* hear you say something like that to him, *ever* again, I will immediately take Owen and walk, and we're *done*. *Period*. No more play, no more sex, no more *friendship*. There are *no* second chances for this—this is your *only* warning. Do I make myself *perfectly* clear?"

Her eyes widen—in a different kind of fear, this time. I harden my heart even more when, for the first time, I see tears in Susa's eyes that I didn't put there from pain or play.

"I'm sorry, Sir."

"Do I make myself *perfectly* clear?" I repeat.

Her head bows. "Yes, Sir," she whispers.

"Do you understand what you did?"

She sniffles. "Yes, Sir."

"Then tell me what you did, *girl*."

"I used the wrong word."

"What happens if you do not speak more carefully to Owen in the future?"

"You'll immediately end things and leave with Owen."

"Eyes on me. Do you understand why I'm so upset?"

She lifts her head. "Yes, Sir."

No, she doesn't. Not really. She *can't*, because I haven't told her about Elsa and what I survived.

Frankly, that's none of her business.

I step closer, so she has to look up to meet my gaze. "This is *not* a game to me, Suse. This is *serious* fucking business. Owen's been through enough hell in his life. When he is with us, *nothing* we do can make him associate us with his mother and what that bitch did to him. Understand? I might spank him, or torture him, or make him hate me for what we put him through physically, but *nothing* I do will *ever* hurt his feelings or make him feel inferior. *Ever.* I will never engage in the bad kind of mindfucks with him, or belittle him. *Everything* I'm doing is designed with the ultimate goal of building him up, including his self-esteem.

"I *let* you play with him. Make no mistake—Owen is *mine* first, the way you're mine. Just like I will never let him do something I thought would harm you, I will not let you do anything to harm him. So let me hear you say it one more *fucking* time so I know you are perfectly *fucking* clear regarding my opinion of this."

She's choking back tears by the time I end my monologue.

Seems that I have finally found *the* thing that can break Susa, her weak point.

Owen's not used to succeeding. Or, at the very least, he's used to not being recognized when he succeeds.

Susa, on the other hand, is completely unfamiliar with failure. I am probably the first person in her life to talk to her like this or dress her down in this way, especially for actions that impact someone else who's more vulnerable than her.

The bastard extraordinaire notes it for future reference and exploitation.

I can barely hear her when she speaks. "I must be careful in how I speak to Owen. Nothing I say or do can make Owen feel bad, or feel like his mother makes him feel. Nothing I do can *harm* him. If I do it again..." She chokes up and I don't interrupt her while she's trying to compose herself. "If I do it again, you'll end things with me and leave and take Owen."

I let those words—*her* words—hang in the air for a moment so I know she's *really* processing what I said and not thinking I'm simply being an asshole.

Don't get me wrong. As much fun as we've had, and as much as I do consider her a friend already—and more—I mean *every* word.

Give me a fucking reason *not* to share him.

Except...I do care about Susa, and I *don't* want to lose her. Not only because of what she can do for Owen, or even because of how Owen feels about her.

But because I'm feeling things for her, too, and that fucking terrifies me.

I finally take a deep breath and let it out before I open my arms to her, and she practically climbs me in her desperation.

"I'm sorry, Sir," she tearfully says. "I'm so sorry."

I close my eyes and inhale, hold it, let it out.

Me, I want to say. *You triggered* me.

If I'm lucky, neither Susa nor Owen will ever need to know anything detailed about Elsa, or the kind of man Sarge used to be, other than Elsa was a bad life choice that didn't work out.

Understatement of fucking *ever*, but I'd rather not taint either of them with knowledge about Elsa and what she did to me, or what I did for her.

That's a clouded darkness that's foul and oily, rotted fish and backed up sewers. It's not the fun darkness Susa and I enjoy playing in, or where I'm slowly teaching Owen how to play.

Even more importantly, that it's okay for him to *want* to play there.

Play being the key word, in Owen's case.

I nuzzle the top of her head and kiss her there. I also gentle my tone when I speak. "Go clean up, sweetie, and blow your nose. We go out *together*. We do *not* tell him about this. *Period*. This is between you and me. Understand?"

"Yes, Sir." She looks up at me and I kiss her, a slow, sweet kiss to let her know everything is forgiven.

Stick, carrot.

I release her so she can go clean up and put herself together. Now alone, I stand by the bedroom door, leaning against it, my head tipped back, eyes closed.

What have I done?

Even though Susa doesn't know it—can*not* learn about it—a chink has appeared in the bastard's armor. One I'll have to carefully conceal from both of them.

Whether or not at some future point it'll allow a fatal wound to be struck in what's left of my soul remains to be seen.

When we return to the living room together, I sit on the floor next to Owen and praise him for obeying me by not moving, making sure I drop him all the way back into subspace before I allow him to go to Susa, where she sits on the couch.

I watch them together. As she folds her body over his, where he kneels in front of her with his head in her lap, I'm shocked at the jealous jolt that shoots through me when she speaks.

"Such a good boy," she softly says. "My *very* good boy."

It's not jealousy at her, for holding Owen.

It's jealousy that Owen can so easily access subspace and still trust her and relish in the freedom of giving himself to her ownership.

It's a trust that was burned out of my soul years ago, and fucking hell, do I miss it.

CHAPTER EIGHT

Susa and I move past that. Fortunately, Owen is none the wiser.

This is one of those incidents that will remain private between me and Susa.

Period.

Besides moving past it, Susa *shows* me in everything she does with and to Owen that she takes my warning very seriously. Not only because she's afraid to lose me, but because she truly cares about Owen.

Worse, she begins to regain and even increase *my* trust in her. I can honestly say I don't just love her, but I'm *in* love with her. To the point that I know we *have* to move forward to the next step.

It's time.

For once, time is on my side, and I've been able to take time to make time. Befriending Owen's father has paid off with him asking me that, if he bought Owen a ticket, did I think Owen would fly out for Owen's little brother's birthday?

I promise to do him one better—that Susa and I will bring Owen out ourselves.

Las.

Fucking.

Vegas.

It's *perfect.*

Even better, it means I can marry Susa before her father's any wiser. Fucking Florida and their three-day waiting period to get married. It's harder to get hitched than it is to buy a long gun.

Three days in Florida—especially in Hillsborough County— means three days that Senator Benchley Evans can find out a twenty-eight-year-old man is marrying his nineteen-year-old daughter.

Might not go over so well with the guy. In fact, I can pretty much guarantee it won't.

But she's a consenting adult, and this is my plan.

Don't get me wrong—Susa's beautiful, and absolutely I see myself spending the rest of my life with her. Otherwise, I wouldn't be doing this.

My plan, however, is for the *three* of us to spend our lives together. The fastest way to do that is to marry Susa, which we won't tell Owen about, for now. Meanwhile, we'll work with Owen to finally sever his last emotional tie to his thundercunt mother.

As soon as we return to Tampa, Susa and I will immediately step up Owen's training and his immersion with Susa both sexually and as a Mistress and slave. Because Owen will see we're the ones who faithfully and steadfastly stand beside him, take care of him.

Love him.

Catch him and hold him and protect him in his lowest, darkest times.

Us.

By the time I force him to choose us or his mother, he won't want to leave us.

Helloooo, Las Vegas.

* * *

I don't tell Owen about the trip until the night before. That's less time for him to stress. Since Susa and I are paying for the trip, he has no excuses to not go.

We fly out to Las Vegas on a Friday afternoon once classes end, and have dinner with Owen's father, step-mother, and the younger brother and sister he's never met. Hell, Owen hasn't seen his father in over eleven years.

After a very emotional talk at their home, where Owen finds out his mother has pretty much lied to him his entire life about everything, Susa and I take him back to the hotel, where the three of us share a bed. Only for sleeping that night, because Owen has emotionally hit rock-bottom now and needs us more than ever.

It kills me seeing him so upset, but this is the only way. His mother is a literal infection in his soul. It's a painful process, I know, but by cleaning it out for good he can start over and be stronger, healthier.

Happier.

Saturday morning, Susa and I, per the plan I outlined to her before we left Tampa, distract Owen in the most obvious and pleasurable way possible.

Orgasms.

It's the first time I allow Owen to go down on Susa, and he does so with gusto. I watch, a thread of jealousy winding through me that she gets to be with my boy in this way, but I rip it out and refuse to let it grow.

This is the way it *needs* to happen. I'll be able to freely love him soon enough.

After we drop Owen at his father's house for the party, with a promise that we'll be back in a few hours to have cake and then dinner, Susa and I go run our "errands."

I want to do some shopping while we're here. Tampa doesn't exactly have a lot of BDSM stores, and this *is* Sin City.

But first...

We have something else to take care of, and that's our first stop. Once we're standing in line in the clerk's office, I take a moment to breathe, reflect.

There is no going back, for me.

Susa's all in, obviously. She understands I'll own her and Owen, and that the plan is for us to bring Owen in as our permanent third for life.

Fortunately for me, Susa sees the benefits of having two guys in her bed every night, and understands that I'm bi and my ultimate goal is a sexual relationship with Owen.

Thankfully, Susa has a Kindle full of...well, fantasies she's about to make reality.

I watch her as we await our turn. Susa's beautiful, nervous.

Scared, but determined, because she wants this, is as hungry for our future as I am.

Looking even more beautiful because of it, in my mind. It makes my cock throb, to see how anxious she is standing in line at the clerk's office while waiting to file for our marriage license.

That she *lets* me see her vulnerable like this. The way I get to see Owen vulnerable.

That's so fucking sexy I don't even have the words for it.

This is the *real* woman, with all her barriers to the rest of the world stripped away.

This is the woman only Owen and I will ever get to see. Not even her precious daddy gets to see this side of Susa.

Everyone else will get Susannah Evans, attorney, or politician.

We get *her*.

Or, in Owen's case, *Her*.

But I mean every word—I'm only doing this once in my life. Once she's mine, Owen's mine. I know this with complete certainty or we wouldn't be standing here right now.

For this plan to work, I can't have Benchley Evans storming in and stopping things.

I need time.

I need her married to me, and then I can bring Owen in, and he's *mine*.

She's a woman of her word. Once we're married, I'm certain she won't back out. Especially once Sir's completely in charge. Once she's mine, I'm not letting her go.

She's my key to Owen.

Don't judge me. I've never lied about being a bastard extraordinaire. I learned at the feet of one of the best mindfuckers there is and, somehow, survived the experience.

Barely.

I was used and discarded, with no thoughts for my future, or Eddie's.

This is totally different. I not only plan on keeping Susa and Owen for life, I plan on dedicating my life to *their* happiness, *their* dreams. Because of them, I once again feel...*alive*.

Meeting Owen and Susa have restored a tiny bit of my faith in the human race. It's restored my ability to love, to *feel*.

To trust.

Unlike *her*, I do have empathy and plan on loving my two pets forever. I'm not in this for some sick game, getting my thrills solely from the manipulation aspect.

I'm in this for *life*.

When I marry Susa, I plan to uphold my vows, and I know she will, too. She's young in calendar age only. Susa is far more mature and knowledgeable about life than many women twice her age. We're going to be a marriage of three, even if the most silent partner is the one who will gain fame first.

Susa knows the plan and wants to enact it, stick with it, carry it through.

Once Owen is mine, life will be perfect. No one—not Benchley, not Elandra—will split us apart.

I won't let them.

It doesn't take long. We get our license, we buy rings...

And then an overweight Elvis marries us.

Hey, I let her pick which chapel.

As I stare down into her eyes while the organist plays "Viva Las Vegas," I can't help grinning. I savor the unfamiliar joy swelling inside me.

Because I've *done* it.

She's mine.

Now it's only a matter of time before Owen's mine, too.

* * *

My plan works, so far. A week after returning to Tampa, I claim Owen after revealing everything and giving him the choice to stay or leave.

He chooses us—meaning he understands he'll belong to *me*.

With that settled, it's time to start enacting part two, which is working toward our law degrees and getting Owen and Susa elected. I feel confident, maybe even a little cocky.

With them by my side, I know we're unstoppable.

Except...

All good plans have at least one downside. It's the give-and-take of life.

I saved three lives and nearly lost mine.

I lived out my fantasies in Germany, and nearly lost my soul.

I gained the man of my dreams—who's in love with my wife.

It is what it is.

Another downside is that I am *not* looking forward to explaining to Senator Benchley Evans that I am now his son-in-law. Doesn't mean I'm going to shy away from doing it. I know how I handle this will set a tone for the rest of our marriage between myself and Susa, myself and Benchley, as well as for the relationship Susa and I both have with Owen.

If it were up to me, I'd consider life perfect with my two pets and maintain the status quo—get our law degrees, go into practice together, and raise kids together, the three of us.

Unfortunately, that isn't going to come anywhere close to making one of my pets happy. Owen could live without politics if he's kept happy in other ways. I know this with all certainty. And Susa would agree to a life in the private sector if I asked it of her, but she would likely grow bitter and resentful over the years as she watched others achieve what she did not.

I'm a bastard, but I'm not an asshole.

Keeping Susa happy will keep Owen happy.

Keeping Owen happy is my priority.

That means politics are in our future, like it or not.

I'm not actually sure which news is going to piss Benchley Evans off more—that I am now his son-in-law, or that Susa and I both now sport *I*s on our voter registration cards.

I guess if he didn't want an independent-minded daughter, he shouldn't have raised her in his metaphorical spitting image.

We're on our way to Tallahassee for a weekend get-together the GOP is putting on for pre-law students. We've been married for less than a month, but finals are over for the semester, Owen and I are moved in with Susa, and we're going to have dinner with Susa's parents tonight at their house in Tallahassee.

There should be fireworks.

We're staying in a hotel, obviously.

I'm driving Susa's car. Owen remains quiet in the backseat as we drive north. Susa acts uncharacteristically nervous, sporadically chatty before sinking into sullen silences as she stares out the passenger window.

I am about to order her into the backseat with Owen to suck his cock and to put both of them in a better mood when Owen softly speaks.

"Maybe I should hang back at the hotel tonight."

I glance in the rearview mirror. "What's that?"

He finally meets my gaze. "Maybe this will be easier if I stay at the hotel."

Oh, no, he doesn't. If anything, having Owen there will help keep *me* focused.

But how to tell him that without looking weak in front of Susa? I settle on the easiest default. "No."

I return my focus to the highway. That should be the end of it, but Owen tries again a few minutes later.

"I don't want to cause trouble, Sir."

"You're *not* going to cause trouble," I tell him. "You're likely going to keep him from blowing up as much."

Susa snorts.

"*What* was that, pet?" Yes, I drop into full-on Master mode, without apology.

She's wearing an adorable smirk that makes me want to pull over right there and spank her, and then fuck her.

"Daddy is going to blow his top. I don't care if it's only you and me, or the three of us, or the entire goddamned Florida legislature standing there when it happens—it's going to happen."

"Is that going to be a problem for you, pet?"

"Not really. Not for me. I'm used to it. House and car are in my name, and he can't revoke the trust. I'm set until well after law school." I glance her way and realize her smile's faded. "I *am* worried about you guys, though. Well, mostly you. He'll probably ignore Owen."

"Me?" I ask. "What's he going to do to me?"

"Remember I told you about the ratfuck he pulled on that guy in Miami-Dade? Sanchez? If you have the slightest thing in your past, he could blow it up into a massive deal and make your future professional life…difficult. At least in Florida."

There's only one thing that could be used against me like that—besides Owen—and I know damn well those people aren't talking. Not without far greater risk to themselves than to me.

Besides, Benchley's reach might be great, but unless he has

contacts in Germany, they aren't even going to scratch the surface of my past. I left no proof anyone could leverage against me. Burner phones and texting apps that can't be traced back to me. No pictures—none that are compromising, anyway—and like hell would I ever admit any of it.

I was young and stupid, but not *that* stupid.

CHAPTER NINE

When we arrive at her parents' home in Tallahassee, Susa doesn't knock, she just opens the front door and ushers us inside, calling out to them.

"Momma? Daddy? We're here."

Poor Owen looks terrified, and I give his shoulder a quick squeeze before following Susa deeper into the house.

It's okay, because part of me feels terrified, too, but I'll never let it show.

Especially not in front of my pets.

Senator Benchley Evans rises to hug Susa as we enter the living room. My girl looks not quite as terrified as Owen does when she introduces us.

"Daddy, this is Carter Wilson and Owen Taylor. Guys, this is my father, Senator Benchley Evans." He's about my height and maybe two of me, a politician's gut on him. Fortunately, Susa seems to more closely resemble the woman who comes to join us.

I go for broke and hold out my hand. "Senator, it's a pleasure to meet you."

He shakes with me, but carefully eyes me as he does, trying to get a read on me. "Benchley."

Owen shakes with him, too. "Sir."

Benchley nods.

"And this is Momma," Susa says. "Momma, Carter, and Owen."

I smile and turn on the charm. "Ma'am." I kiss her hand, and Owen follows suit.

She smiles, delighted. "You boys can call me Michelle."

Benchley gave his daughter his blue eyes and his brass balls. "SusieJo talks an awful lot about you two boys," he says. "I hear you're all roommates, now, huh?" He chuckles. "Sponging off my daughter, are you?" His smile doesn't touch his eyes.

As Susa rejoins me and Owen, standing between us, I see Benchley's gaze focus on her left hand, then mine, on the rings we wear, and storm clouds quickly build in his eyes.

Busted.

That's fine. I wanted to do this sooner rather than later, anyway.

"Actually, I pay my own way," I say. "Between my disability pension and my scholarships. The truth is, Owen's *our* roommate." I drape my arm around Susa's shoulders. "We're married."

Ooooh, here we go.

Michelle frowns, obviously confused. "What—"

"*WHAT?*" Benchley thunders.

I'll give Susa all due credit. Owen is darn near cowering behind us now, but Susa straightens even as she presses herself against my side. "I'm registered as an Independent now, too. I've left the GOP."

It takes every ounce of will I have not to burst out laughing.

My girl is wicked smart. She just derailed her father's brain for a moment. Benchley stands there, *literally* with his mouth gaping open as he stares at her.

I couldn't be more proud of her in this moment if I tried.

Michelle finally finds her voice. "What do you *mean* you're *married?*" her words bear a shrill, sharp edge.

"What do you *mean* you *left* the GOP?" Benchley demands. "You *can't* do that!"

Michelle wheels on her husband and actually stomps her foot. "*Benchley*! Will you *please* focus? She fucking *married* him!"

Susa gasps. I've gathered from what she's told me about her parents that her mother, a retired college professor, wouldn't say *shit* if she had a mouthful of it. Susa got her mouth from her father, in addition to her cunning, political savvy, and cut-throat instincts. Her mom, however, is usually gentle, soft-spoken.

That her mother's dropped an F-bomb likely means she's the more dangerous of the two, at this moment.

"*When* did this *happen*?" Michelle demands.

"The weekend before I came up for the fundraiser," Susa admits. "We took Owen to Las Vegas to reunite with his father, and we did it there."

Her mom takes a step forward, but Benchley's hand shoots out and catches her arm. If the woman wants to take a shot at me—eh, with her fists—I'll stand there and take it like a man.

But I'm sure Benchley's mind is thinking that a) he'd rather be the one hitting me, and b) how horrible a 911 call to their house and Michelle being arrested for battery would look in the papers when he's eyeing his own run for governor, and beyond.

Benchley looks at Owen, then me. "You two—*out*. We want to talk to our daughter. *Alone*."

"No, Daddy," Susa says, stepping forward, her hands on her hips. "This happens with all of us, or none of us. Owen's our friend, and Carter's my husband. I don't need to explain my rationale to you."

"Oh, yeah, you kind of do, Susannah Joleen!" he roars.

Damn. I watch as she crosses her arms over her chest, a slow, sly smile filling her face, and I realize *this* is the future attorney, the future politician.

The future governor of the great state of Florida.

And *I* married her.

"Daddy," she says, her voice low and slow. "The trust is safe. Everything's owned by that. We're going to do a postnup after we pass the bar—"

"You didn't even sign a *fucking prenup*?"

But he doesn't rattle her in the slightest. She's apparently used to this side of Benchley Evans. "—*if* we feel we need it. I love Carter, and he loves me. I actually proposed to *him*. We're all registered as Independents now, we're going to work on running for lower offices first, then we're going to get Owen elected governor with me as his lieutenant."

"Over my *fucking dead body*!"

"That can be arranged, Daddy!" she roars back.

He flinches, as does Michelle.

Fair enough, because so do I, and I reach out to Owen to steady him, too.

I've never seen this side of Susa. *Fuck*, I didn't know she *had* this side. Apparently, neither did her parents.

I also realize I'm now uncomfortably erect, and don't dare reach down and adjust where my cock's painfully wedged against my fly at an angle that's pinching me.

Thank god I'm wearing jeans and not slacks.

Susa steps forward and jabs a finger at her father. "All my life, you raised me to be independent, to fearlessly go for what I wanted without apologies, and to find what makes me happy. Well, what I want is Carter, and to help Owen get elected, and get myself elected. *That's* what makes me happy.

"Now, I'm sorry I'm disappointing you and not staying with the GOP, but this isn't a shocker to you, admit it. I've told you plenty of times I'm not happy with them holding on to platform planks that try to limit women's healthcare rights and the right to choose. Not to mention the disturbing number of racists who seem to be congregating among their ranks. *Your* GOP is stuck in the

Dark Ages, Daddy, regardless of *your* personal beliefs. It was never *my* GOP. And you know I do not agree with the Democrats on more than a few of their fiscal and foreign policies.

"So *here's* the bottom line, Daddy—*deal* with it. I'm *not* divorcing him, I'm *not* getting an annulment. I'm nineteen, and you and Momma got married when you were both eighteen, and here you still are."

"We were *both* eighteen," he counters, "and neither of us had a pot to piss in. How do you know he's not going to divorce you or rob you blind?"

"Because he wanted a prenup to protect me," she lies, "and I said no. Everything we bring to this marriage is exempt from a divorce. I already checked." That last part is true, though.

I guess it shouldn't surprise me that she can so easily lie to her father, but it is a vital skill for a politician.

Maybe I misjudged my girl, underestimated her.

"Sir," I say, taking over as I reach out and touch Susa's shoulder, "I'm sorry this is such a shock, and happened so quickly. I take responsibility for that."

"Damn fucking *right* you will!" he roars.

"*Daddy.*" Susa's voice bears a dangerous edge that sounds like she's taken a page straight from Sarge's playbook. "Settle the fuck down, *right* now, or we're leaving."

Michelle gasps. "Don't you talk to your father like that!"

"Oh, I'm going to talk to the Senator like that," Susa says, meeting her father's glare head-on and without cringing. "If I was your son and came home with a wife, would you be acting like this?"

"If she was, what, ten years older than him and had no prenup? Probably, yeah."

"Then I guess if you wanted to make all my decisions for me, you shouldn't have raised me to be self-sufficient and given me the means with which to do it."

"So how much have you blown through of your trust, huh? Don't you come running to me when you run out of fucking money!"

She angrily yanks her phone out of her back pocket, opens an app, swipes to something, and jams it in his face. "You see that, Daddy? You see that fucking bank balance? What does it fucking say, hmm?"

His eyes widen. "What the *hell*?"

"What?" Michelle asks, stepping in to look.

I can't help it—I'm smirking, and use their distraction to reach down and finally adjust myself.

I know exactly why they're shocked, because when Susa showed me and explained it, I was pleasantly shocked, too.

"In case your math skills are rusty, Daddy, yes, I've actually *increased* the value of my trust by two *hundred thousand* dollars in the last six *months*. I did some research and made some excellent stock choices and then sold them. So I'd say I'm doing okay right now." She shuts the phone off and slides it back into her pocket. "And Carter doesn't get a say about that, either."

She's right. While we know each other's finances, one of my rules was that, for the two of us, the actual management of our money is a joint venture with the person whose account it is getting the final say. That excludes purchases. I have veto powers. Together, we support Owen. The other can veto what we feel is a poor decision that will cost money, but as far as smart investment to increase our savings, that's off-limits.

In fact, I've taken Susa's advice and started retooling my own savings and retirement accounts. Plus, the small retirement account we started for Owen is already making tiny gains. She obviously knows her stuff. If she wasn't going to be an attorney, I'd be urging her to think about becoming a stock broker or something.

Hey, I'm a bastard, but I'm not an idiot. I'm happy to admit Susa is an expert in this area, and both Owen and I are learning a lot from her. Instead of her going out and partying in high school, she spent it learning, researching, and building her trust, which her father gave her control of at age sixteen. It's part of the reason she was upset at Benchley for overruling her decision to live in a dorm this year. She'd been looking forward to a "normal" life, for a change.

Fortunately, it all worked out for the best.

Michelle is crying now. "Honey, can we *please* talk about this like adults?" She sends a withering glare my way. "*Alone?*"

"No."

"Are you pregnant?" Benchley asks, full-on death glare at me in progress.

"No, Daddy, I'm not pregnant. That's not going to be a problem."

I ignore the pang I feel over that but refuse to let my emotions show or give anything away.

"What about school?" Michelle has devolved into tearful pleading.

"I'm still going to school. We all agree that school is our priority."

"Then why did you *fucking* do *this*?" Benchley roars, back to thunder.

"Because time is never your friend, and it's never on your side," she softly says. "That's what you told me. And Nana always told me to take time to make time, or I'd regret it." She glances at me over her shoulder. "Carter's a decorated war vet. He nearly died saving his men. He wants to be an attorney, and he wants to help me get elected as governor."

"Then why did you quit the GOP? What the *hell* am I supposed to tell people…"

And…

And…

AND…

We stand there for the better part of thirty minutes with her parents repeatedly circling around the same issues.

Honestly? I'm not so sure that Benchley might be more upset about Susa switching party affiliation than he is about her getting married. As I read him, when she showed them her trust's bank balance, that seemed to mentally slide the man into a different track.

Michelle is still pleading with Susa to talk to them alone, and Susa's still refusing.

Finally, Benchley scrubs his face with his hands and sounds defeated. "If you were a *real* fucking man," he says to me, "you would have fucking called me and talked to me about this first."

Susa crosses her arms again, her voice returning to that drop-dead fucking sexy growl. "How many years did *you* spend in the Army, Daddy? How many car bombs did *you* throw yourself in front of to protect your men, hmm?"

His eyes widen, and I'm again simultaneously hard and trying not to burst out laughing. She's got him, and he fucking knows it.

She steps forward and actually forces the man back a step. "Don't you *ever* question his manhood again, *Senator*," she says. "Because he's got a Purple Heart and the scars to prove his bravery. Suck it up. *Both* of you. I love you, but this is *done*. Are we having dinner, or do we need to leave?"

I reach out and gently lay my hand on her shoulder and call my sweet little Hellhound back to my side.

"Susa," I say, "as you both are well aware, is very independent. I asked if she wanted to take more time and have a formal wedding, and she didn't want to waste the money on one. Now, I know this isn't perhaps how you envisioned gaining a son-in-law, but if it means anything, my parents have been married for over forty years, and I don't take my vows lightly."

"What do your parents think of this?" Benchley asks.

"They don't know yet. I wanted to wait until after we told you, which I wanted to do in person, when we both could be here."

"And what does your father do for a living?"

"He's a retired lieutenant colonel," I say. "Army. I have six brothers, all currently serving or retired, two of them killed in action while I was still in high school. I'm the youngest."

That softens Michelle a little. "I'm sorry for your loss."

"Thank you. I spent nearly eight years in," I add. "I always wanted to be an attorney. I'm not going to apologize for falling in love with Susa. We're lucky, and we know it."

Owen's spent this entire time silently standing there and feeling extremely uncomfortable, from the way his hands are shoved deep in the pockets of his slacks. I know this is a two-pronged issue for him, both the tenor and tone of the conversation, as well as the subject matter.

He has to pretend he's just Susa's friend, just my friend, not that he's in love with her and belongs to me and Susa.

Unfortunately, that's when Benchley finally focuses on Owen. "Well? Do *you* have anything to say?"

I tamp down my rage, but before I can move to defend him, Susa steps in front of Owen, her arms behind her to hold Owen in place. Back to the Hellhound growl. "Don't you *dare* attack him, Daddy. He's our friend, and he's our family."

"Family?"

"We've…adopted him," I say. "His mother's abusive, and I don't want him to jeopardize his scholarship by having to get a job. I can afford to pay his share of the bills, and yes, Susa can show you bank statements where I pay in to the household account. We asked Owen to move in with us because we love him. I'm loyal to the people I love, sir. Owen really helped take care of me this semester when I had trouble because of my pain."

"What are you, a junkie?" Benchley asks.

Susa launches another verbal fusillade, but I simply unbutton the top two buttons of my shirt and pull it and my undershirt off over my head in one movement before I turn.

Benchley falls silent mid-sentence, and Michelle loudly gasps.

When I turn back, I'm staring the man in his eyes before I pull my undershirt and shirt back on. "Had three guys shot in an ambush. Insurgents rolled a car bomb at us, and I threw myself on top of my guys to protect them."

That's not the full story, but it's as much as they or anyone else will ever get from me. "No, I'm not a junkie. I can't tolerate opioids, actually. So I live with my pain." I tuck my shirttails in. "I believe Susa asked you a question, sir."

They're still both trying to process what I know they just saw on my back. I hate going shirtless around people I don't know. I only tolerate shorts because while the backs of my legs are scarred, it doesn't look as dramatic as when seeing the wide swath of scars on my back.

Owen was the first person who got to see my back, other than medical personnel, since leaving the rehab center. Last year, I never took my shirt off around my roommate, at least not when he could see my back.

Susa sometimes lies in bed behind me, her fingers slowly tracing my scars, her lips following the contours. I won't deny that it is one of the things that melts me about her. The first time she saw my back, she didn't act horrified, or pretend it wasn't there. She treated me matter-of-factly.

As my lover and wife, she's shown me that my physical scars don't scare or repel her.

If only I could show her all of my emotional scars and be certain she would feel the same way.

Michelle's hugging herself again. "I'll go check the roast," she quietly says. "It should almost be done." She heads off to the kitchen.

Susa focuses on Benchley. "Truce, Daddy? I promise I'm getting my law degree. I'm going to make you proud of me, I swear."

I don't understand what nerve that strikes with him, but I see him flinch. "I've *always* been proud of you, SusieJo."

"Then please be proud of me now. Give Carter a chance." She smirks. "Hey, I ran a credit and background check on him, if that means anything."

He finally laughs. "Goddammit, honey." He finally opens his arms to her for a hug, but as he holds her, he's glaring at me.

He's not done with me yet, I'm sure.

That's fair, because the bastard extraordinaire is going to spend every opportunity I can get to find something I can use against him to get him to back the fuck off. Just because he's her father doesn't mean I won't ruin him if he pushes me too far.

Or if he tries to go after Owen.

CHAPTER TEN

Now

Benchley and Michelle are not handling waiting well. As Susa approaches her due date and we cut back all of our public appearances, they're over at our townhouse nearly every evening after work, and it's driving Susa crazy.

She's actually threatened to move in to the guest room at the Florida Governor's Mansion, if they don't back off. Meaning security would be there to keep them out.

Hey, my sweet little Hellhound is perfectly capable of dealing with her parents without my help. But Susa is their only child, and this is their only grandchild.

I can't blame them, but like hell will I contradict my pregnant and very emotional wife.

#bastardextraordinairenotidiotextraordinaire

Owen's actually stopped by tonight on his way home from the office, and he brought Chinese food with him because Susa asked him to stop and get it, knowing he'd be dropping by anyway.

Governor or not, our boy loves Susa, and like hell will he say no to the mother of his child.

The obstetrician we're using schedules us after-hours appointments, and we always make sure Owen is there and inside first, his security detail vehicles moved and not visible before we arrive. So far, no one's caught on.

If anyone does, we're prepared to defend our decision to have Owen there, up to and including revealing he's the baby's biological father, if we're forced to.

Hopefully we won't need to go to that length. The video loop of Owen breaking down as he gave his statement when her plane first went down humanized him to his state. They saw the distraught friend, not their governor.

I'll remind people of that, if we're ever questioned. It's no secret that Owen and I are best friends.

Susa hired a private Lamaze instructor who signed an NDA and came to the townhouse for our lessons so Owen could be a part of them.

Now it's just a matter of waiting for Petey to decide he wants to join us.

Of *course* our best-laid plans go to fucking shit. I'm out of the office and on the other side of town on a Wednesday afternoon at meetings with lawmakers from all over the state when I get a 911 text from Dray on my work phone.

I immediately excuse myself and leave the room to call his personal cell from nine.

"What's wrong?"

He's laughing. "Um, well, Governor Taylor literally just carried your wife downstairs, and we're getting into a car to go to the hospital. Her water broke while we were in his office and they were on a conference call with Governor Forrester of Tennessee. He says congratulations, by the way."

I hear her yell, "*Give* me that," and then she's on the line. "Can you *please* order *someone* to let me walk?"

I laugh. "*No.* Give Dray his phone back, pet. I'll meet you at the hospital."

She grumbles, but hands Dray the phone, because he's back.

"Do you want me to stop by your place and the mansion and grab clothes for all three of you? He literally scooped her up in his arms and carried her out to the elevator when it happened, so...*yeah*."

He doesn't need to draw me a picture. "Yes, please. Our go-bag is right inside the front door at the townhouse. I know Owen has one, too, ask him where it is. Meet us there."

"Yes, sir."

I dash back inside. "Sorry, gentlemen," I say as I dump all my shit into my laptop bag, "but I'm leaving. I'm about to become a dad." I grin as the room erupts in applause and cheers.

It takes me about twenty minutes to reach the hospital, and they quickly get me checked in and where I need to be. Someone's given Owen scrubs to wear, and Susa's in a hospital gown. He's sitting in the hospital bed, behind her, letting her squeeze his hands as she breathes through a contraction.

When he sees me, he starts to move but I shake my head. "You stay right there," I tell him as I start rolling up my sleeves and loosening my tie. I lean in and kiss her. "How are you, sweetheart?"

She glares at me as she growls, and I laugh. "Okay, then," I say.

One of the nurses starts to talk to Owen, apparently realizes who, exactly, he is, and then turns to me. "Um...did you want to switch places with Governor Taylor?"

"No," I say as I remove my tie and toss it onto my laptop bag. "I'm having a really bad pain day myself," I lie. "She needs him there." I pull a chair next to the bed and sit there, one arm on Owen's leg, my other hand holding Susa's hand. "Breathe, sweetheart."

She starts crying. "Don't let them make him leave," she tearfully begs. "I need you guys, *please*."

I look at the nurse. "You heard the lieutenant governor. Let's get him a wristband, too, please? He's family. He's the baby's godfather."

She nods. "I'll see what I can do."

Dray appears with our bags, and I point to him. "Take him with you," I tell her.

"What'd I do?" Dray jokes as he sets the bags down.

"Governor needs a wristband, too." I hold my hand up to show him the one they gave me, which matches Susa's and our arriving son's, once he's given one. "See that he gets one."

"Yes, sir." He follows the nurse out of the room.

I know he'll do it or die trying. With that handled, I focus on my two pets again. Owen looks at me, and I see the tears in his eyes.

"*Thank you, Sir*," he silently mouths.

I squeeze his leg, long and hard, in reply.

* * *

Susa's labor goes on into the night. Benchley and Michelle are more than a little miffed that Susa wants Owen in there and won't let them in, but when she angrily snaps at both of them over the phone that she doesn't want them standing around and staring at her vagina, I think that changes Benchley's mind.

If they're going to argue why she's okay with Owen seeing her, they don't bring it up now.

I'm sure I'll hear about it later, though.

That's fine.

For now, we're doing all we can to help her through this. She gets into and out of bed, but now the staff has been told about my pain. I've changed into comfortable shorts and left my shirt off long enough that everyone could get a really good look at my scars.

Now they all seem to understand why, when Susa moves back into the bed, I'm happy to have Owen there instead of me.

It's in the early morning hours when we finally hit the

homestretch and they have her start pushing. Owen and I are flanking her, our arms behind her and holding her hands as she bears down. Finally, she gives one more push, accompanied by bone-crushing squeezes from her hands and a loud cry of her own before she slumps back against us.

And we hear our son cry.

We both lean in, kissing her, each other, not giving a shit in this moment who sees us. Dray and Gregory have stayed with us, filming and taking pictures for us with our cell phones.

This is for *us*. We'll take a picture for the public later.

"Dad," the doctor says. "Did you want to cut the cord?"

I look Owen in the eyes. "Go cut the cord, Owen," I softly tell him.

He's really crying now, and yeah, fuck, so am I. "Really?"

I nod. "Really."

He does, returning to us and me pulling him in, all three of us, our foreheads touching as we cry.

This is a literal damn *miracle*. Compounded, in many ways.

Like fucking *hell* am I excluding him from a second of this in any way. I don't care how I'll have to spin it later—this is his soul on the line. His happiness.

This is one of the few times, for now, that we'll be able to freely and openly love our husband.

And if any word of this gets out? Well, we *are* attorneys. We will *own* this motherfucking hospital with a HIPAA lawsuit.

They bring Petey over to us and lay him on Susa's chest, and fuck, we're all crying again. He has Owen's eyes and a downy, dark fuzz of hair on his head.

We ask Benchley and Michelle to wait until daylight, at least, to come over, that we'll hold off posting any pictures or releasing official statements until they've met their grandson, and they finally agree. I'll Skype with mine once it's daylight and I know they're awake.

We haven't decided how to handle Owen's parents yet. They'll drive up tomorrow, because Susa and I are like adopted kids to them, but I'm leaving the decision to tell them the full truth up to Owen.

I actually hope he does, because I think it would help his soul to have someone else besides Dray and Gregory who knows this secret. I know they wouldn't tell.

I would tell Benchley if I didn't honestly worry he might use it against me somehow.

As the craziness dies down over the next hour or so, and Dray and Gregory leave, it's finally just the four of us for a few minutes. Susa's been holding Petey and trying to get me to hold him, but I waited.

I wearily drag myself to my feet and get my cell phone ready. My lie about my pain levels really isn't a lie anymore, but I'm not going to complain considering Susa just pushed a seven-pound five-ounce baby out of her body, and, oh yeah, survived a fucking *plane crash*.

"Owen," I quietly say, "hold your son."

I won't get many chances to say things like that to him.

I *need* for him to have *this*. I *need* a few things to be firsts for *him*, *not* me.

There will be another goddamned media circus surrounding us for a while.

I need my boy's soul soothed *now*, while I can.

I need to put *him* first.

I *need* to know he's going to be okay, because I won't hesitate to sacrifice everything to make sure he is, even if it means publicly revealing the truth about Petey's parentage to heal Owen's spirit.

I can now add *father* to the list of things I am, but Owen is still *mine*.

I need him to understand that does not change, and never will change.

Susa hands Petey off to Owen, and I take pictures, then switch to video. "Welcome to the world, Peter Benchley Taylor Wilson. Smile for Daddy, Petey."

Owen's blinking back tears as he stares down at his son. "Hey, buddy," he whispers. "Welcome to the world. Love you so much."

Sure, we'll take some public-friendly video later of "Uncle Owen" holding him, but like I said, this is for *us*. For *our* family.

As much as we can behind closed doors, our son will know Owen as one of his fathers, not as "just" an uncle, like one of our brothers.

And you can better believe that, from this day forward, I will make sure Owen gets to spend at least a little time with him every day, as long as he's in town. Because this is a dream come true for me, too. A day I never thought I'd ever see.

I had no idea how much I *needed* this miracle until he was here, with us, in the flesh.

To see my boy holding *our* son.

I feel like I can finally take a deep breath again. Like maybe the bastard and Sarge can finally…go away. At least for now.

I end the video and walk around the bed so I can stand between Owen and Susa and take a selfie of the four of us together. Then I take one of me and Owen, our heads together and staring at our son.

And Susa smiles as she takes the phone from me and snaps a picture of me kissing my boy as he holds our son. I do the same for her.

I know I will spend hours privately smiling over these pictures, and will turn to them when alone, especially if I have to be away from Tallahassee.

These pictures will always remind me of what's important.

Of *who's* important.

For the first time in my adult life, I finally understand what inner peace feels like.

CHAPTER ELEVEN

Now

It's October, almost one year before the general election that will hopefully put Susa in the Florida Governor's Mansion. It's been an eventful three years both personally and professionally. We've seen our state through a major hurricane, enacted important education and gun reform, and other items that have helped our state and its residents.

And we're also now the parents to Thomas Gerard Taylor Wilson—Tommy.

One of the tasks we need to complete by the end of this third year of Owen's second term is narrowing down the field of lieutenant governor candidates for Susa's run next year. I know it's early, but I want them thoroughly vetted.

Yes, I'm asking Benchley's help for this. In fact, before we even sit down to talk with any potential candidates, I've run the list past Benchley for his perusal to make sure he doesn't have any dirt on them. That eliminates three candidates from our short-list almost immediately. One for a domestic violence 911 call in another state, but which was never prosecuted because his wife refused to testify, one for irregularities on a campaign finance disclosure form during a county commission race, and one who it turns out has three different mistresses, in addition to his wife.

When I find out that it's obvious his wife has no clue about the mistresses, I ratfuck the bastard myself, dropping an FYI call to one of my favorite reporters at the *Orlando Herald*. They take only a week of tailing the guy to get compromising pictures of him with another woman.

Who wasn't one of the three Benchley already knew about.

The good news is, the man's not *our* problem.

Personally, I'm really gravitating toward Ethan Hamilton. He's an Independent, and has spent two terms in the Florida House after two terms as a county commissioner in Sarasota County. Thirty-six, single, divorced—amicably, by all counts—and no kids.

He's reported to be a nice guy, has an MBA, worked his way through college before going to work for a commercial real estate company.

Even better, the guy's not bad-looking at all. Reminds me of Owen, in many ways. Hot, but doesn't come off like he even has a clue he knows it. Self-effacing, friendly smile, the kind of guy you wouldn't mind having a beer with after work, and he'd likely make you feel like he really does want to be there with you. Big, hazel eyes, expressive.

I assign Dray and Gregory the job of having dinner with him while Hamilton's in Tallahassee, to get a feel for him before we officially approach him with any kind of an offer. If I personally meet with the man at this point, everyone will be looking hard at him.

If Dray and Gregory don't sign off on him, knowing us as well as they do, then we won't even bother taking things further and he'll be quietly crossed off the list.

I have no interest in people talking behind their hands about why someone didn't make the list if we don't select them early on. Once it's closer to the time to file for the primaries, sure, people would expect us to have a short-list.

But whoever we pick, I want that person to be someone hungry for the job, someone who will use what we've done with Owen's two terms to carry through Susa's two terms and then continue during their own terms.

Someone who will not try to undercut Susa at every turn. Someone who will have her six and work *for* her, *with* her. Someone who will understand he needs to wait his turn, and, in return, we'll help him get elected.

We're talking political *dynasty* kind of stuff.

We have the momentum, and I want to put as many safeguards in place to keep our work living on past our term in office. It'd mean nearly a quarter of a *century* of our plan helping our state.

Our trick of placing the lieutenant on the ballot rubbed off on our opponents for Owen's re-election run, and all of the GOP candidates, and most of the Dems, had their lieutenants listed during the primary.

Which backfired on two candidates, one from each party, when it turned out the lieutenants had problems with their financial disclosure forms, weaknesses their opponents ruthlessly exploited in campaign ads.

I knew we wouldn't be able to hold that particular advantage in that election, but it really didn't matter because I think everyone pretty much expected Owen to win after what Susa went through.

The day after Dray and Gregory have dinner with Hamilton, Dray comes to my office that afternoon and shuts the door.

I sit back. "Well?"

Dray drops into one of the chairs in front of my desk and slowly nods. "I really like him."

"What'd Gregory think?"

"He likes him, too."

"So he makes the short list?"

Draymond Garcia is a handsome mixed Latinx. He has gorgeous green eyes a different shade than Owen's. They're even more striking with his flawless, dark brown skin. He's six-five, and while not as muscular as Owen, he's still imposing in his own way. He's carefully studied me, and his brother, how we carried ourselves, and I've seen the skilled lawyer's persona change and grow over the years we've worked together.

I am flattered and honored that he mimics me, and it frustrates the shit out of Susa that he's mastered both my smirk and arched eyebrows.

And that he will rat her out for panty infractions in a heartbeat.

I know the man is a sadist, and that he and Gregory have a relationship not unlike the one I do with my pets.

But Dray turns that gaze on me now. "He *is* the list," he quietly says.

I turn that over in my mind. Like me, Dray enjoys being the power behind the throne, and he's proven himself—and his loyalty—to us all over the past eight years, and even before now. He has no desire to be elected. He'd much rather be working in the shadows. How do I know he's loyal?

His brother, Samuel, is one of the three, along with Trent and Eddie.

I *literally* could call Dray to help me dispose of a body, and I know he'd pick up shovels and lime on the way, along with lattes and some Xanax to help us out and keep us calm.

I settle back in my chair and motion for him to continue. Even Benchley admires him and tried to hire him away from us for one of his friends who wanted to run for state Senate.

"He's *it*," Dray insists. "His background and financials all check out. I talked to people who've worked with him personally, and they say he's a nice guy. He's got the look, he matches us on platform and message, and he's *solid*."

"Keep going." I know there's more, and that he's leading with his pitch just proves it to me.

"He's eager to run Independent, and he said he'll happily be lieutenant for eight, then run and keep our initiatives going."

"And?"

"Gregory can be his chief. He can do it."

I let the silence lay there for a moment before I finally say it. "So how big is his cock? And I'm assuming he's a bottom?"

He tries not to smile, I'll give him credit for that. Finally, he throws back his head and laughs before looking me in the eye. "He'll keep *all* our secrets, Chief. I personally guarantee it."

I think about it for a moment. For Dray to succeed, I have to let go. He's good, he's talented, he's smart as fuck, and he's driven.

He's *hungry*.

"Run another background check, *deep* background, just to be sure. Run it past Benchley again. As long as there's nothing there worse than a parking ticket, then we'll take it to Susa and let her sign off on him."

He stands and leans in to shake hands with me. "Thanks, Chief."

I don't release him immediately. "Remember—you're *personally* guaranteeing him. I'm trusting you, Susa's trusting you, and Owen's trusting you."

He nods. "He's going to be governor eight years from now."

"Okay."

Once I'm alone, I chuckle. I know what Gregory and Dray did last night.

They did Hamilton.

CHAPTER TWELVE

Then

I've developed a habit over the years of picking up stray bits of info and storing them away for digesting later. Sometimes for use immediately, sometimes in the distant future.

One such stray nugget is gleaned from a cocktail party at the start of our second year at the Tampa law firm.

Susa is working another section of the room, as she always does, while Owen and I stand pretty much in a corner, because it's where I feel most comfortable, so my back's not to the room or the door. It's also where poor introvert Owen feels most at ease.

Right then, the biggest thing on my plate is figuring out how to gain Benchley's support and public endorsement for Owen's upcoming county commission run. It's still too early to file, and we don't want to signal too far ahead and give people advanced notice.

Despite Susa's best efforts to talk the bastard into endorsing Owen, Benchley is still sitting on the fence, irrationally hung up over the *I* on Owen's voter ID card. But I know if Benchley throws his weight behind Owen, we would win. The likely GOP candidate, the incumbent, is pretty much despised now. There's no way a Democrat, unless they're a racist drunk, could lose in an even match, but it would be close. Running the past numbers, however, I spot a trend.

If we run a fiscally conservative platform and hammer Owen's opponents hard over infrastructure, including traffic, storm water drainage, storm prep, and school performance, Owen could split the vote enough to capture the swing voters who don't stay loyal to either party.

The incumbent has just barely survived an audit over spending county funds to redecorate his office to the tune of eighty grand, and paying auto expenses for what turns out to be his wife's personal car. He claims it was miscommunication with staff and filling out the wrong forms, he reimbursed the county, and then it dies out in the onslaught of more pressing news both locally and nationally.

Still, he's likely going to be turfed out in the primary, but it'll be a bloody fight in the process.

However...if Benchley weighs in and supports Owen in the primary, it would sweep in enough GOP votes from people disgusted with the incumbent so as to give Owen a huge boost. Since we have a closed primary state, it also means we'll have a tactical advantage if several GOP candidates run for the incumbent's seat in the primary, splitting local party support across several candidates.

If I can get Benchley to support Owen, or even get him to sway the local party to pull their support from the incumbent and put it behind Owen as a protest—exactly the kind of statement that Benchley enjoys making—that would be the first stepping stone to getting Susa elected Governor.

Even Benchley would have to admit that.

I use events like tonight's cocktail party to network and bounce ideas off people. Also, to introduce Owen around. He tends to do well at these kinds of events, especially if I'm there. It allows people to meet him in a more relaxed, one-on-one kind of setting. I need him to learn how to have an "on" mode in public. He's getting there, but this is why I have to slowly build his tolerance. Thanks to his bitch of a mother, I not only have to teach him how to be "on," I'm having to deprogram the negative feedback he heard most of his life following some sort of event like this. He was used to blending in and remaining hidden in plain sight. Susa and I have to teach him how to draw the good kind of attention onto himself.

There's a few bigwigs from local politics in attendance tonight, including Kelly Fortuno, an elderly man who was a two-term Hillsborough county commissioner, a two-term Tampa city commissioner, a two-term Tampa mayor, and who now sits on the county's planning and zoning committee.

Years ago, he also worked as a deputy county administrator under one Benchley Evans. So of course he feels it appropriate tonight to regale me with hysterical stories of my wife's childhood. Considering the guy is in his late seventies, I go with it, laughing where appropriate.

"Yeah, sometimes I even went camping with them." He shakes his head. "Wasn't there that one weekend, though."

It was currently myself, Owen, and Kelly in our tight little group. "What weekend?" I ask, my antennae twitching with the hint of something juicy, even perhaps at Susa's expense.

"When that guy shot himself." He scowls, his brow furrowing as he tries to remember the details. "Oh, what was his name. Morgan something-or-other. Head of public works, at the time. City of Tampa, not county."

He glances around and leans in closer, dropping his voice. "Guess he got a girl pregnant." He leans out, nodding knowingly. "*Young* girl." He keeps nodding. "Teenager. And he was a *married* man. Well, married until his wife took their kid and divorced the sonofabitch."

Anger flares through me and I quickly school it, keeping my voice calm, I hope. "I hadn't heard any of that." I wonder if there's something from Susa's past that she hasn't revealed to us. As far as I know, she's never been molested or assaulted.

Except by me, and that was consensual.

"Oh, Susa might not even remember it. Probably not. She wasn't even ten when it happened, I don't think. Confessed in his suicide note about what he'd done. Guess he forced himself on the girl. I'm talking young teenager. She had the baby, if I remember correctly. He would have gone to jail for it, that's for sure, if he hadn't saved the state the cost of a trial."

I want to know more but am frustrated by one of the senior partners walking up to talk to Kelly. Owen arches an eyebrow at me as I pull out my phone and quickly type a note to myself with details about what Kelly told us. I'll have to research it later.

Yes, I have a good memory, but I'm not an idiot.

If for no other reason I want to talk to Susa and ask, for my own peace of mind, if she'd ever been victimized by the creep.

In fact, I've almost forgotten about it by the time the three of us finally get out of there two hours later. Owen is driving tonight, and I turn in the passenger seat to glance back at Susa.

"Guy we talked to tonight, Kelly Fortuno. Said he used to go camping with you and your dad sometimes."

Her brow wrinkles. "I think so. Why?"

"He started to tell us an interesting story, but we got interrupted. About a guy who killed himself one time while you all were camping. Do you remember that?"

Her eyes widen. "Oh, my god. I haven't thought about that in years."

"So it did happen?"

"Yeah. Why?"

"What was the guy's name? The guy who killed himself."

"Wheedon. Martin Wheedon, I think."

"Morgan?"

"Yeah, that's it. Morgan Wheedon. Why?"

I've already pulled my phone out and am adding info to my original note. "He said the guy got a teenaged girl pregnant."

"*What?*"

I look back at her. "Yeah."

She stares out the window for a long moment, an uncomfortable tightness filling my gut. This started out more as a marriage of convenience for me, but don't get me wrong—I would kill or die for either of them. I meant my vows to her, and to Owen. Owen might be first in my heart, but I quickly came to love Susa, too. The thought that something like that might have happened to her at such a vulnerable age makes me sick and angry.

"Pet?"

"I'm...thinking, Sir." But she doesn't look away from the window.

I give her the time she needs and a few minutes later, she turns back to me. "I'm wondering if that was Rebecca."

"Rebecca Soliz Martin?" I ask.

"Yes, Sir." She apparently doesn't realize she's dropped into full-on pet mode, and I'm not about to tell her, either. "She stopped going camping with us a few months before he killed himself."

"Did he ever molest you?"

"No, Sir. Fortunately, that's one experience I never had. I think people were too afraid of Daddy. I mean, I had boys get handsy in school every so often, but nothing I couldn't handle. Why?"

Relief fills me. On my phone, I'm already running a web search for the guy's name, and it takes me no time to hit pay-dirt. "I was just curious. You know me, I hear something, I want to research it. So who did you talk to tonight? Anything juicy to report?"

I let her go on about her discussions while I'm staring at a *very* interesting color photo that was run with one of the newspaper stories about the man's suicide. Rebecca wasn't named, but the investigation into man's death was quickly closed as an obvious suicide because of the note and the "young victim's" age and situation.

Morgan Wheedon was recently divorced, had light blue eyes, pale skin and freckles, and hair so red he could be one of the Weasleys from Harry Potter.

* * *

Because I can't leave this alone, I do more digging over the next couple of weeks, until an interesting puzzle starts to untwine itself before me. I have to make sure I don't disturb any hornets' nests in the process, but when I go to visit Doris Norman at her nursing home, I take flowers, pastries, and some other gifts I hope the woman enjoys. I haven't seen her in several months and feel a little guilty that I haven't been visiting her with Susa.

But only a little.

I wouldn't be a bastard extraordinaire if I let something like a little guilt slow me down, much less stop me.

She's eighty-two and David Norman's widow, in addition to having worked as Benchley's receptionist during his tenure as county administrator and county commissioner. From that time period, she probably knows where quite a few bodies are buried.

I used to think that was just a metaphorical expression, but now I'm not so sure.

Mentally, the woman is still sharp, even if her frail body fails her. She has severe osteoporosis and has broken her hip twice in falls, along with a heart condition, and she can't live independently anymore.

We have a lovely visit. I wait until the end, when I know she's exhausted, to bring it up, after I pull my cell phone out and glance at the time before propping it up on its end on my thigh.

"Ran into Kelly Fortuno the other night at a cocktail party, and he said to tell you hello."

"Oh, isn't that lovely? I always did like him."

"You know, he mentioned something about a camping trip years ago. Someone killed himself, but for the *life* of me now, I can't remember the guy's name."

"Oh, you mean Morgan Wheedon. *Phhpt.* Good riddance. They did everyone a favor by putting one in his skull."

"'They'?"

She looks around as if to make sure we're alone—which, of course we are, since she has one of those little private apartment suites—before she drops her voice. "Benchley, David, and Chris took care of *that* worthless, perverted sonofabitch." She nods at me before sitting back in her recliner.

Benchley is the only one left alive from that list of names, that much I know. David and Chris were older than Benchley. Both men died mostly natural deaths, if you count, respectively, lung cancer from smoking and liver cancer from drinking as "natural."

"'Took care' of him?"

She nods. "Helped him along, so to speak. He raped that girl and she got pregnant. When she told her daddy who did it, he immediately told Benchley."

"Her father is Edward, right?" I interrupt, but wanting it out there.

She nods again. "Right. Edward, Benchley, Chris, and David were all good friends. Benchley told Edward not to call the cops, and to let them handle it." She smiles. "And they did."

"Did they, now?"

"Yep. They got him drunk, forced him to write the note, and shot him with his own gun. Benchley pulled the trigger while Chris and David held him. Made it look like a suicide. Poor Rebecca, she had to go live at her aunt's house in Orlando for a long time when she had that baby. Missed almost a whole year of school. They told everyone she went overseas to study. When she married John Martin, he adopted her son. The boy must have been six or seven by then."

"How come I never heard about any of this before?" I don't try to bullshit her too much. She's still sharp for her age, and I've pushed the envelope already. She's tired and she likes me and she likes talking *to* me. She also loves Susa.

I doubt had I come right out and asked her about all of this at the beginning of our visit that she would have admitted it.

#yesImabastard

"He was a rapist," she says with venom so fierce her words could almost dissolve flesh. "No one missed him. His ex-wife and daughter were better off without him. Wasn't the first bastard he sired with a teenager, either, but the other girls before Rebecca were older and, somehow, he skated through. Sonofabitch probably would have gone after Susa next, if they hadn't stopped him. The city wanted the story to go away, didn't want people to know they had someone like that on staff, so they had their city attorney talk to the sheriff and medical examiner up where it happened to get the death certificate signed and the case closed in just a couple of days." She mimes wiping her hands. "Nice and tidy."

"How did Benchley know they'd get away with it?"

"Because of Susa. She used to share a tent with Rebecca on their camping trips. Benchley bought a new, bigger tent so he could put Susa in there with him. Had a divider in it, like two rooms. Susa told the deputies Benchley was in the tent with her when she heard the gunshot, and Chris and David, of course, vouched for each other, because they were sharing a tent. The new tent was David's idea. Susa liked to sleep in her own tent, so Benchley needed a way to make sure she could vouch for him. Benchley pretended he didn't know anything about Rebecca being pregnant, or what Morgan did, when Benchley invited him to go camping with them that weekend. Told Morgan he'd heard about a job opening up at the county, and wanted to talk about it with him that weekend."

"So Benchley lured him there?"

She shrugs. "Call it what you will. I say it saved taxpayers the cost of a trial. Between the suicide note, Rebecca's statement to police corroborating the facts about the rape, and Susa saying her dad was in the tent with her, police wrote it off as a suicide. Case closed. No reason to suspect otherwise."

"When did you find out the truth?"

"Oh, I suspected for years. David finally confessed it to me after he got sick the last time and we knew he wasn't going to make it." She sadly smiled. "Bless his heart, he asked me if it made him a horrible person, and I told him no, he was my hero. Always had been."

I reach for the box of tissues on her coffee table and hand it to her so she can dab her tears.

"I miss him so much," she softly says.

"I'm sorry, Doris. Of course you do. I didn't mean to dredge up bad memories. I'm sorry."

"No, it's okay." She sighs. "He really was my hero." She shakes her head. "Told me Benchley asked the bastard if he'd touched Susa, and the guy swore he hadn't."

"Did Benchley believe him?"

"Yeah. They all did. But he confessed to the other girls he'd been with, some of them not much older than Susa." Her expression hardened. "David told me he was convinced Susa would have been in his sights if they hadn't taken the guy out. Definitely would have been other victims. Man was *sick*. Guess his wife was only seventeen when he married her, and that was because she got pregnant. He was twenty-nine at the time, and her father told Morgan he would marry her, or he'd file charges against him."

I decide to turn the mood around. "I'm shocked Benchley didn't hire a hit man for me."

She smiles. "He's not fond of you, but he sees how much Susa loves you. I think that's why you're still alive. Still, might not want to go camping with him."

I chuckle. "Had enough of roughing it in the Army, thanks…"

By the time I leave a short while later, I have her laughing and smiling again.

And as I sit in my car and watch the video playback on my phone of Doris telling the story of how Benchley, Chris, and David murdered Morgan, I smile.

This is my fulcrum on which to balance a lever plenty long enough to allow me to play Archimedes to Benchley's immoveable stone that forms his loyalty to the GOP.

CHAPTER THIRTEEN

Then

Two days after my lovely little chat with Doris, I'm driving to Brandon that afternoon when Susa and Owen assume I'm still in depositions for a case.

I didn't lie to them. I simply blocked out extra time on my calendar and didn't tell them I wasn't at the deposition.

I *would* be lying, however, if I said part of me isn't relishing this confrontation with Benchley. We both have similar goals—get Susa elected governor. But I need to get Owen elected first, because I refuse to allow Susa to run on the GOP ticket, either.

Benchley will, of course, argue that she should simply register GOP, problem solved, and she can ride on his coattails.

Except...no. Because that would sink her into the morass of dark money pouring in over the transom with little way to control it or even vet it properly.

I don't want that.

Not for her, and definitely not for Owen. Despite being Benchley Evans' daughter, Susa has scruples and integrity she must have inherited from her mother. While Owen's secret dream was to be governor, Susa's secret dream is to make a name for herself.

The best way to do that is run her as an Independent instead of GOP.

Also, it's a way for me to give a *fuck you* to Benchley, success outside his precious party.

What intrigues me even more is what will I find as I dig deeper into Benchley's past? How many other *literal* bodies might I uncover as I start exploring?

Right *now*, I need to let Benchley know I have this info. It's a tricky balance, though. Could go either way. If I over-play my hand, he might decide to retaliate in ways that can't even be traced to him. Benchley is as much of a bastard as I am. More, even, because he has money, power, and a history in county and state government.

I want to tweak him just enough to force him to reluctantly do my bidding, and yet allow him to still lie to himself that it's his idea.

I meet with Benchley at their Brandon house while Michelle is out. In fact, I set up the appointment yesterday so he could send her out, allowing us to talk in private. Probably for the best. Michelle only tolerates me because she knows her daughter's happy. I hold no illusions that she "likes" me.

She wants to wring my neck with her own hands for how I married Susa.

I'm sure Benchley is wondering what this meeting is about, and maybe he even privately hopes I'm coming to offer him some sort of buyout deal in exchange for divorcing Susa.

Okay, the way I worded my request to meet with him—keeping it secret from Susa, implicating it's to do with Susa, and wasn't a meeting I really wanted to have but knew I had to—*might* have led him to think that.

#yesImabastard

"What's this about?" Benchley asks once we've settled in his home office.

I waste no time metaphorically smashing his hopeful expectations that I want money in exchange for a divorce or annulment. "Tell me about Morgan Wheedon."

He's good, but not better than I am. I catch the twitch in his left eye. "Who?"

I melodramatically sigh and save us at least ten minutes of his bullshit and bluster by pulling out my phone and playing the video for him. When it ends, I return the phone to my shirt pocket, where it sticks up, just a little.

"Yes, I've backed it up in multiple places, Benchley. And yes, I've taken precautions. Anything happens to me, this and other stuff ends up all over the place."

He glares at me even as he's reappraising me. It takes him the better part of five minutes to speak, and I wait him out. "What do you want?"

I smile and lace my hands behind my head. "I want you to publicly support and endorse Owen's county commission run for your old seat. As a senior member of the state GOP, I want your *official* endorsement for his run as an Independent. I want you to twist arms and put bugs in ears and call in favors. I want every applicable ratfuck you've got used to his benefit. I want you campaigning for him, showing up at town halls to introduce him, shaking hands and filming endorsement ads. I want the local branch of the GOP to support Owen, *not* the GOP incumbent or any of the other primary candidates. I'm talking from the *primary* on, not just in the general."

His gaze narrows. "You're insane. How's that going to look?"

"The incumbent is a dirty shithead, and you know it. How's it going to look if I start stirring up ghosts and Susa puts together the fact that you used her as your alibi to murder that guy?"

"You'll destroy her chances to be elected governor if you do that!"

I shrug. "Won't hurt Owen's chances, though."

Lesli Richardson

His eyes widen. "You'd throw her under the bus *just* to get me out of the way?"

I smile. "In a heartbeat."

"Wheedon was a rapist!"

"And Susa might be cutthroat, but she also has very strong ethics. Her father or not, she'd still go to the police with this evidence, even at the cost of her own political aspirations, and you damn well know it. So you're going to go along with our plan. You're going to help us get Owen elected to the county commission as an Independent. Then, in four years, he's going to run for state Senate, for what will then be *your* old seat, and you're going to endorse him there, too. From the primary on."

He's literally slack-jawed. "You're fucking serious!"

"Damn right I am. Just because Susa's my wife doesn't mean I won't fuck you over. You're a pain in my ass, until I know you're going to do what I tell you to do. Would you rather be sitting in jail and knowing I not only put you there, but that I own your daughter's affections? Or would you rather keep your freedom? You're an attorney. I don't need to tell you that there's no statute of limitation on premeditated murder."

"I can't endorse an Independent for my Senate seat!"

"What do you care? You're term-limited out now and will have already moved on. After one term as a state senator, Owen's going to file to run for governor, with Susa running as his lieutenant governor. Play your cards right, it'll be at the end of your second term as governor." I pause. "Or, you can be doing time in Starke by then. Your choice."

He sits back in his office chair and stares at me for several long, silent minutes. "You're a crazy fucking bastard," he finally says. "You know that?"

I grin. "Yeah, I've been called worse, though. I take that as a compliment." I let my smile fade. "I put myself between a car bomb and three of my guys. *You* don't fucking scare me, and you

112

never have."

He rocks back in his chair as he reappraises me. "Why not run him for a House seat instead of Senate? That guy in your district is term-limited out, too, and there really isn't anyone good to run in his place."

"Because that Senate seat was *your* seat. *Your* endorsement and active support will have more impact that way, especially later on. You were popular, had good poll numbers. It's going to be lost to a Democrat this time around, anyway. It'll be a GOP bloodbath in the primary, when they frag each other trying to win it, and it'll stay blue next time around when they do the same shit again."

"Bull*fucking*shit, it'll flip blue this time!"

I slowly shake my head. "I've already run the numbers, Benchley. You won the seat because of your strong Hillsborough county ties, and the bulk of the voters in that district are within the county limits. They remembered your name. This county traditionally trends liberal in voting, and you damn well know that, too. Between a heavily split GOP primary field shredding each other, and the Dems only putting forth one candidate in their primary, you're going to have a populace who will be happy to check the box under the Democrat rather than any of the GOP assholes.

"Your endorsement of *any* of the GOP candidates will not only be lost in the blood mist of them eviscerating each other during primaries, it'll cheapen your reputation. Especially if your primary candidate loses. Your best bet is to not endorse *any* of them and sit this election out. Means your future endorsement of Owen, an Independent, will be even more powerful. Doubly so if you're serious about running for governor. Means you're serious about bringing people together and working for unity across the aisle, not just tribal partisan politics.

"Then you can run for a second term as governor, endorse Owen for his state Senate run at the same time, and when you're term-limited out, Owen will run for governor and you, the incumbent, will endorse him. Again, it looks good, a GOP bigwig endorsing an Independent? Must mean you know some serious shit about the GOP candidate, if you won't endorse them. It's what you *won't* say that will have as much impact in those races as what you *do* say. Add to that fact Susa will be Owen's lieutenant, and no one with half a brain will question why you've endorsed him for governor. You'll have people tripping over themselves sucking up to you, thinking you can get them access to Owen through Susa."

He stares at me for a long, angry silence, his lips pressed in a tight, thin line.

He knows I'm right. Maybe he was in denial, or hoping he could pull a miracle out of his ass, who knows?

He's already run the numbers but didn't realize I had, too, *and* that I see the writing on the wall far better than most pols do. Having someone he despises as much as me put it all out there means he can't ignore the facts any longer.

The moment he breaks he slumps in his chair and blows out a long breath. "Fuck you, Carter," he grumbles.

"I take it we have a deal?"

He scrubs his face with his hands. "Yeah, fine. *Fuck.*"

"You know I'm right about this. Consider it a karma chip." I stand, pulling my phone from my pocket like I'm checking the time. "This works out perfectly. You're governor for two terms. If you don't fuck up, that is. Then we slide Owen in for two terms, followed by Susa. Think about *that*. Twenty-four *years* of solid influence in Tallahassee, if you count two terms for each of you. With both you and Owen stumping for Susa, she's guaranteed the win no matter who runs against her. Meanwhile, you run for national office, if you want."

I smile. "*There's* your legacy, Benchley, and one you can be damned proud of. First father-daughter governors. Add in Owen, and it's a true political dynasty the Bushes and Kennedys would kill to emulate. Plus, Susa wants to go national after two terms in Tallahassee."

"What's she going to run for first? Before Owen runs for governor?"

"I'm probably going to put her in for a term in the state House after Owen runs for the state Senate. Meanwhile, she's going to be building lots of connections. She won't need to waste time running for a bunch of lower offices before her gubernatorial run if she's already spent eight years as lieutenant governor, and has both her father's endorsement as well as Owen's. Your buddies will back her, Independent or not, because they'll know you can deliver juice to them."

"That's a lot of ifs, Carter."

I shrug. "Call me an optimist."

"There's a lot of things I'd call you," he darkly says, "but an optimist isn't one of them."

I head for the door. "I know you wish she'd married Owen, but let me tell you something." I turn. "If she had, you could pretty much forget about her being elected to *any* office. Admit it—you know damn well you wouldn't have supported her over a stronger male GOP candidate, your daughter or not."

He looks like he'd rather punch me, but he finally nods, and I continue. "The *only* way this works is the way we've set it up." I tip him a two-fingered salute from my temple. "You're welcome."

I smile as I close his office door behind me. As I show myself out, I hit the *stop* button on the video camera, where I'd been recording our meeting from right after I played him the video.

Stupid fuck.

I don't give a fuck how pissed off he is at me. All that matters is he's agreed to go along with the plan. I won't tell Owen about this, and I won't tell Susa.

It'll be our little secret.

Granted, had Wheedon not been a repeated child rapist, I might have turned Benchley in myself to get him out of my fucking hair and ratfuck the GOP by painting them with the same brush, but this is better.

Much better.

This is something I can use to our benefit.

It means Owen's nearly guaranteed to win and, officer of the court or not, I don't have to hurt Susa, or her chances for political office, by turning her father in for premeditated murder.

All I have to do is keep Owen moving forward and doing what we tell him to do.

In retrospect, I sometimes wonder, despite how outlandish I know the thought is, if Benchley's heart attack a mere three weeks before the general election was his own kind of *fuck you* to me. Because Michelle forced him to retire from politics at the end of his Senate term.

Doesn't matter. News about his heart attack might have even gained us a few sympathy votes. Owen wins the general by twenty-two points, biggest win any Independent candidate has ever managed in any Hillsborough County Commission race.

I suppose a better man might wonder if the extra stress and work I heaped on Benchley by pressuring him to stump for Owen contributed in some way to his heart attack.

But I am not, and have never claimed to be, a better man.

I am *absolutely* a bastard.

Benchley will never know how much of one.

Hopefully, neither will Susa or Owen.

CHAPTER FOURTEEN

Before the Bastard…

I am nineteen and turned loose for the first time in a foreign country as an adult. I am back in Germany, finally, and damned glad to be here. My German isn't fantastic, but I speak it better than many of the other soldiers, mostly because I learned it as a kid. Certainly better than any of my brothers' German. I lived here for four years, and still remember a lot.

There are things that fourteen-year-old me learned hints of while living here before, as a military brat, but couldn't investigate before we moved back to the States at the end of Dad's hitch here.

Partly because of my age and lack of freedom back then, and partly because of my fear of my parents—especially my father—finding out. I had no clue who might have known me through my older brothers, of which, at that time, I had three stationed here.

Now, I'm an adult.

And I wanted to know all those things previously denied to me *now*.

I don't understand why I'm so drawn to this lifestyle. I wasn't abused by my parents while growing up. We were disciplined, yeah, but Mom never had to spank us. We were just…terrified of her. Maybe Park or Charlie might have been, but they were already teenagers when I was born.

By the time Mom got to me, she had keeping order with her six other sons down to a science.

And we were all scared she might bring Dad into the mix, when he was home and not on deployment.

I hated scrubbing toilets and floors, and would do anything to avoid that punishment. Our homes might have been crowded and definitely not expensive, especially if we lived on-base somewhere, but they were always clean and tidy.

And we *always* felt loved. Our birthdays were always recognized, we spent as many holidays as possible together, when everyone was home. And while my older brothers might have teased each other or me, god help anyone that tried to fuck with one of our brothers. The Wilson boys would dogpile the motherfucker. We were a force of nature.

Mom and Dad made time every day for each of us individually, even if only a few minutes, to sit with us and talk to us about our day. Meals were family time, with everyone sitting down and talking. When Dad was home, we did morning PT with him, and when he wasn't, it was Park or Charlie, or sometimes Gene, who led us on a morning run from when I was old enough to keep up. Every day, regardless of weather, before school.

It was funny that Dad was willing to go easy on us in that regard, but Mom insisted on it. Said it was the only way to help us burn off the excess energy. As an adult and Army soldier, yeah, now I can see her point. It was a way to help keep us in line, a routine for us.

As my brothers started leaving home for college and, later, enlisting, our numbers grew smaller, but Mom and the rest of us kept up the routines. As many of us could gather together did so for holidays.

It devastated all of us to lose Pete and Tom, but I think I took it even harder than my other brothers, because they'd been the next youngest to me. Tom was only two years older than me, and Pete was four. By then I knew I did not want to enlist, definitely didn't want to make it my career, but knew I needed to. It'd be the only way to keep the peace in my family. It would have been seen as an insult to their memories to not enlist.

Not going in never crossed my mind, so I rebelled the only way I felt I could, by going straight in from high school and not doing ROTC and college first.

I didn't want to be an officer. I wanted to get in, earn enough for college, and get out and be *done.*

Tonight, I have a forty-eight hour pass and money in my pocket when I walk in the nightclub. I know Jace isn't in Germany this month. He's off in Italy or some shit. Gene is back in the States for three months. Dad's currently stationed in the States, too, even though due to his command he frequently travels over here and spends weeks at a time.

No one to stumble across who's actually related to me.

No one even knows I'm here. My best buds, Gohber and Kenney, they tried to get me to go out with them tonight, but the shit they want to go do is stuff me and my friends did after school when I was fourteen and living here.

I *need* to do this tonight.

This nightclub is far enough from the base that I'm not completely concerned about running into someone. It has the rep I'm looking for, and at this point, if I run into someone here who knows me, they're likely here for the same thing I am. That means they'll hopefully take a *don't ask, don't tell* approach, or risk their own extracurricular activities being exposed.

There's only so much porn a guy can wank to before he needs to feel the real thing. I know three things for certain about myself—I'm most likely bi, even though I've never had an actual sexual experience with a guy, I'm apparently attractive to women, and I apparently need a dominant woman to really enjoy myself in bed.

The five girls I slept with between high school and now wanted me to take charge in bed, and…that's just *not* doing it for me. The only way I got over with any of them was imagining them taking charge of *me*.

The nightclub is located in a three-story warehouse in an industrial area that looks deserted this time of night. No sign to advertise its presence, but you can feel the bass thumping through the walls from inside nearly half a block away. You need to know you're looking for it to find it. This isn't the kind of establishment you randomly stumble across when looking for a tourist-friendly *Biergarten*.

This is the kind of nightclub that caters to a certain specialized…clientele.

Which is why it's located where it is.

The music is some sort of EDM electronica shit that I couldn't care less about. The drinks aren't too pricey, and the ambience is concrete industrial neon grunge with a touch of leather and latex. Think if IKEA finally hit rock-bottom after coming down from a three-day meth high, and you're close.

But all of this *why* I'm here. I joined a website for kinky people and found a local discussion group nestled within its electronic walls. I don't participate on that website—I do nothing but lurk from the browser of a burner phone I bought specifically for this purpose.

But this club's been mentioned plenty of times.

There are people from all walks of life and all age ranges, dressed in everything from black jeans to full-on latex and leather dresses and corsets. I catch a few interested glances from women as I make my way across the main space on the lower floor to the bar, but I'm not interested in most of the women I see, no matter how gorgeous some of them are. Besides, once they get close enough to spot the chain collar I locked around my neck just before paying my cover charge and entering the club, they turn and walk away.

That's fine. I'm looking for a particular type of woman.

The type of woman I'm looking for likely won't hesitate to approach me, and will likely approach me *because* of the collar.

I grab a soda and, after showing my red wristband to the bouncer at the base of the stairs to prove I paid the extra cover charge and know what I want, I make my way upstairs. I also know from my research that's where the real fun can be found.

The particular wristband I'm wearing will actually get me up to the third floor.

The place is a little on the warm side, and a haze of cigarette and vaping smoke creates interesting patterns in the lights. Up here, there's an actual live DJ playing different music from downstairs, better music, and apparently reading the energy of the space based on how he's studying people from his raised perch in a corner near the stairs.

There are seating areas up here, black vinyl couches and ottomans sprinkled here and there, and low tables. Curtains hanging from the ceiling and folding, free-standing screens create temporary and flowing spaces and prevent someone standing at floor level from seeing straight through to the far side of the huge space.

Up here, people are wearing more in some cases—full-on latex body suits, leather gimp suits complete with hoods. Or less, in other cases—rope chest harnesses, bustiers without an undershirt on, leaving nipples exposed, or the occasional man in a jock and hood and wrist and ankle cuffs.

And nothing else.

I'm more interested in getting a look at the women who are with the lesser-dressed men. There are some gay couples in attendance, but they're in the minority, and that's not really my jam. Although I have already considered contacting a male Top as a possibility, if I can't hook up with a woman. Not to sound like an asshole, but I *know* I can get laid.

What I think I *really* need, but I won't know for sure until it happens, is to get spanked.

And what I also don't know is how long I'll be here in Germany before I'm shipped out to a combat deployment.

As I take all this in, my cock thickens and hardens, and I fight the urge to wildly plunge into the space. I know I need to scope things out first. I might not even meet anyone here tonight, but at least now I know I have found the right place and can return accordingly.

It's still early in the evening, just barely eight. That it's already so busy bodes well. The group on the website said this Friday would be particularly busy earlier than usual because of a couple of Dominatrixes who'd be showing up tonight.

It's going to be a demonstration, of sorts.

A rhythmic thudding noise strikes my ear, just under the music. I slowly wind my way around the outer perimeter of the space and follow the noises until I realize I need to make my way inside the maze. I follow the sounds to one curtained "room" and see a woman flogging another woman on an X-shaped frame I know from my research is called a St. Andrew's cross.

Hellooo.

My cock has gone from interested to a painfully raging hard-on.

This is *definitely* the right place.

Wanting an unobstructed view of their scene, I move around the people gathering to watch. The woman on the cross is dressed only in a G-string, and there's a tidy pile of clothes on the floor next to the cross. Her brown hair is pulled up off her back into a messy bun, which reveals the leather collar buckled around her neck. Leather cuffs around her wrists are clipped to rings on the uprights of the cross.

The woman doing the flogging wears a leather corset, a short leather skirt, and knee-high leather boots with three-inch heels. She's tall to start with, probably five-ten, at least, in addition to the heels. Her long, red hair hangs down almost to the middle of her back, and her tight clothes don't leave much to the imagination in terms of her body. She's fucking gorgeous, the leather hugging her slender curves.

I can't tell how old either woman is from my vantage point, but I'm nearly desperate to have a chance to talk to the Dominatrix after they finish. That means I stay right where I am and hope I get my chance. She uses a variety of implements on the woman's back, ass, and legs, from floggers to canes. They're speaking German, and while my high-school German didn't cover sexy-time situations, I can understand most of what they're saying, and what I don't sort of makes it through with the context.

As I watch the scene, I find myself wanting to drop to my knees, and I haven't even gotten a good look at the Dominatrix's face. But I have a mind full of memories and porn and really want a chance to make some of that come true. I don't know how, yet, but I'm hoping she'd be willing to help me out with that.

The commanding tone the Dominatrix uses while topping the woman has hardened my cock to a painfully erect level I've honestly never felt before.

They're almost done when I feel the hand on my shoulder, startling me.

"You look...interested," she says in German. Her icy blue gaze pierces straight through me and makes my cock throb even more. She has long, jet-black hair braided down her back and is clad in a black latex corset and latex skirt.

I nod. "*Ja.*"

Her gaze narrows and carefully looks me up and down before she switches to English. "You're American?"

I nervously nod. "How did you know?"

When the toe of her patent leather stiletto pump touches my right sneaker, my cock twitches. "Those are worn," she says. "Can't buy that brand here, except at the PX, and you've had them a while. I work with a lot of Americans."

"Oh."

She cocks her head as she looks at me, studying me. "Army?"

I nod.

"How old are you?"

"Nineteen."

A slow smile spreads across her face, making me shiver. "First time at a place like this?"

"Yes, ma'am."

She touches the collar around my neck with one perfectly lacquered finger. "Does that belong to anyone in particular?"

"No, ma'am."

She looks at my wristband, her gaze narrowing a little. She wears the same wristband.

There's a bag at her feet, a small rolling suitcase, like a carryon size, black. She points at it. "Bring that." Then she turns and walks away.

It takes me a second to realize that was an order, and I scramble to comply, grabbing the suitcase's handle as I scurry along behind her.

Like hell am I going to say no.

This is my dream come true, and losing Pete and Tom taught me early that life is short, sometimes brutally so.

That means I need to make as much of this life as I can, while I can.

And I plan to.

CHAPTER FIFTEEN

Now, Four Weeks Until the Gubernatorial Primary

When I first met Owen and Susa, I would've told you the three worst days of my life were, starting with the first-place tie, the days I learned my brothers died, followed by that day in the desert, when I threw my body over my men and I nearly died. The day of the school shooting later became a close contender.

Later, that worst-day designator also became tied with the day I received the phone call that Susa's plane went down.

Everything in my life is placed in context to those events.

I'm alive.

My wife is alive.

My husband—and I consider Owen my husband, even if he isn't in name or legal standing—is alive.

Our children are alive.

We're all reasonably healthy.

I would, without hesitation, lay my life on the line to protect any of my loved ones.

So when the next hit comes, four weeks before Susa's primary election in her run for governor, it literally catches me off-guard and threatens to destroy everything we've worked so goddamned hard for.

And it's from *my* fucking past.

A past I'd assumed dead, buried, and living only within my nightmares.

Even though my job is in Tallahassee, at Owen's side, I still have ongoing work for the Tampa law firm, which means time spent down there, on occasion. I hate the times I have to travel alone to Tampa for work, because it means I literally can't reach out and touch those I love while I'm away from them. I can't walk into Owen's office and lock the door.

I can't walk into Susa's and do the same.

I can't go home and hold our sons.

I have to sleep alone, which I rarely have to do anymore.

Sleeping alone is nearly always accompanied by nightmares. Owen's busy running the state, and Susa's busy with her work and the campaign, which means I have to go alone.

I definitely was *not* prepared to receive a terse phone call from my father-in-law, asking me to stop by their Brandon house that afternoon.

As in, he wants me there ASAP, even though he doesn't couch it in those terms.

He doesn't need to. I can speak subtext as well as the next politico. Since he never summons me like this, I have a really bad suspicion I need to get it over with quickly. I didn't even realize they were in Tampa this week—I thought he was up at their Tallahassee home.

I excuse myself and head there to find him alone at the house.

"Where's Michelle?" I ask after he lets me in and gives me a quick handshake in greeting.

"Out. I sent her on a grocery run. You're welcome." He's leading me through the house to his office.

Those last two words fill me with growing dread. "Why? What happened?"

No reason to beat around the bush or engage in time-wasting

bullshit. Whatever this is must be worse than bad, and likely has something to do with Susa's campaign for governor. Benchley's been in the game longer than I have and wouldn't call me over like this for something petty or stupid.

It must be something serious that threatens what we've built.

Don't get me wrong—I hold no illusions that my father-in-law views me more as an adversary than family. But he tolerates me because I've proven myself and my love for Susa and our boys.

Also, since that tape I have on him has never so much as leaked, he knows I'm a man of my word. We have never spoken of that day since it happened, but we both know it's still there, and it has guided the path of our relationship ever since.

After he closes and locks the office door behind us, I sit in one of the chairs in front of his desk and he takes his seat behind it, before leveling a dark glare at me.

No preamble. "Tell me about Germany."

"What?" Although my mind is already pivoting, heading there, skimming through everything and quickly zeroing in on what I hope he's not talking about but already suspect he is.

There's a tablet on his desk. He punches the home button to wake it up and quickly swipes through to something, then hands it over for me to read.

It's an e-mail.

Interesting information to share about your son-in-law. I'm sure you wouldn't want anyone to find out about it. Had a unique "relationship" with him for a while in Germany years ago. Let's talk. I need a few things, and I'm sure a gentleman such as yourself can supply them.

I'm positive it's sent from a throwaway e-mail account. While the e-mail isn't signed, I already know who it's from just from the wording.

Goddamn that bitch.

Ancient, murderous rage and seething hatred course through me. Yet I'm careful not to show any emotion. I don't know for *sure* if the e-mail is from her, no matter what my gut tells me. I find it hard to believe she wouldn't approach me directly with a demand considering our history together, and I doubt it's Eddie. He'd contact me directly if he wanted to fuck me over.

But considering I saved Eddie's life, and what else we survived together, I'm nearly certain it's not him.

At least, I *hope* it's not him.

If it *is* him, we have far worse problems than I thought.

It's most likely her, or someone who knows her, and who is trying to leverage that knowledge against what they feel is a vulnerable soft spot.

I return the tablet to him. "I take it you haven't responded?"

"Do I *look* stupid, son?" He switches it off and sits back. "Well?"

I lean back in my chair and lace my fingers together behind my head. "Well, what?"

"Don't leave me blindsided."

"Why? What are you thinking of doing?"

"Well, I'm not paying them, if that's your first concern." He points at his face and circles his finger. "Again, *not* stupid."

"Then what are you suggesting?"

"For starters, you tell me what the *fuck*. Secondly, I hope your passport is in order."

"Why?"

"Because your ass is going to Germany to personally handle whatever this is. Tomorrow."

I'm careful not to give anything away. "If they're in Germany."

"It originated from there."

That catches me by surprise, and I frown. "How do you know that?"

"Because I already ran the info past a... Let's just call them a friend of mine." He smiles. "I'm old, but—again—*not* stupid. I'm also connected. No, I didn't send him the text, only the headers. The person who sent it didn't disguise their actual IP address, they just created a throwaway account. No attempt to hide who they were beyond the e-mail account."

"I thought you didn't know much about technology."

He smirks. "After my last *experience* with you, I educated myself. Especially since I had time to spare stuck in a bed after my heart attack."

"Ah."

"I rarely repeat the same mistakes twice, son." He slides a piece of paper across the desk to me. He's already tracked down the flat address...and her name.

Fuck.

He's earned that point, and I'll graciously concede it to him.

I feel a small measure of relief that it's not Eddie, though.

I sigh as I fold the paper in my hand and crease it, slip it into my shirt pocket to deal with later.

"I assume from the look on your face you know who this bitch is?" He sounds all too satisfied with himself.

I'm not used to being at a loss for words. No doubt in my mind now that it's her. There is no other way Benchley could have connected her to me, unless the e-mail is from her.

I guess my ass is going to Germany.

I slowly nod.

I guarandamntee you, there will be at least two unhappy people in Germany upon my arrival there. Me, for starters.

And most assuredly *her.*

* * *

When you leave the past firmly in the past, the last thing you expect is for it to rise up, smack you in the goddamned balls, and risk it fucking up not only the present that you've so carefully constructed, but the comfortable future you anticipate, as well.

I always knew my father-in-law was a bastard, too, I just didn't know how much we truly had in common. Although it took over forty years for our paths to mirror each other.

Before I leave to return to the Tampa office, Benchley's already made several phone calls with a throwaway cell phone, using Signal to further mask his trail, and he's put a basic plan in place to give me what I've asked for to make this go away.

Funded the...mission.

Because as far as I'm concerned, this *is* a covert ops mission.

One in which I plan on terminating my target with extreme prejudice.

He sits back. "I'm guessing you have one or two contacts of your own there still?"

I slowly nod. "I do."

"They can help you?"

"They can." I'm going to have to make a similar call to Eddie, but I need my own burner phone with Signal enabled, and don't have one with me. Didn't think I'd need one. While I would normally call Eddie with my personal phone, I would prefer no trace to me on this one, if I can avoid it. Although I can come up with a public-friendly cover story without much effort, if forced to do so.

"I want this handled, Carter," Benchley says with more grim determination than I've ever seen him possess. "I don't give a shit *how* it's handled, as long as the loose end is tied up in a way it can *never* unknot itself." He stares at me. "Am I making myself clear? I'm cashing in that karma chip for you, like it or not."

He's finally speaking the unspoken.

I nod.

"That money is from a Caymanian account," he continues. "Untraceable. If you need more, you'll have to let me know."

"I won't need more." The money he's given me is plenty. I know Eddie will be happy with the boon. It's not nearly enough to make up to him for the past and broken promises, but he won't turn it down, I'm sure.

Benchley nods.

"We done?" I ask.

"You need a plane ticket."

"I'll book it shortly. I need to…make arrangements."

He harshly laughs. "You mean set up your alibi."

"Fuck you, Benchley." For over twenty years I've wanted to say that to him. I knew I had him by the balls, but I didn't want to press my luck.

This is as good a time as any to finally be able to say it.

I know he won't expose his daughter over this. Not now, not this close to her goal. Plus, my level of bastardism is far more advanced than his. Early on, I was willing to sacrifice Susa's political career for Owen's, but now that she's so close to finally getting elected, Benchley will do anything to protect her chances.

He smirks. "You have balls, I'll give you that." His smile fades. "Don't think I don't know those boys are his. Question is, did *you* know it, or did you plan it?"

I wasn't expecting that left-field question. He's expecting to rattle me, take advantage of his brief advantage over me, but it won't work.

"Does it really matter?" I ask.

"It does to me."

"I'm listed as their father on their birth certificates."

"No one in my family or yours has eyes that shade of green." He's trying to stare me down now.

I take a slow, deep breath and don't blink. "Making allegations like that is beneath you, Benchley. Ask me to my face what you've been dying to know and get it over with. You've still got balls, don't you?"

"I believe I just asked." He smirks. "She did well marrying you."

"Thank you."

He relaxes in his chair. "Owen doesn't make a move without you telling him first. At events, he's always glancing around, looking for you if you aren't there at his side." He studies me. "When I chewed her out over marrying you, she made a comment about not worrying about her getting pregnant accidentally, because it wasn't an option. I remember her saying it again that day in the car, after we met with Rebecca. I didn't pay much attention to that, back then. I thought she was being young and stupid. You had a vasectomy before you met her, though, didn't you?"

"Yep."

"What happened to the doctor records about your vasectomy?"

"Only one other person knows about that besides Susa and Owen." Technically two, but like hell will I fucking give him that much info. As far as he knows, Eddie is one of the three, just like Dray's brother.

"Who?" he asks. I lift an eyebrow and he groans. "Fuck me. Does she have proof?"

"No. I had it done there under a fake name and paid cash."

He grumbles, unhappy, but knows there's nothing left to play on that particular line. "So was it IVF? Do I have to hunt down a doctor's office to pay off people to delete records? Or did it happen the old-fashioned way?"

I meet his gaze head-on. "Like you said, my boy doesn't do *anything* without me telling him to." I let that rest for a beat. "Neither does my girl." Hopefully that shuts him down.

His eyebrows lift. "Ah." He slowly nods. "That explains a lot. So it's that way, then?"

"Yep. Is that a problem? Because it seems like I've proven myself and my love for both of them over the years."

"Nope. Just been wanting to know." He levels a finger at me as a smile creases his face. "You're good, though. *Damn* good. I give you every bit of credit for that. Not so much as a *squeak* from anyone in the capitol. You run a tight ship."

"Of course I do." I pick at a crease on my slacks, tug it back into place.

"Until now."

Rage I haven't felt in years is simmering over this hiccup. "I'll take care of it."

"Awfully careless of you."

"It wasn't supposed to be. I can assure you, there isn't anything else like this out there, either."

"Except you three. And now two boys to protect, as well."

"We're a team. We're going to get her elected."

"You can't guarantee that."

"Can't I?" I tip my head as I study him. "Unless you're going to suddenly decide not to back her. You and I both know you can sway the entire party to vote for her."

"I'm not in office any longer."

"Cut the bullshit, Benchley. You literally know where all the bodies are buried. How many ratfucks do you have waiting in the wings to drop on people who don't follow your 'suggestions' to support her and Owen?"

His gaze narrows as he slowly nods. "You might not be wrong about that."

"Then let's work together. We both want her elected governor. Hate me or love me, I honestly don't give a fuck how you feel about me. All I care about is her happiness, and Owen's, and that includes our boys."

"We *are* working together," he says. "That's why I'm giving you a chance to cover up your shit instead of hiring someone else to do it and ratfucking *you*."

"Don't bullshit me, Benchley. You want me to cover up my

own shit so *you* don't have one more loose end hanging around out there that might come back to bite *you*."

He wears an evil smirk as he sits back in his chair. "Who says you can't read minds, Carter?"

CHAPTER SIXTEEN

Then

I follow my latex-clad wet-dream come true as she winds her way through the diaphanous maze. We arrive at a door on the periphery of the space, probably across the huge room from where the stairs to the first floor are located.

There's a man sitting on a stool here, and he looks at our wristbands before opening the door for us and allowing us to pass. I realize there are stairs inside, and I gulp what's left of my soda and drop the cup in the garbage can next to the door before plunging into this stairwell after her.

I follow her up the dimly lit stairs, unable to stop myself from looking up her skirt as we go, but it's too dark for me to see if she's wearing panties or not.

My cock is still rock-hard, aching, probably leaving a wet spot in my briefs.

I'll be damn lucky if I don't come before we finish climbing these stairs.

Her steps are smooth, measured, confident, her long legs trim and gorgeous, her posture perfect.

Everything about this woman is like something out of one of my darkest fantasies come to life.

It feels like she knows that, too.

The suitcase is heavier than it looks, and I carry it with both hands, using the top and side handles and praying the damn thing doesn't bust on me and embarrass the hell out of me, or make her mad at me. Behind us, the music from the second floor fades as we approach another door and she opens it, not waiting for me and forcing me to turn and catch it with my side and shoulder or risk it crashing into my face.

This space is still large, but the ceiling is lower than the floors below, maybe ten feet instead of the more cavernous warehouse feel. The lighting is much dimmer, in shades of red and purple, from small lamps on the floor in various places and pointing up at the ceiling, which is painted black.

This space is less populated, but I expected that, too. I had to pay a much more expensive cover charge to get this wristband. Apparently, certain Dominatrixes and Doms are allowed access and get a cut of that extra fee. They draw in more customers for the nightclub.

There are no vertical dividers or curtains in this space, but there are couches, mattresses, spanking benches, and more crosses. Short pieces of iron bar hang from chains in various places, and when I spot a woman whose wrists are attached to one, I realize what they're for.

The man with her holds a riding crop and is standing in front of her, fucking her as he smacks her ass and backs of her legs with the crop.

I somehow manage not to trip as I follow the woman across the space. There's a man in a latex hood strapped down to a bench and getting fucked by a Dominatrix wearing a strap-on. I try not to slow down too much as we pass that scene, but I can't help watching. When the unnamed woman I'm following glances over her shoulder at me, I suspect her path was deliberate to gauge my response.

Yeah, I'm desperately horny now.

Another woman is bent over one end of a couch and being brutally fucked at both ends by two men wearing masks that cover only their eyes. From the welts on her ass, I'd say she's already had a beating.

All that, and more, I try to take in as I catch up to the woman and realize we're stopping by a bench similar to the one the man being fucked by the strap-on is restrained to.

She smiles at me and points to the floor. I set the case down and drop to my knees.

The laughter…

I'd kill to keep her laughing like that.

She reaches out and ruffles my hair. "You're adorable," she says in German. "I meant for you to put my case down, but you seem to know what you are."

"Yes, Ma'am."

"Elsa." She holds her hand out to me and I take it and kiss the back of it. I'm not sure if that's what she wants, but it feels right, so I'm going with it.

"Carter," I say.

"You will address me as *Mistress* or *Ma'am*." Those two words she says in English, but the rest is German.

I nod. "Yes, Mistress."

"Here are my rules, Carter. You do what I say, when I say it. You be a good boy and amuse me, and I might give you more. When do you have to be back?"

"Sunday night."

"Excellent. Depending on what happens between now and then, I might give you a phone number. Do you have a disposable phone?"

"Yes, Mistress."

She tips her head. "You are prepared. Why?"

"I…I need secrecy. Job, family."

"So do I. If I decide to give you my number, I will give you specific rules on when you can call me. If I call you, I expect either you answer or text me a response. I will give you safe codes to use to mean certain things. If you have to leave the area, you will let me know, and then notify me when you return. Are those rules you can abide by? If not, we can still play, but it will only be here."

I eagerly nod. "Yes, Mistress."

She points a finger at me and circles it. "Strip. All the way. Except for the collar. Leave that on."

I'm...*trembling* I'm so fucking nervous. I didn't even feel this goddamned nervous the first time I had to jump out of a fucking plane. But my cock remains hard even once I'm naked before her.

She nods and has me spin around so she can see my entire body. "You can have marks on your ass?"

"Yes, Mistress." Those I can hide. I share a bathroom with seven other guys, but we have shower curtains.

"Have you ever been with a woman before?"

"I'm not a virgin, but I've never done...*this* before. I've wanted to for a long time, though." I'm so nervous I can barely remember how to speak German. I'm stumbling over words, my pronunciation sloppy.

She snaps her fingers and points at the floor, and my knees automatically unhinge.

"Hands behind your head, fingers together." She puts me in the position she wants me, my knees obscenely wide, back straight. "This is *Ready*. When I tell you *Ready*, I want you in this position. Understand?"

"Yes, Mistress."

I don't understand the evil smile on her face, at first. She steps in close and runs the top of her right shoe along the underside of my cock, getting pre-cum on it.

"*Tsk*. Someone is very eager tonight." She taps her foot. "Lick that off and make it shine again."

I'm head-down before the sound of her words die in the air. She laughs as she reaches down and shoves on the back of my head. "This is *Worship*. Head to the floor, or licking your filth off my shoes, whatever I tell you. When I order you into *Worship*, I want your head down, back round, and that gorgeous little ass of yours nice and exposed. And to stay there until I order you otherwise."

My tongue has licked up the pre-cum from her shoe and I'm desperately wiping at it now with my hand. I snag one of my socks from my pile of clothes and start polishing the patent leather, finally relieved when it shines again.

She pulls her foot away and examines my handiwork while I remain in position.

"Excellent." My cock throbs as I process her praise.

I hear her open the bag and rummage around in it. Then she walks around behind me and I flinch when something taps my ass. "Hold still."

I bite back a cry as pain slams into my left asscheek, then the right, one impact each. When she circles around me again, I see her holding a riding crop.

"Well, you seem to have decent tolerance. *Ready*."

It takes me a second to process that's the order for that kneeling position, so I'm slow to rise. She circles behind me and two more impacts strafe my ass.

"Pay attention. When I order you into a position, I want no hesitation. *Worship*."

I drop down again. We do this for several repetitions, the riding crop striking my ass when I move too slow for her liking. I'm back in *Ready* when she nods. "Better." She looks around and calls someone over. A man in a latex body suit runs over and drops to his knees in front of her. He's sitting up on his knees, but in a more relaxed position than I'm in for *Ready*.

"This," she says to me as she points at him and the position he's in, "is *Release*." She taps the top of my head with the riding crop. "You, *Release*."

I move into it and she nods. "Good." She taps the other man. "*Allegiance*." He spreads his knees, his left hand on his thigh, his right flat on the floor, back rounded and head bowed but not on the floor like *Worship*.

She taps me on the head. "*Allegiance*." I assume the position and she nods, then dismisses the other man.

We spend the next several minutes going through those four positions.

Then she taps me on the head. "On the bench. Facedown."

With more than a little fear, I comply. She quickly binds me to it with straps already attached to the table. Then she walks around to my head and grabs my chin, making me look her in the eyes.

She's smiling. "I like your cock, boy. You were gifted. When we finish here, if you please me, I'll let you worship my pussy. If you please me with that, I might consider rewarding you by letting you fuck me. But that will mean you pay me by coming home with me tonight and serving me first. Deal?"

My throat is so dry, between passion and fear and eagerness to do whatever I have to do to please her that all I can do is nod and barely whisper, "Yes, Mistress."

Her thumb strokes my cheek as she smiles. "Excellent. I've been looking for a new boy. Depending on how well you do this weekend, I might make you my new pet. Would you like that?"

I nod again. "Yes, Mistress."

"Excellent." She buckles a ball gag into my mouth and walks behind me, where I can't see her. "Let's begin."

* * *

I can look back on the nineteen-year-old boy and see how fucking dangerously innocent I was. Unlike Susa, I really didn't know who or what I was.

I'm simply eager to please, which is why I think I connected so hard and fast with Owen. One of the reasons, anyway.

I'm not given a safeword, or options. I'm guess I'm lucky I don't wake up in a hotel room tub full of ice and missing a kidney or something.

After she beats me to screaming tears, she softly, gently soothes me by rubbing my head and telling me how good I am. Then she unfastens me, attaches a leash to my collar, and leads me, naked, over to a couch where she rides my face until she's satisfied.

No, she isn't wearing panties.

She also shaves her pussy, which, to me, is an amazing discovery.

It wasn't even midnight when she leads me outside and to her car, which sits parked a block away. I am...

Gone. In a sweet, deep haze that feels better than any buzz I've ever had from drinking, that's for sure.

We head back toward the base, and a tendril of fear races through me until she speaks again. "I have a flat. I work on base." She smiles. "You and I both need secrecy. I think we will get along just fine."

She lives on the third floor in a converted warehouse building. Her loft is spotless, exquisitely decorated. It looks like something out of a movie, and perfectly *her*. Based on the building and the loft's size, I know it's fucking expensive. She must be making good money.

I carry her bag for her and put it in her bedroom, which is walled off from the rest of the space and has a folding door for privacy.

"Strip. When you are in my home, unless I've specifically told you otherwise, you will always strip."

"Yes, Mistress." I quickly obey. My cock has remained mostly hard through all of this.

She snaps her fingers and points at the floor. "*Allegiance.*"

I immediately drop into the pose despite my knees protesting.

I hear her walking around, humming to herself, sounds like she's getting undressed. She puts on music. When she finally returns to me, I feel her snap a leash to my collar and she tugs. "Up."

I follow, and she leads me over to the bed. "Hands and knees." There are some things on the bed, but before I can look and see, she blindfolds me.

I hear the snap of a glove. It feels like she sits on the leash, because now I'm pinned and can't move. "Because I know you will be able to come again quickly, I am going to milk the first one from you. Expect I will do this a lot. Do not move while I do this, in any way. If you resist me, we are done. I expect complete obedience from my boy. Understand?"

I swallow hard. "Yes, Mistress."

"Good boy," she coos.

I jump a little when her lube-covered finger presses against my asshole, but I force myself to remain in place. Her other hand closes around my cock, but she doesn't stroke me, she just holds it. It's taking everything I have not to fuck her hand, but she told me not to move.

I'm struggling to process the sensations as her finger in my ass seeks something, finally finding it. The hand holding my cock tightens even more as she begins rubbing my prostate.

Clenching my fists helps me hold still—barely. I gasp from the sensation, never having felt anything quite like this before. There's the humiliation of having her hand up my ass—my face feels like it's as hot as my beaten ass—the pleasure of her hand around my cock, and the strange feeling of what she's doing inside me.

I cry out when the orgasm hits, but it feels weird, not as satisfying in some ways, but it lasts longer, feels...deeper, somehow.

"Good boy," she coos again, sounding pleased. Another conflicting emotion to process later. I'm gasping, trembling when she finally releases me and her hands disappear. I stay in position as she leaves the bed and I hear the sound of water running.

She returns and sits at the head of the bed, catching my leash and tugging. She's fucking gorgeous all naked, her hair still braided but a flat stomach and perky, full breasts.

I know what she wants and automatically go for her pussy while she holds the leash close and tight to keep me where she wants me. Her other hand rests on my head, massaging, sometimes fisting my hair, as she talks me through it and improves my technique.

Once I've gotten her over again, she sighs. "Excellent." She hands me a condom. I was so focused on her I didn't even realize that, yes, I'm hard again. "You will fuck me until I come. Only then may you come. If you come before I do, you will *not* like the consequences."

Needless to say, I'm a good boy and manage to leave her sated, a smile on her face before I'm allowed to finish.

Then, keeping the leash on me, she allows me to curl up in bed with her, where we both fall asleep. At the time, I'm thinking I've finally found Heaven.

If I'd known that night what future hell lay in store for me, I definitely wouldn't have slept as well as I did.

CHAPTER SEVENTEEN

Now

I'm no longer the naive nineteen-year-old.

I'm a father, a husband.

A lover.

A combat-hardened veteran.

Except right now, as I sit back in my first-class seat and await our final approach over German airspace, I'm none of those things.

Right *now*, even though I'm not here on official business, I'm still Carter Edward Wilson, chief of staff to the governor of the great state of Florida.

And one very pissed-off man. Especially since I didn't even have time to return to Tallahassee to see my family before making this journey by flying out of Tampa. At least Susa and the boys have Owen while I'm gone.

This trip, however, forced me to lie to Owen and Susa, and that...

That *enrages* me.

The promise I'm forced to break—to not lie to them. I realize it's a lie for the greater good, and to protect them, but it doesn't matter.

Because of that fucking bitch, her actions, it's indirectly

impacting my pets. She's fucked up enough of my soul and my life, forced enough lies out of me by her actions—forced me to break too many promises already.

Took my dreams.

I will show her zero mercy when I finally find her. I could have, at any time, burned her with her job, or ruined others' careers, and I didn't. I walked away from her, and yet, because of her and her actions, Eddie and I nearly died.

I had to break a promise to someone who deserved better from me.

And now, this.

My past was meant to stay in my past. I took careful steps, even back then, to ensure something like this would *not* happen.

Ever. Burner phones and anonymous chat apps. Taking every precaution.

Mostly because I was afraid of word getting back to my father or any of my brothers.

That's no longer my fear, because I'm no longer a nineteen-year-old kid, yet any of this information coming to light at this juncture would cause problems for those I love most.

So now, *here* I am.

After my flight lands, I've made several errands before arriving at Eddie's. He's home when I knock on the door of his flat a little before three p.m. local time. He lets me in with a grim smile, shaking hands with me before closing the door behind me. Part of me is glad he didn't go for a hug.

Part of me is…not.

I follow him inside, glancing around as we walk. Not the largest or ritziest place, but I'm used to American excess. He still has a limp, even this many years later.

Then again, on my bad pain days, so do I.

We've stayed in touch over the years, yet there remains a distance between us that I know rests on a foundation of secrets and memories. I once loved the man like a brother—more, even—and still do, I suppose.

It was...complicated.

It still is complicated.

Then again, I wasn't on the receiving end of a lot of the worst shit, and he was.

The man I am now regrets I allowed myself to be used by her back then. I still harbor a hidden, simmering rage at her for what she did to us, put us through, used us and especially Eddie for. Not only the sadistic giggles for herself, but how she weaponized me against Eddie.

Fortunately, Eddie blames her totally.

I know at least some of the blame lays on me.

Because I didn't say no.

Because I left him behind instead of begging him to leave with me.

Because I didn't have the guts to stand up for us, for him, and to blow the whistle on everything.

This whole flat is maybe the size of our master suite at the Brandon house, and it's downright spacious by average German standards. But from the high-dollar electronics in his living room entertainment center, and the posh leather couch, I know he's doing okay for himself.

We sit down with two fingers each of Macallan, neat. "Do I get the story now, *sir?*" he asks, the last word snarky by design and coaxing a smile out of me. I remember that snark, his deliberate goading in formation or around others, which would make me take it out on him later in return when we could sneak away in private.

At the time, a game I didn't mind, and downright reveled in.

So did he.

I shove aside dusty old memories and tell him the story of why I'm there. He's one of the few people I'd trust with this intel, and only because he knows her.

Actually, he's the only person I'd trust with this, because I'd prefer to go to my grave without confessing any of it to Susa, or especially Owen.

He slowly nods after I sum up what I know. "So what do you think that bitch wants with you after all these years? What's her end game? Money? Or something else?"

I shrug. "I don't know. The way we parted company, I assumed I'd never hear anything from her again. *She* dumped *me*."

"Yeah, I remember." He should, because he was there. Then she dumped him.

And then we *really* got fucked over. I think, at the time, losing her tore him up a lot more than it did me. I was far stronger in some ways.

Which is why he ended up belonging to me.

He studies me. "You haven't talked to her?"

"Not yet."

"Did he reply to her e-mail?"

"No. It's been less than forty-eight hours since he received it. He's not replying, unless I can't handle this now."

"What's your excuse for flitting to Germany on short notice, should anyone ask me?"

I smile. "I have an old buddy from when I was in the Army who needed me."

He snorts as he tips his glass for another sip. "You're not wrong."

I know he means it differently than I do, and pain arcs through my soul that I can't be who he needs now. "Oh." I reach into my pocket and hand him the key for the safe deposit box that I took out at the bank before making my way to his place, along with a business card with the bank's name and address. On the back I've written the box number.

He turns the key over in his hand. "Did I ever say thank you?" he quietly asks.

He doesn't need to clarify. He's one of the three.

At least, in that *one* way, I was able to balance my karmic scales with him a little. It doesn't make up for the years lost between us, or what might have been, or what I didn't do, but he is alive, and the world is still a better place with him in it.

For that, I will *never* regret what I did.

I don't regret that I saved the other two men in the process, but they weren't the main reason I threw myself over the three of them that day.

Eddie had been hit and was down, along with Dray's brother, and Trent.

When we'd dragged them behind cover so the medic could triage them, Eddie had ended up in the middle.

I would have done it again, too. In a heartbeat. They were my guys, and I still lost Gohber and Kenney that day. I'd have thrown myself over them, too, if it would have saved them. I was in command.

They were my guys. Them and Reynolds, the third man who died that day.

I nod. "Before I was shipped back to the States. You were so out of it, though, you had no clue what you were saying." I grin. "Fortunately, that's the excuse I used to explain your rambling to the nurses. Even more fortunately, they believed my ass, or we both would have ended up in the stockade, or with dishonorable discharges."

The ghost of a smile curls his lips as he nods again, his eyes on the key. "Sorry, *Sarge*."

My damned cock *still* wants to twitch remembering what he used to look like on his knees in front of me with his lips wrapped around my cock and tears streaming from his eyes as I face-fucked him. And that's been, what, over thirty years in the past?

A past known only to myself, this man here, and the bitch I'm about to pay a visit to.

Maybe in a different world, a different time, Eddie and I would have ended up together. But we were too much of a reminder to each other of dark and evil times we really didn't *want* to remember. It might have poisoned us, eventually, if we literally hadn't killed each other first with our dark version of "play."

Plus it doesn't help that most of my nightmares that aren't about the desert feature Eddie, in some way.

Over our years in the desert, I discovered I *liked* hurting him too much, and he hated how much he liked me to hurt him…and how much he *needed* me to do it and keep doing it, even after we were free of *her*.

Especially then.

Except it would have hurt both of us too damned much to completely sever all ties to each other. There was too much love there, even if we couldn't admit it.

"This won't come back on me, right?" he asks. "I'm semi-retired and live a quiet life. I've stayed under the radar all these years. I don't need to wind up on it. That's mainly why I stayed over here in the first place after I got out. The…job opportunities. Lot of clients in Eastern Europe. I never did local work, but I don't want to risk going back to the States, if I can help it."

The kind of contract work Eddie did after leaving the military perhaps fuels his own bad dreams. Or, maybe not. The bell curve of Eddie's morals arced in different directions than mine, and always has. He once joked that if we were playing *Dungeons and Dragons*, he'd be a *chaotic neutral* alignment with a decided bent toward *neutral evil*, and I'd be classified as *lawful evil*.

I can't exactly say he's wrong. Eddie has always followed the money, ever since what we went through and I told him what I'd found out. He'd honestly had no clue, and she'd never given him a penny, either.

Then there's the fact that I *am* a bastard, thanks to what we went through with her.

"I was never here," I say. "Unless I need to be *here*. If so, we stayed in, did a lot of talking, and did some drinking. You sounded distraught on the phone when we talked yesterday, and I was worried about you. I currently have the resources to help out an old friend." I shrug. "PTSD is a real bitch."

"Again, you ain't wrong." He settles back on the couch, his gaze no longer meeting mine. Neither of us break the silence for several minutes after he pours us refills and we sit there, sipping and remembering.

"What's your timeline today, sir?" he asks a little too quietly, and this time with no snarky emphasis on the last word.

My heart squeezes, old memories slamming against my mental bulwarks, ancient and barely tamed demons howling to be unleashed, the bastard extraordinaire sooooo fucking tempted.

So tempted.

The smell of gun oil and sweat and dusty damned desert comes to mind. The sound of his knees rubbing in the dirt as I quickly fuck his throat, tears streaming from his eyes before I paint his face with my cum and then smear it all over with my hand. His strained gasp as I let him jerk off while I do it and make him lick up any he got on me in the process after he sucks my hand clean.

I actually have to take a breath, because those memories have my cock aching so damn hard it's literally painful now. I hadn't forgotten what this feels like, but I have to remind myself that most of the fucking nightmares I've had in my life were created by what that bitch did to me and Eddie both.

Owen's made me a better man, because loving him forced me to learn how to be…gentle. Tender.

How to use my evil side for good instead of…well, the obvious.

"I'm sorry," I gently say. "I can't. I have to go back to my hotel. I told the boys I'd video chat with them before they go to bed." It's a lie I know he'll believe and understand. It's also far less cruel than the truth, which is that I made promises to others that I'll absolutely keep, and yet not the one I made to him.

I left him behind.

He slowly nods. "Yeah. It's okay. I get it. Just...putting it out there." I watch the rise and fall of his chest. His gaze is still fixed on the inside of his glass, and the better bastard that I am wishes I could at least let myself offer to hug him.

I can't, because I won't be able stop there if I do, and I damn well know it.

So does he.

I never could stop myself with him once we got started.

Ever.

He didn't want me to, either.

Which led to a lot of close-calls, but made being stuck in the desert a little more tolerable, at times.

"IVF?" he finally asks.

I'm watching him as I nod. "Owen. He's my best friend." From our conversations over the years, Eddie knows a little about Owen, barely more than the public does.

Eddie will believe this, though, and it won't hurt him and therefore add more guilt to my already overflowing plate in the process. Because, contrary to what you might think, I can and do feel guilt about some things.

Feeling it, and not letting it stop me, are two different beasts entirely.

With Eddie, I don't want to add to my guilt. I already carry enough where he's concerned.

"What'd you tell them?" he asks. "Your wife and your friend?"

I know what he means. "The truth, basically. That I stupidly got a vasectomy for a woman I was in love with, and it didn't work out."

He softly snorts and drains his glass before setting it on the coffee table. Then he pockets the key and the business card and stands, heads for what I assume is the bedroom.

When he returns a moment later he's wearing latex gloves. He's carrying a nine millimeter with a magazine in it and an extra magazine, both fully loaded. He sets them on the coffee table in front of me, as well as a cheap-ass, battered switchblade that's seen better days, and an unlabeled bottle of oxy tablets. Probably fifty in the bottle.

He's done damn good with only a day's notice.

Then again, this kind of request, to someone like Eddie and the work he's done over the years, is probably akin to asking the average person to grab a quart of milk and a loaf of bread from the store on their way home.

"Gun's untraceable," he says as he strips off the gloves. "I cleaned and wiped down the gun and all the rounds myself, and both mags, before I loaded them. I wore gloves the whole time. When you're finished with it, break it down, if you can, then drop it. The knife, too."

"I'm hoping I don't need either of them," I lie as I stare at the bottle of pills.

"Well, just in case. You don't know what you're going to be walking into with *her*." He points to the pills. "I wiped the outside of the bottle, and the cap. Don't be stupid."

"I won't."

He sits back in his chair. "When you see Elsa, give that cunt an extra little 'fuck you' from me, too, huh? Remind her I told her karma's a bitch."

"I will," I swear.

And I will.

His smirk holds no humor and a lot of *really* old pain.

That's how I know I can trust him—he hates her even more than I do, but for different reasons.

Related reasons, but different ones.

Which is why I can never admit to him how much I enjoyed a

majority of the things I had to do to and with him during our time with her, before I realized the truth of what was going on.

It's also why I *definitely* can't reveal to him the deeper truths about me and Owen.

And it's why I know that while Eddie would still *absolutely* comply—and enjoy it—if I grabbed him by the throat, slammed him against the wall, kissed him, and ordered him to his knees, I won't.

I *can't*.

Not just because of the two pets I love awaiting my return, and the promises I've made them, but because Eddie *would* comply and play with me and…I'd enjoy it too damn much. There's a dark side of me I will *never* let Susa or Owen see, no matter how well Susa mistakenly thinks she knows it.

A side of me that Eddie knows well.

Better than Susa does.

I'm am *absolutely* a bastard, but the older, wiser bastard knows some secrets are best left lost to time, and that darkest side of me needs to be one of them. I can never again allow it to see daylight. Which is why I went so far as to rename the positions.

One less tie to that darkness.

All Eddie knows is I'm protecting my wife, our two sons.

Susa's fledgling political career.

My best friend and his career.

My own career.

My *family*.

The one thing Eddie knows I always wanted, and yet also knows *she* took from me.

As far as Eddie knows, my reaction to the e-mail Benchley received is logical when weighed against what Eddie thinks he knows about me and what we mutually survived, back then.

Not meaning the day in the desert—meaning *her*.

"You think she just wants money?" he asks. "Or someone

using her for a bigger score?"

That possibility had crossed my mind, too. "I don't know. But I'm going to find out shortly."

CHAPTER EIGHTEEN

Then

Two months into whatever *this* is with Elsa, and I'm over at her place any time I have a few spare hours. I text her my schedule at the beginning of every week. Then, on a daily basis, once I know when I'm free, I text her and wait to see if I'm summoned.

When I'm not summoned, I find myself aimlessly surfing porn or going for a late run. Otherwise, I sit there wondering what was wrong with me that she didn't want me that night.

But when I *am* summoned, it feels like I'm in heaven. She quickly trains me for what she wants me to do, stepping things up every few times together, until I'm her perfect, willing pet. It's a mix of pleasure and pain, and using pleasure as positive reinforcement to take more pain or…other things.

She even takes me to a few events where she knows we won't run into anyone from the base, vanilla events like concerts or soccer games.

I'm made to feel special when I'm with her. I lavish her with devotion, despite her reminders to me not to fall in love with her, that I'm her pet and she's my Owner.

I don't even care. I'm happy for whatever I can get from her.

I know that she goes to the nightclub on a regular basis, because she makes no secret about that. But because of my schedule, I don't feel I have a right to ask her not to. Not that I think that would go over well, anyway. There's no claim on her from me—that was declared by her in the beginning. Besides, I'm not always free to go to her, and I belong to her.

Continuing our relationship is my agreement to her terms. She is the one who gets to set the terms, not me.

We use condoms, and her orders are that I'm not allowed to date or sleep with anyone. If I have that kind of time, it's reserved for her. Because I belong to her.

I'm a *pet*.

I'm her *favorite* pet, according to her, but I'm still a pet. As such, that means I don't get certain rights.

She's trained me to love being fucked with a strap-on, because she's a tricky damn bitch. I'm nineteen—I can get it up in a stiff wind. She uses alternative ways of making me come so that when she allows me to fuck her, I can last for a while. She feeds me my own cum, makes me amuse her by sucking it off a realistic dildo and giving me lessons on sucking a cock that way.

I try to not think about what that means, because if I ask, I risk being turned away.

I don't want to lose this. I...*can't*. She's become a damn *drug*.

I *need* it. I need *Her*. I need the sweet silence that settles in my brain when I'm with her and doing nothing but focusing on exactly what she tells me to focus on, whether it's taking her pain or giving her pleasure. I find my every spare moment is focused on her, thinking about her.

I know that she plays with others. I try not to feel jealous over that, because this is what I signed up for. For all I know, I could wake up tomorrow to find out I'm being shipped out to some FOB in Afghanistan or somewhere.

I don't feel I have a right to…complain.

At least, that's what I keep telling myself.

Following orders, unfortunately, is something I'm pretty good at.

The longer we do whatever *this* is, the more she puts me through, and the more she starts hinting that I *will* be playing with her and her other pets at some rapidly approaching time in the future. Pets who also have a vested interest in secrecy.

How me reaching that point would make her so proud.

One evening, when I let her know I'm free, I'm summoned to her place and immediately stripped and hooded, my wrists cuffed behind me. She sits me on the end of her bed and spreads my legs wide, strapping leather cuffs to my ankles and then attaching them to the bed frame so I can't close them.

She smiles at me. "You are allowed to come tonight as many times as you want. This is a reward for being my *very* good boy." Her hand rubs my head through the hood and I feel the drop into subspace hit me. All she has to do is rub my head and I'm…*gone*.

"All you have to do tonight is not talk, orgasm, and if something is put in your mouth, you suck it. You may moan or make noises like that, but you do *not* speak unless I ask you a direct question. Do not embarrass me tonight, boy. This isn't just a reward—it's a test. If you wish to keep doing what we're doing, then you'd better obey me and impress me. Do you understand me?"

Fear tightens my gut. "Yes, Mistress," I whisper, unable to speak any louder than that with my growing terror.

I guess I knew this day would come.

She looks so happy, and when she laughs…it *melts* me. "Such a *very* good boy." She kisses me—something else that rarely happens and I treasure it when it does—then buckles a blindfold into place around my head.

Music starts, and only a few minutes later, I hear a knock on her door.

I swallow hard, force back my fear…

Pray I don't fuck this up or embarrass her.

I hear a nervous-sounding man's voice, and Elsa's voice drops into Mistress mode. They're both speaking German, and the man sounds like a native speaker.

I try not to listen, but I can't help it.

Context tells me this guy is another of her "pets," but it sounds like he gets off on humiliation. I hear their voices draw near and the sound of him stripping at her command.

Behind me, the bed dips, and Elsa's voice softly speaks next to my right ear. "Good boys get rewarded," she reminds me, her hand rubbing the top of my head through the hood. "Bad boys, on the other hand…"

I hear a yelp, followed by the feel of warm breath on my cock.

A man's stubbly cheek rubs against the inside of my thigh.

From what I can feel of her body against mine, her arm over my right leg, I'm guessing she's fisting his hair and forcing him to choke down my cock.

She presses her face against the side of my head, the hand on my head rubbing, her voice telling me what a good boy I am…

I don't last long. She chokes the guy on my cock, and a weird kind of pleasure fills me when she degrades him, tells him I'm a *real* man compared to him, which is why she's making him suck *my* cock.

Over the next however long it is, I'm sucked off twice more by two different guys. Despite my fear, nothing is put in my mouth except for her fingers, which I eagerly suck. Once the last guy leaves, she releases me. I'm trembling, my back and shoulders aching from having sat up like that for so long, but the pain made the pleasure feel that much sweeter. Once she pulls the hood off me, she kisses me deeply.

"There. See? Good boys get rewarded. You did *so* good. You

made me so proud by how good you were."

I can't help it—the wild-eyed pleasure in her eyes is my undoing. "Thank you, Mistress."

* * *

This becomes my new routine. Over the next couple of weeks, I'm only allowed to come when I'm restrained on her bed and faceless, nameless men are sucking me off. I'm either sucking fingers—usually hers, but one time a man's—or a dildo. I eagerly suck that when it's presented, because it makes her laugh, and usually I'm so horned up I can't help it. Some of the guys are obviously skilled at what they do. Some are not, and I can tell they're getting off on the humiliation of her forcing them to do it.

She allows me to go down on her and make her come at the end of the nights, but by then I'm usually too drained to do anything but get her off.

I sleep like a fucking rock, though.

I start to notice sometimes that, when she kisses me during these sessions, her mouth tastes like beer or hard liquor. She always offers me drinks, but I stick to water or soda. Sometimes I see her take pills, but I don't know what they are. One day she sees me watching her and smiles. "Xanax," she says, shaking them with a smile. "They keep me calm."

After several weeks of this, there finally comes a night in this routine where it's two men who arrive instead of one. They're the first of the night, and I'm not sure how to feel now that I've noticed I get hard in anticipation when she straps me down in this position, and even more hard when I hear a knock on her door.

The men are speaking German and sound like native speakers. I gather from the context they're a Master and slave couple, but the slave sounds like he's inexperienced.

This time, it's not a dildo that slides into my mouth as my cock is swallowed, but a condom-sheathed cock.

I pretend it's a dildo and savor Elsa's laughter even as the guy blowing me is being choked on my cock by her hand in his hair. I guess I should be glad she made the guy I'm sucking use a rubber.

When they depart, she leaves me restrained but pulls the hood off and kisses me deeply. Then she smiles and strips, gets me hard again, and rolls a condom on me before she straddles me and fucks me. Her eyes bore into mine and a gorgeous smile fills her face.

"You were perfect, boy," she tells me. "You did so good. I can tell how much you enjoyed that. I cannot wait to begin the next stage of your training. You want to make me happy and be my good boy, don't you?"

I'm lost to her and those gorgeous blue eyes. "Yes, Mistress, I want to be your good boy." She's always horny after these sessions, and it's all mixed up in my head now.

Later, she frees me and allows me to cuddle in bed with her, and I feel...

I guess I'm happy.

Right?

* * *

The first time I fuck another man, I don't know it's Eddie.

I didn't know *who* it was, at first, and he didn't know it was me, either.

It's the following week when my next stage of training begins. When I'm summoned to Elsa's that evening, I'm not taken to the bedroom immediately. Elsa had hooded, blindfolded, and gagged each of us as soon as we arrived. I assume after the fact that Eddie arrived first and was in the bedroom.

Then she played music loud, and over the next hour or so tortured us and worked us both into a frenzy as she ordered us to beg her for relief. I'd thought she was simply making me wait between activities the way she sometimes did when she played with me, leaving me and ignoring me for a while before coming back and paying me attention.

In retrospect, the fact that she's playing with two of us at the same time explains everything she did that evening. I do know she loved anything we said or did that put her front and center of our attention and affection.

A total narcissist.

Having two of us desperate and begging, focused on her and unaware of the other's presence, must have been a huge turn-on and ego boot for her.

I have no clue about any of that at the time, though. All I know is after spending time rubbing her feet, being allowed to lick her pussy several different times, and going through every position she ordered me to assume, as I kneel there on the cold floor, naked except for the cuffs, hood, and blindfold, I think my balls are going to explode. I am beginning to wish she'd strap me to the bed and let me come, even if it's another guy sucking me off.

She clips my hands behind me, hooking them to my ankles, and forces me to remain in that position as she reaches in and plays with my balls, my cock, delivers cane strokes to the bottoms of my feet and the backs of my legs.

"There is someone else here," she reveals after our ball gags were once again put in and she turns down the music. "You're both being remarkably good boys right now. I'm very impressed." Her hand settles on my head, rubbing me even through the hood, and what little fear had filled my brain from the revelation that we weren't alone vanishes.

"*Such* good boys. So good that I want to reward you both. But reward still must be earned. Show me how well you can beg to be fucked, and I'll let both of you come."

I am *desperate*. I hunch over as low as I can with my wrists bound the way they are and plead to be fucked. I'll gladly take an ass-fucking to be allowed to *finally* be able to bust a nut, even if it means jerking off while she fucks me.

I have no idea who the other guy is. With both of us gagged, it's just muffled, mumbled gagspeak. I can make out words, barely, but not his voice.

What I *can* hear, like bright, crystal sunlight, is *her* laughter.

Pure amusement.

I crave hearing that, making her laugh like that, nearly as much as I crave making her smile or hearing her say *good boy* to me.

"I can't decide," she finally says. "I know! I'll flip a coin to decide." I finally realize she's speaking English and fear hits me, because I wonder if that means the other guy can't speak German.

Like…what if he's another guy from the base?

To this day, I have no clue if she really flipped a coin or not. I don't know what criteria she used to decide who was on top, if it was just random choice, or because I had a bigger cock and she wanted to watch me fuck him—I don't know.

I'll never know.

I don't even *want* to know how she decided, because it really doesn't matter.

"Excellent," she says, followed by the sound of her preparing. I hear her moving stuff around, the sound of a pained male grunt, and then I flinch when I feel her hand grip and stroke my cock.

I can't help moaning.

"Yes, my very good boy," she softly says. "My *special* boy. You're my favorite, you know."

My heart races over her words as she keeps my wrists clipped behind me, but unclips them from my ankles and makes me crawl on my knees until I bump into a naked leg, which startles both of us guys.

I quickly realize from what's happening that I'm the "lucky" one. She rolls a condom onto my cock and helps me into position between the man's legs. He's on his hands and knees, too. She holds my cock to line it up with his ass, and maybe this is the moment the first hints of my bastard side emerge, because I'm so goddamned horny that I don't even care if she's lubed him or not.

"You may put your cock inside him, but hold still once you do. Be my good boy. Do *not* start fucking him yet, or your positions will be reversed."

Her hand disappears. Me and the other guy both moan as I press forward, maybe harder than I meant to, but god*damn* his ass is hot and tight and it's grabbing at my fucking cock. It takes every last ounce of fucking willpower I have not to plow him.

I'm biting down on the fucking ball gag now more to hold back my needy groan than anything. I sense her right next to us, doing something, and then the guy groans again, his ass twitching around my cock.

She unclips my wrists. I instinctively reach forward, my hands on his ass, his hips. I realize his hands are clipped behind him, and I hold on to them, pinning him there.

If he's like me and enjoys the way she uses a strap-on, then he'll love that.

I think his happy-sounding moan is in response to me doing that.

I hear her whispering something to the other guy, then another long, loud moan from him.

"You may fuck him, boy," she tells me. "Make it last as long as you can, because unless you decide to suck another one from each other, it's the only one you're allowed to have until next time I let you play."

Fuck.

I don't even have time to contemplate that. I start fucking him, realizing at least she lubed the poor bastard. I suspect from how eagerly he's fucking back against me that either he likes being on bottom, or she's jerking him off at the same time, or maybe both. The two aren't mutually exclusive.

I slow down, wanting this to last, but Elsa's a bitch. She strokes him in a faster rhythm that's making the guy's ass clench around my cock and getting me too close to the edge too damned fast.

Fuck it.

I know what she said, but I'll risk it. Lights go off behind my eyelids when I finally explode, grinding hard into the nameless man as she gets him over and his body squeezes me.

Laughter.

Her laughter.

Even though I *just* came, I feel my cock twitch already.

Especially when she reaches over and rubs my head through the hood. "Good boy," she says.

CHAPTER NINETEEN

Now

I leave my suitcase back at the hotel just outside the airport, in the room that I've booked for two nights. Between my stop at the bank and my visit to Eddie's, I return to the hotel and change from the suit I wore to take out the safe deposit box and deposit into it the cash from the wire transfer I accepted there.

In Western countries, men wearing five-thousand-dollar suits and ten-thousand-dollar watches don't usually earn a second look in a bank. Especially a bank such as this one, who has a very...specialized clientele. But the jeans and sneakers I'm currently wearing damn sure would have met with resistance and extra scrutiny from them.

The suit ensured my transaction was handled quickly, discreetly, and even if they were asked about me later, these people will swear that they can't recognize me for certain, no matter what their security camera tapes might show.

That's one of the things Benchley learned about that particular bank before using it for the wire transfer.

They came highly recommended by friends of his.

Elsa's building is older, not in the best neighborhood, and doesn't appear to have any CCTV cameras out front. Here, a man in a five-thousand-dollar suit would stand out like a pile of dogshit in a buffet line.

Fortunately, I thought ahead and opted for jeans and sneakers and left the watch in my suitcase. The damp evening is quickly turning chilly, so the jacket I'm wearing to hide the gun doesn't look out of place. Neither does the knit cap pulled low over my ears. Along with the cheaters I purchased in a drugstore, worn low so I can look over the tops of them, it should be enough to throw anyone off.

I study the building for a few minutes before I time my steps so I hurry and catch hold of the front door for a woman with two young toddlers and her arms full of groceries. In my other hand, I carry a paper grocery sack with a bottle of vodka in it.

"*Guten Abend*," I say as I smile and hold the door for her.

She offers me a hesitant smile as she herds her children ahead of her. "*Danke.*"

Fortunately, the mom lives on the second floor, while I'm walking up to the fourth. The formerly red carpet in the hall is threadbare and filthy and now a rust-hued shade of brown in most places. The building's interior is twice as dingy as the exterior. I smell stale cigarette smoke and have a strong suspicion there might be a meth lab somewhere within, based on the chemical odor.

Not my problem.

There's not a lot of noise on the fourth floor as I walk down the corridor to where Elsa's flat sits, the last on the left. There are no cameras on this floor, as far as I can tell, although there was one inside the lobby downstairs. Except, based on the building, I'd be willing to bet that one's not even working. Or, if it is, it's likely not recording to anything, or being monitored by anyone.

I unzip the jacket, take out the nine, and knock with my left hand, being careful not to smash the bottle against the door as I do. I remain mostly turned to my right, like I'm looking through the small, dusty window at the end of the hall. I keep the gun held down along my outer right thigh where others can't see it should they peek through their viewfinders.

When she opens the door, I shove it, hard, taking her off-guard. Before she has time to respond, I've got the gun in her face.

"Don't," I whisper in German. I've decided to speak German tonight, because the sound of English might raise suspicions and cause people to pay more attention than they would otherwise. I quietly close the door behind me and lock it, and I'm extremely pleased to see she now looks absolutely fucking terrified.

"You alone?" It feels weird speaking German now, like this, especially with her.

Tears roll down her cheeks, but she nods.

I cock the hammer and touch the muzzle to her forehead, even though she likely doesn't see I have the safety on. "Truth. Someone steps out of the bedroom, I'm killing them, and then you."

"I'm alone," she hisses. "I swear!"

The place is a dump and smells like an ashtray. It's a far cry from the large, spotless, stylish loft she used to rule her small kingdom from. I march her down the short hallway to the living room, make her take a seat on the sagging sofa.

I remain standing.

She's gained at least a hundred pounds since I last saw her, no longer the thin, angular Dominatrix who could command fear and loathing even while making someone beg for more. Her clear, ice-blue eyes now look rheumy and bloodshot. The perfectly coiffed black hair is now a mousy brown that's more than half grey, a little oily-looking, and pulled back with an elastic band from her puffy face. She wears a ratty brown cardigan sweater with the sleeves pushed up to her elbows. Her old T-shirt has stains on the chest, maybe ketchup, and her sweatpants have a rip in the left knee. Where her hands rest on her knees, I see blunt, chewed, unpainted nails. On bare feet, her toes are also unpainted.

This is not a woman I recognize from my nightmares. It both relieves me and threatens to allow a tendril of sympathy to take hold.

I remember the sound of the colonel locking the door behind me, sooo many times.

I remember the sick feeling in the pit of my stomach as I accepted money and stowed it, uncounted, in an envelope for her.

I remember whispering to Eddie the few German phrases I was able to teach him so I could soothe him.

I remember the sounds of Eddie's tears in the darkness.

I remember the nervous look Eddie and I exchanged at the clinic before I went first so he wouldn't feel so nervous, a decision that took one of my dreams from me, and thus I remember who, *exactly*, this woman is.

I remember the countless times Eddie came to me during our years in the desert, the mix of lust and loathing he always wore when I gave him what we both needed.

And thus I yank that tendril of sympathy out by the roots and douse it and the ground beneath it in napalm before mentally setting it aflame.

Burn, baby. Burn.

I stare at her for a long minute, giving her plenty of time to feel terrified, even though I've eased the hammer down. "Don't make me ask," I quietly say.

She knows better than to try to bullshit me. "I didn't want to do it!" Even her voice sounds sloppy now, a little slurred.

"Didn't stop you, huh?"

The needle tracks on her arms are relatively fresh, which validates one of the many theories I'd considered during the flight over.

Not that it was much of a stretch to go there in the first place, knowing what I knew about her.

"I owe someone a lot of money," she finally admits. "I

wouldn't have *really* said anything."

She's lying. She *absolutely* would have gone through with it, and she's only fooling herself if she believes otherwise.

I *know* this narcissistic bitch. I lost my heart to her once, not even counting the other things she almost stole from my life. I'm not about to let her steal my happiness—times two, if you count both Susa and Owen, and I *do* count them—no matter how low she appears to have fallen.

"What proof do they have?" I ask.

Now she looks nervous, a tell she always had when caught in a lie. "They...don't. Just my word that I'm getting them money. I have two weeks."

Ooooh, honey. You done fucked up. "*Why* do you need the money?"

I can see her debating what version of the truth to tell me and spot the moment she realizes none of them make her look any better.

She opts for what's probably as close to the actual truth as I'll ever get. "I borrowed money from my employer. I needed to quickly repay it, so I...took out a loan."

I can't help the snort that escapes. "You stole money, then hit up a loan shark to replace it before your employer discovered what you did and had you arrested."

She glares at me, but the fire quickly flickers out of her expression and she glances down. "*Ja.*"

"Fucking sloppy, Elsa. Why'd you steal the money in the first place?" I already know that. The answer is all over her arms.

"I borrowed it over a long period of time. Then they replaced their financial officer unexpectedly and he wanted to do a deep audit of their books when he took over. I was not expecting that." She glares at me. "I hurt my back about ten years ago. The doctors won't give me pain meds. You of all people should understand. I researched you before I contacted you. I know about your injuries.

169

The *war hero*." She manages a little half-hearted sarcasm for the last two words that makes me want to pistol-whip her.

I resist that urge—barely—because it would fuck up my plan.

And no, I don't understand, honestly. I live with my pain. She always was a wuss. A hangnail was a dire emergency to her.

Ironic, considering her former pastime.

"Uh huh. So you thought you'd be out of there long before their previous financial officer left, and no one would be the wiser?"

She nods.

"And you were hoping my father-in-law was going to open a dialogue with you for you to, what, fill in some nearly thirty-year-old blanks and give you cash without any proof?"

"I was going to record a video and send to him. I have that picture of us in Berlin together. That's the only one."

There's only one that I know of, because pictures were the exception, not the norm. "From the World Cup game?"

She nods.

"We're dressed. In public." And she now looks nothing like that young woman, except for her eyes, and even those barely resemble her current state. Eddie took one of me and her, and I took one of him and her.

Now she looks triumphant and I know for certain that this, combined with her not masking her IP address, was an act of sheer desperation.

"But it proves I know you!" she insists.

She has a point, albeit a very tenuous one. Maybe in her current state of mind she's convinced herself it would pay more.

At the time, we were both very careful. She was a civilian contractor with security clearance who worked for the DoD. I was active military and didn't yet know exactly what my future was, but I knew I didn't want it to include naked pictures cropping up if my law career took off. My father was also still active military, a high-ranking officer, as were some of my brothers.

It's that very relationship to all of them that delayed my unit's deployment in-country as long as it did.

Well, that, and the fucker Elsa had in her pocket, although I didn't put that together until later.

I didn't want my actions negatively reflecting on my father or brothers and risk getting me excommunicated from my family, much less thrown in the stockade or out of the Army.

At the time, the arrangement we had worked for both of us.

Until I fucked it up by falling in love with her, and then letting her twist me around for her own sick amusement and profit before she discarded me, after making me and Eddie both go through a cruel loyalty test that I didn't realize at the time would alter the course of my life.

Had I known her other faults, at the time, I never would have gotten involved with her. At least, I'd like to *think* the stupid kid I was wouldn't have gotten involved with her.

Who knows?

In the years since I last saw her, it seems her demons have grown much larger than extra doses of Xanax and day-drinking could keep in line.

"Where is it?" I ask. "The picture?"

"In my bedroom. On the dresser."

"Where'd you send the e-mail from?"

She glances toward the small table and I see an old laptop there.

That'll go with me.

"How many other former boyfriends and clients have you tried to hit up?"

Resignation fills her features. "You were the first and, hopefully, the only one I'd need."

The past almost three decades have *not* been kind to her. I am a bastard and a horrible human, but I want to stand here and gloat over that. She's rubbing at her arms now, notices me noticing her, and she tugs the sleeves of her sweater down to cover the needle tracks.

"Something wrong?" I ask.

"I was going to go out before you arrived."

I pull the bottle of vodka—her favorite brand—out of the bag and set it on the table.

I also don't miss how her eyes light up.

"Maybe that'll help." I take the bottle of pills out of my left pocket—I don't know if she's put it together yet or not that I'm still wearing gloves inside—and shake it before I toss it to her.

Her eyes widen, her hunger unmistakable before she looks at me again and tries to school her expression.

Too late.

She frowns. "What's the catch?" she asks.

"I needed to know everything you had on me."

She seems to have forgotten I still hold a gun on her. She gets up and grabs a glass from a drainer sitting on the kitchen counter. I'd almost expected her to grab a knife, but she's so hungry for the booze and the pills that she doesn't bother trying for false bravado.

Then, she pauses. "Do you want a glass?"

"No. Still not a drinker." Which is a lie I feel zero guilt about telling.

She shrugged. "I was assuming. Sorry." She returns to the couch, cracks the seal on the bottle, and fills the glass, leaving the cap off of the bottle.

She opens the pill bottle and shakes two of them into her hand, considers it for a moment and adds a third, then washes them down with vodka.

I can*not* believe I once stuck my dick in this woman.

I cannot believe I once surrendered my heart—and control of my body—to this woman.

There are a *lot* of things I cannot believe I did with, for, and to this woman.

Things I cannot believe I let her do to me...or let her have others do to me.

Worse, the things I let her make me do to others, especially Eddie.

Ironically, one of the reasons I fell in love with Owen—and Susa—is due in no small part to her.

You'd think I'd feel thankful for *that*, at least a little.

You'd be wrong.

CHAPTER TWENTY

Then

Elsa keeps us hooded all evening, until after she has us sixty-nine, with me on top and pinning the other guy down.

From the way she's been talking to him, I get the impression he is more comfortable on the bottom in more than one way.

I'm not sure which of us is more horrified, him or me, when she unhoods us at the end of the evening and we recognize each other.

It's Eddie, one of the guys not just from base, or my fucking unit. Oh, no, that'd be a coincidence, sure, but it's worse.

He's in my fucking *barracks*. He's one of the guys I share a bathroom with. He's my age, or close to it. While I'm not close to him, like I am Gohber and Kenney, he seems like an okay guy.

I had no clue about this side of him.

"Oh, it's like you two know each other, hmm?" she asks.

The two of us nod.

From the way her eyes narrow, I can tell she knows more than she let on in the beginning. "Ah, good. I can see you two will get along just fine." She smiles and rubs both our heads. "You'd *better*." The smile fades. "Because you are going to want to get along just fine if you want to stay my pets."

Once she releases us for the night, we leave together. Downstairs, before we exit the building, I hold out an arm to stop him. "Dude, do we need to talk? I feel like we should...talk."

"About what?" He looks at me but his eyes don't meet mine. "You heard her. I'm not fucking this up. I'm not going to say anything. Don't fuck me over, I won't fuck you over."

We return to base in silence.

With my duty schedule, I'm not going to get a chance to see Elsa for a week. And then she's going out of town for a week, and I struggle with thinking about who she might be going with or what she's doing, because she doesn't volunteer any details.

I know better than to ask.

I don't know if Eddie gets to see her or not before she leaves town, because I don't ask him.

We do *not* talk about this.

At all.

As in, we don't even *look* at each other if we don't have to.

Fortunately, it wasn't like the two of us hung out a lot before. Except now it seems like we're put together every time we fucking turn around, whether it's being assigned to the same duty schedule, or ending up at the same table for chow.

It's been four days since I saw her and I'm crawling the walls. I'm horny as hell. This has been the longest stretch in a while that I haven't been allowed to come, but rubbing one out doesn't feel...right.

Not when she told me to be her good boy. I'd do anything to obey her.

Pleasing her makes *me* feel good, even if I go through misery in the process.

When I send her my usual good-morning text on day five, I don't get the expected *good boy* response.

Are you horny, boy?

Holy shit, I could drill for oil with the goddamned boner I've got. I've had cold showers aplenty.

Yes, Mistress.

And have you behaved yourself?

Yes, Mistress.

She replies a moment later.

Because you've been a good boy, and you're my Alpha pet, I am going to give you very special permissions. E will come to you at lunch time. He is now your beta. You may fuck his mouth. I have already given him permission to pleasure himself while you do that. Just for today, though. I want a text from you both once it's done.

I have to re-read the message several times, because my cock's now so hard I can barely think straight.

It takes me several tries to tap out a typo-free response.

Yes, Mistress. Thank you.

You know what? At the time, I *honestly* didn't think any farther than *Hell, yes, I'm allowed to come!*

Yes, she was already planting the seeds from which the bastard was to grow.

* * *

We do it in my room because it's farther from the main

entrance to our area and quieter. I lock the door behind Eddie. He doesn't say a word to me as he unfastens his belt and shoves his briefs and ACUs down before he drops to his knees, waiting.

He won't meet my gaze and his cheeks are red, but his cock is hard and he opens his mouth as I unfasten my belt and my ACUs and shove my briefs down when I step in front of him.

Okay, then.

I'm not even attracted to the guy, but my aching cock and throbbing balls could give a shit. I grab his head and…go.

Meanwhile, he starts jerking off.

I close my eyes and think of *Her* while I fuck his mouth. Ten minutes later, he's wiped up his mess and left—without ever having said a word to me, but then again, I didn't say anything to him, either.

And for the first time in days I feel like I can *think.*

I text her.

Done. Thank You very much, Mistress.

Her reply hardens my cock.

My VERY good boy. :) Good boys get rewards. You may use beta every day at lunch like that while we're apart. I will text you both when to stop. He is allowed to make himself come, but from now on, he must lick it up. Feed it to him, if you must.

Fuuuuuck me. My hands tremble as I reply.

Thank You very much, Mistress!

* * *

It takes me three days of being a nice guy when I use him to realize he actually gets off harder on it when I'm rough and talk to him, call him a good little slut, refer to him as beta, things like that.

Once I start doing that, he's usually moaning and I have to choke him on my cock to keep him quiet, which makes him come harder.

Which makes *me* come harder.

Day eight of this new routine, and I realize my life is revolving around wanting lunch to hurry up and get there so I can get relief. We both always text her after we finish, and that day brings the next development.

Good boy, Alpha. Because you two pets play so well together, you may play together twice a day, and you may fuck beta, if you want, or use his mouth. His choice for the first time, yours for the second. He is not allowed to refuse you. He still must clean up his mess.

Jesusfuck, what the *hell*? I really don't have any other answer I can text her, because just reading and re-reading the text has me throbbing.

Thank You, Mistress!

Eddie shows up at lunch and locks the door. Without a word, he puts down a condom pouch, turns his back to me, shoves his ACUs down, and gets on his hands and knees. I can barely get mine open, between how hard I am and how much my hands are shaking.

He's already lubed himself.

Okay, then. Here we go.

Later, I show up at his room around nine and fuck his mouth. I accidentally discover I like having him up on his rack, his head tipped back over the edge and cushioned by the mattress, because I can really pound him into it and he comes even harder. I also found

I can last a little longer, and he can more easily take me deeper that way.

After three days of that, she changes it up again.

Since beta is being so good, it's time to reward him. Starting today, and every other day, he may use your mouth or ass one time for pleasure instead of his hand, if he chooses. You may still use him as you were. Remember, good boys swallow.

Um…
Oh, boy.
I have no options.

Yes, Mistress. Thank You.

She replies immediately.

That's my very good Alpha. :)

Keep in mind, other than what I say to him, he still has not said *anything* to me during our "play." The only thing he mentions is a time or place. Sometimes that's through texts on my burner phone.

There are no conversations, no pillow talk, no canoodling—nothing.

Not to mention we're probably breaking all sorts of regs doing this.

Okay, we're *definitely* breaking them.

But the furthest thing from my mind is my Dad or my brothers or anything but making *Her* happy and getting off. That's *it*.

I'm just wondering what kind of reward we're going to get from her when we're finally able to see her again.

That day, for our lunchtime meet-up, he blushes as he points to my mouth.

I don't hesitate, and I lie on my rack, tip my head back, and get comfy.

Now he's almost…well, shy. He's actually having trouble getting it up, and I can see him grow more frustrated.

I feel bad for the guy.

I finally hook my hands behind his thighs and pull him in and take over, sucking him down. He almost falls over, but braces himself on my rack and finally gets hard.

I realize the more I take charge of this, the better he does, so I pull off, flip him over so he's lying on my rack, then stand, going down on him like that.

He's like a changed man and gets hard immediately. I fist his shirt in my hand and pin him down as I get him off—yes, I swallow—and he seems to need a minute to recover.

The look he gives me when he lifts his head… Like something between awe and wide-eyed wonder.

Yeah. I don't understand it either, or why it twists my insides in good ways.

Or why I keep my hand on his shirt to hold him in place to kiss him.

He hesitates at first, then starts getting into it. Guy's not a bad kisser, actually.

I crawl up his body and leave him pinned there as I unfasten my pants and then fuck his mouth right there, making him lick my sac and…

I belatedly realize we're going to be late if I don't finish up. I'm eating a granola bar for lunch as I text her a few minutes later, once he's left.

Thank You, Mistress. I kissed him while we played. I'm sorry I didn't ask if that was allowed first. I didn't think about it.

Good boy, Alpha! You are absolutely allowed to kiss your boy.

I read her text several times.

Okay, then.

*   *   *

From that moment on, things were…different between me and Eddie. Like something had shifted. He started hanging out with me, Kenney, and Gohber, joining us for morning PT and meals, all of that. Became one of the guys. Some of our play happened off-base, like in a park or in the bathroom at a bar with Kenney and Gohber out at our table—risky stuff we should've known better but did it anyway.

I took great pleasure in taking my pleasure from him, and finally got him to admit he liked it better when *I* was in complete control, even when going down on him.

Blowjobs were usually logistically easier than fucking, which we didn't do nearly as often, and thus became the norm.

It was over three weeks since we'd last seen Elsa, a Friday, when she responds to my morning text.

Can you and beta come over tonight?

I don't know Eddie's exact schedule, but I can go, and tell her that.

Good boy. See you at 7. No playing today. If he can make it, arrive together.

That's how the two of us caught a bus and rode together, chatting about any- and everything, but constantly catching each other's gaze and knowing we were both thinking the same thing—we were horny and excited to be back with her.

When we arrive, we both strip and drop into *Worship* at her command. I'm beyond excited to see her, and I'm sure he is, too.

"There's my good boys," she softly says. "I'm very proud of my Alpha and beta. You took good care of each other while I was gone." She rubs both our heads, and…

Oh, fucking *thank* you.

The sweet, mellow bliss fills my head. I'd missed it so goddamned much.

"I have a *very* special treat for my two good boys tonight," she says. "We need to get you ready."

That means hoods, blindfolds, and leather cuffs buckled around our wrists and ankles.

She puts me on my back across the bed, my legs hanging off, feet on the floor. Thankfully, it wasn't a very tall bed. My arms are over my head and she clips the wrist cuffs together and fastens them to the bed frame. Eddie is put on the other side of the bed, facedown, his wrists clipped behind his back, his ankles hooked to the frame and keeping his legs spread wide.

I find this out later.

But our heads are next to each other.

Kissing distance.

And Elsa pushes our faces together. "That's right, just like that. I want you both to show me how much you like that."

So we do. Like I said, he's a good kisser.

I hear a knock on the door, and my cock twitches in response.

I don't know about Eddie, but I'm beyond hard now.

"What's going on?" he whispers. He sounds worried. I listen. It sounds like four men, and I swallow hard.

I've learned Eddie doesn't speak a word of German. That's when it hits me for the first time that, if she's been doing stuff with him like she does with me, he has *no* fucking clue what's going on, unless she's speaking English to him.

It'd actually started feeling…friendly between me and Eddie. We'd started finding a kind of groove between us.

Now, I'm not sure how we're supposed to act except...obeying her.

I wish I could see him, look into his eyes. But I kiss him and nuzzle his nose with mine, hard with the hoods but we manage it, because I can't reach him with my hands.

"It's okay," I whisper. "Just obey Mistress."

"Okay."

They're all apparently Tops, but one of the guys does go down on me.

I find out why my legs weren't tied down when someone grabs my ankles and shoves my legs up and back to give them access to my ass.

Fortunately, Elsa lubes both of us.

There's a strange push-pull in my soul as we lie there and get used. My body is loving the pleasure I'm feeling, because if I'm not being sucked, Elsa's jacking my cock while someone fucks me.

And she's kissing me, telling me how good I'm being, even when a cane and a paddle get used on my ass, and hear Eddie receiving a similar treatment.

Even when I end up with a cock at both ends—check first spit-roast off the list—I feel Elsa's hand on my head or my cock, and she's telling us both in English how proud she is of us and how good we're being for her.

Eddie ends up shifted away from me a little, and some of the sounds he's making…

Okay, some of them are definitely a guy enjoying what's going on.

Then there are other sounds, and, honestly? I'm glad Eddie *can't* understand German. They're not just humiliating him, they're really dredging depths I'm not comfortable with.

That's the night when I finally learned a truth, after she unfastened our restraints and told us to kiss and cuddle on the bed while she saw her "guests" out.

My blindfold had slipped a little, and I could see under it.

I saw the wad of bills she pocketed.

I didn't know, at first, how Elsa could work at the mundane government job she held and yet still afford to live where she lived and the manner in which she lived.

She told people in polite company that her family had money.

I was fucking naive.

The reality, of course, is far darker.

She wasn't a whore. That would have been too debasing, too demeaning for her.

No, her sideline business, I soon realize, is a very specialized and expensive service—whoring out *others*. To a very particular clientele.

Others like me and Eddie.

CHAPTER TWENTY-ONE

We were young and stupid and in love with the woman. What can I say?

At least she assured us that, when guys fucked us, they used condoms, and she had checked their test results. That they were "carefully screened."

Is that bullshit? I don't know. I'm just glad I didn't end up pos. The only credit I'll give her is that she did seem to be very careful about that. I guess she had her own health to think about and her reputation to consider.

I was soooo stupid. Young and horny are *very* bad combinations for making good decisions, I've since realized.

Sometimes, women were part of the equation, usually with their submissive men, who were allowed to fuck us or be blown by us while the women also got off with us somehow. Or, sometimes I was used to fuck the guy, depending on the particular dynamic the couple had.

Regardless, Elsa would usually start those times by horning us up, praising us, telling us what good boys we were, and teasing us until we were begging for relief. On the back side of the session, more praise.

I thought this was…well, okay, I knew it wasn't "normal" but I didn't realize it wasn't healthy or, technically, consensual.

To me, if it wasn't rape, it was consent. I had no fucking clue beyond that. Rape—bad. But what we were doing wasn't *that*, right? I mean, we were *agreeing* to what we were doing and having done to us.

Weren't we?

Hell, she got both of us off. We were never left hanging on those nights.

The more Eddie and I did, though, the more Elsa pampered us. The more attention she paid to us. The more time she spent with us.

The more she praised us.

It made it far more comfortable for us to ignore the dark thoughts that would creep in sometimes. Made it easy to ignore the times that we weren't that keen on the activities, because she always made up for it in other ways.

Give and take, right?

This went on for the next couple of months. Eddie and I had fairly regular schedules now and usually had weekends off, even though we had to stay close to base. When we both received full forty-eight-hour passes, Elsa made plans to take us to a party in another town, a private house party, where we'd be spending the night.

Yeah.

Except we were the party favors, for men and women.

We spent that whole weekend blindfolded and had no idea who was doing what. Elsa was there, and I understood more of what was going on than Eddie did, obviously.

There was a guy who seemed particularly interested in me. I never heard him speak English, but he didn't sound like a native German. Sounded older.

Liked to spank me with his bare hand. I'm pretty sure he fucked me a few times over those two days, and I know I blew him at least once.

He rubbed my head the way Elsa would.

Don't get me wrong, Eddie and I both had a blast that weekend, but I still didn't tell Eddie about seeing Elsa accept the money that day.

Maybe I should have.

I *definitely* should have confronted Elsa about it, except that whole *I was young and dumb and definitely in love with her* stupidity.

No clue how much she was paid for our services that weekend, and part of me doesn't *want* to know. We were never offered any of the money. She pretended that didn't happen, although from some stray comments I heard, I'm sure that she was paid, and it apparently wasn't the first time she provided "entertainment" for a gathering like that. I tried not to think about it and stay in the moment.

I think maybe she forgot I spoke German, because when it was just the three of us, she always spoke English for Eddie's benefit.

Eddie and I were both moving kind of slow the next day, Monday morning, and that's when shit happened.

We were both summoned to the colonel's office that morning. I'm sure the *oh, shit* look on Eddie's face matched mine as we headed over there.

There are a few memories that will forever live with me, some of them big, some of them small. Memories positive and...not so much.

Sensations, smells.

Sounds.

As we stand at attention in the colonel's office and he walks behind us to close his door, the *snick* as he throws the lock will forever stay in my mind.

The sound of his footsteps as he walks behind us and stands there so close I can feel his breath against the back of my neck.

But it's the next word he whispers, in very familiar-sounding German, that makes me realize exactly how deep a world of shit the two of us are in.

"*Worship.*"

I know the wide-eyed horror in Eddie's eyes matches mine as he stares at me before we both drop to our knees.

* * *

We now belong to the colonel. Maybe "belong" isn't the right word, because it's clear Elsa still claims ownership of us.

Priority access, maybe?

Rentals?

Oh, we still go to Elsa's several times a week, but Eddie and I get used to being fucked over the colonel's desk at least once a week, usually at night, or blowjobs, if he doesn't have the time for more.

The thought of saying no doesn't cross our minds. For starters, Elsa arranged it. Apparently, the colonel is a "friend" of hers.

Secondly—fucking colonel, *duh*.

The colonel seems to prefer me over Eddie, and I get summoned more often. We're not allowed to come when we are with him, either, so we're left frustrated and horny on the back side of those encounters. Unless we can get alone time with each other, sneak away somewhere on base to give each other relief. I've gotten really good at fucking Eddie's mouth fast and busting a nut in a variety of locations. Sometimes he doesn't get relief then, and has to wait until later.

But that's now one of my perks as Alpha. Elsa allows me to use him after I've been with the colonel, and Eddie's never allowed to refuse me.

The benefit to this strange dynamic is that apparently the colonel doesn't want to share us with other men. We're free to play with each other, and Elsa has women who sometimes use us, so at least there's that.

As the months tick by, I realize we aren't getting deployed. Before, I assumed somehow my Dad—and the fact that I had two brothers who were KIA—gave us a little bit of protection.

Now, it's obvious the colonel is likely keeping us there because he doesn't want to give up his toys.

I don't know what excuses are being used, but Eddie and I share secret glances any time we hear someone talking about it— and giving thanks for it, because, seriously, *none* of us actually *want* to be sent to a goddamned desert.

Not like we can say, "Yeah, the married colonel likes secretly fucking us too much to deploy us. You're welcome."

But Elsa is like a new woman with us. Sweet, loving—and, as crazy as this sounds, I'm not jealous of Eddie. Maybe in the beginning I was, but going on a year into this insanity, and now he's my buddy. He definitely is a bottom, but I find I like topping him. Sometimes Elsa has me top other men or women for her, and that's okay. We can fuck or be fucked by the women, but with the men, sexually, we're limited to using hands or strap-ons or other toys on them.

Or the men using those on *us*, except men are allowed to blow us.

When topping women, and most of the men, I have to tone things back sexually and physically.

Unlike with Eddie, who wants and needs a heavy level of play from me, both sexually and physically.

I'm enjoying it, too. He brings out something dark in me I never knew was there before. I start to discover after some of our more intense sessions that it leaves me feeling quiet and calm in a way that I only used to feel before and after Elsa took control of me.

And I really like that, too.

It's like the best of both worlds. I can submit to Elsa and enjoy that, and also enjoy what I do to Eddie or others. When it's just the two of us with Elsa, she frequently makes love to us, and it reaches a point where it feels natural for it to be the three of us.

We don't ask Elsa about the colonel. He becomes a mostly unspoken topic. Apparently, he clears with her when he calls for one of us, because she always knows about it before we go and sometimes it's her texting us to send us to him, especially after hours.

We do as we're told and think of the reward it's going to earn us with her later, when we see her again.

All she tells us early on is that she's made an arrangement for us with him, and if we're smart, we'll go along with it. That it will make *our* lives easier.

To enjoy the special perk of being appreciated by an officer such as him.

That it means we're afforded, by him, a level of protection we might not otherwise enjoy.

We thank her, of course, because there really isn't another option, in our minds. And we do feel…thankful.

Let's see, getting fucked in the ass versus getting our asses shot at or off.

Yeah. That's a no-brainer.

Meanwhile, she takes us places on the weekends, like World Cup games, or museums, or concerts.

It's feeling…

Comfortable.

It's a melancholy feeling, though. This can't last, no matter how much the thought of this ending one day tears me up inside. I won't be in the Army forever. I know Elsa isn't interested in something permanent, even though this sure *feels* permanent.

Eddie and I work on rank promotions, though he plans on staying in longer than I do. And Elsa starts talking to both of us like maybe she does want to make this permanent.

I'm a stupid kid. I don't stop to think about the fact that she's whoring us out to a colonel or others.

I mean, I *do*, but it's just easier *not* to think about that part of things. Not when we're with her and she smiles at us, praises us.

Tells us what good boys we are.

Her laughter.

I focus on the fact that she nurtures us and makes future plans—except one.

She does *not* want children.

Over the next several months with Elsa, I find myself going from really wanting kids to not wanting kids. So does Eddie.

I find myself nodding when Elsa says how nice it'd be if we had vasectomies, then we wouldn't have to use condoms with her.

Hello, frog. Meet pot of cold water.

Don't worry, it'll get warmer.

Then the suggestions become more solid nudging on her part. Eddie and I are *really* starting to think maybe she actually *means* forever when she offers to pay for our vasectomies.

"How far would you go for me to prove you want me for life?" she outright asks us one afternoon.

Eddie and I exchange a glance. Somewhere, during the past few months, I realize the answer is *anything she wants*. We've been doing this with her for over a year now, working on our second year. The colonel definitely prefers me, because I might end up being used by him a couple of times a week and Eddie none. Eddie is now the backup and usually only summoned if I'm unavailable because I'm on duty.

I've actually started thinking about staying in Germany when I get out, maybe going to college here instead. I'm fluent in German now, and have been improving my vocabulary, my pronunciation. They have attorneys in Germany, right?

One night, after she's made love to us and once again *tsks* how inconvenient it is that she can't dispense with condoms with us, I finally take a deep breath and say it.

"I'll do it."

Once I've agreed, so does Eddie.

Of *course* Elsa manages to get us a week's leave each. She drives us to the appointment, pays the doctor at the clinic cash, and fills out our paperwork for us. I notice she uses fake names for us.

We spend a week off, both of us recovering at her place, with her literally fucking *babying* us, cooking for us—Jesus, I didn't even know she knew *how* to cook, because usually Eddie and I do the cooking when we're with her—and making promises with and to us.

It's not long after that when the bottom falls out.

CHAPTER TWENTY-TWO

Now

I stare down at this woman, this nightmare generator who's been an invisible emotional vampire in my soul for nearly half my life. "Eddie says fuck you, by the way. And to remind you he told you karma is a bitch."

Elsa chuffs out what's supposed to be a laugh, I suppose, but the booze and pills are already hitting her hard.

"You're still with *him*?" she slurs. "He can go fuck himself. He was *horrible* in bed. He tried, but he was never much good. He was too needy. He was much better suited to be a fucktoy, not a boyfriend." She tries to focus on me. "Unlike *you*. You were...amazing, *boy*. You were always my favorite, special boy." She sadly sighs. "I always did regret letting you get away."

I refuse to let myself think about the guy I was or what that guy felt for her back then.

The things that guy didn't merely willingly do for her, or let her do to him, but who *begged* for them at one time, simply to make her happy and earn her praise. To earn her smiles, her laughter.

Or how that guy once would have *killed* to hear those words from her—that she regretted letting him go.

That guy no longer exists, and hasn't for a long damn time.

That guy's death birthed Sarge and the bastard extraordinaire, who are the same man, basically. One is enlisted, one's a civvie, but they're just different names for the same damn guy.

I hold up the gun and motion with it. "You need to take a few pills, Elsa."

She's trying to focus on me. "What?"

"Pills. Take three."

"I took some."

"No, you didn't. You were going to, but you got distracted by what we were talking about."

She giggles. "What were we talking about?"

"That you are in pain and need the drugs to help you. That's why you stole the money, isn't it?"

"*Ja.*" She sighs, opens the bottle, and shakes three more tablets into her palm. Then she swallows them and chases them with vodka. She doesn't bother putting the cap back on the pill bottle.

I still wear my gloves. I pick up the bottle of vodka with my free hand and top off the glass for her. "You look thirsty, Elsa. You should have a drink."

She doesn't bother arguing with me. I don't know if she's compliant because of everything hitting her system, because she knows I mean business because of the gun, or because she's simply ready to follow this path now that she understands her only decent chance to free herself from it has evaporated.

Because if she borrowed from the kind of people I'm reasonably sure she borrowed from, based upon the kind of people I know she used to know…

Well, this is a *far* kinder fate than they'd have in store for her.

She's got great tolerance, I'll give her every bit of that. I wait a few minutes and talk her into swallowing four more pills.

Then I lean against the wall and wait. "This is also for Eddie," I tell her. "He deserved better than what you gave him."

She stares at me, but I think we've hit the point of no return. Her eyes look glassy and she tries to speak, but it's just slurred sounds, nothing intelligible.

I smirk. "Eddie would come to *me* after I left you, Elsa. He'd visit me at night for comfort. You didn't drive a wedge between us, you only brought us closer. *I* was there for him. He came to *me*. His loyalty was to *me*. And I took care of him after you got rid of us. He was *mine* after we were deployed."

I'm not sure how much she's processing now, and I don't care. "I have a life now you can only *dream* of. I'm powerful, I'm rich, and I have a family. I could have been yours if you'd just stayed loyal to me and Eddie. I was thinking about staying in Germany, you know. I would have worked my *ass* off to take care of you after I got out and went to school. We could've made it work. But you never gave a shit about us. You *used* us, until you couldn't easily control us anymore. It took me a lot of years, but this is satisfying, seeing you used up and broken."

I walk over and lean in. I want her to hear this. "I am loyal to *my* pets," I softly say. "I *love* them. When *my* pets are threatened? I will kill or die for them. Guess which option this is."

It takes another ten minutes for her to pass out, slumped forward on the couch.

I set the gun down on the coffee table and ease her onto her side with her face pressed into the cushion, then grab a throw pillow. Her system's so numbed by the narcotics and booze that there's barely any reflexive response, just one of her legs kicking a little.

All the times toward the end, when I was bent over the colonel's desk, when I'd fantasize about doing something just like this to her—only to feel horribly guilty about those thoughts because narcissists are master manipulators of their victims.

Here I am, getting to do *exactly* what I'd wanted to back then.

I take little satisfaction in this now. It was much preferable imagining her...

Well, like *this*. At her lowest point, reduced to a nothing existence with no one in her life to love her, while I have nearly achieved the apex of my success and happiness both professionally and personally.

But no way in *hell* will I let this cunt's evil hands so much as indirectly touch my Owen, my Susa, or my boys.

Or Eddie. Because she likely would have gone after him next.

She fucking turned me into the bastard I am today. My reward for the penance I did back then, and the nightmares I suffer as a result, is Owen, Susa, and the boys.

My blessings.

The dark filth of her soul will *never* foul their lives or taint their existence.

I am not the literal or metaphorical boy she once owned, and I refuse to be him again.

Ever.

Alpha died in the dust of time and memories when Sarge took over.

The bastard extraordinaire rose from those ashes like a phoenix.

The bastard also has no trouble burning everything down to get what he wants and needs.

After she's gone, I roll her onto her stomach with her face pressed into the cushions.

A good man might have waited until she passed out and simply taken the photo—and her phone and computer, just in case—and left.

However, I am not and have never claimed to be a good man.

Sarge has always been a bastard extraordinaire, thanks in no small part to the woman in front of me.

I am the creature she made and molded and forged. Frankenstein's monster.

There is poetic justice in the fact that I get the literal final word. This is for me, for Eddie, and for all the others she fucked over, whose hearts she shit on, and whose lives she tried to or succeeded in ruining.

For the happiness she tried to take from me a second time.

For the children she denied me as a bullshit, narcissistic loyalty test.

* * *

I remove my gloves and don't touch anything with my hands except her lighter. I use that to burn the picture in her bathroom, holding it over the toilet, and I flush the unrecognizable ashes, using a hand towel to hold the handle. Then I put my gloves back on, wipe the lighter clean, press her fingers to it, and return it to where I found it.

One problem solved.

Her phone I switch off, remove the battery from it, and slip it into my pocket. Her laptop also goes with me, stuffed in an old messenger bag I find on the floor by the table. It's after dark and I'm almost two miles from her flat when I stop in a wooded park at the edge of a river. I keep my gloves on. After glancing around to make sure I'm not being observed, I toss the phone and battery into the water. Then, after walking a little farther, I quickly break down the nine and toss the slide in. I continue walking along the bank, thumbing rounds out of the magazines into the water, toss the magazines themselves, then the barrel, and the frame. The switchblade.

What to do with the laptop?

I'm damn sure not keeping it, and I need to make sure it's as unattractive a salvage project as possible.

I walk into a copse of trees and remove the laptop from the bag. Opening the computer, I stomp the screen and keyboard with my heel, grinding dirt and rocks into it. I probably have a little too much fun doing that, thinking about the hell I endured.

Then I flip it over and jump on the back side of it, making sure it's trashed, before righting it and peeing on the keyboard.

That should hopefully discourage anyone from trying to recover the contents of the hard drive.

I dump it back into the bag and toss it in a large garbage container behind an apartment building on my way to a bus stop.

Like I said, I have never claimed to be a good man.

But at least tonight I will hopefully sleep well with that particular nightmare generator permanently excised from my life.

CHAPTER TWENTY-THREE

Then

It's been twenty-two months since I met Elsa that night in the club and my world—and asshole—was expanded.

Am I in love with her?

Absolutely.

I don't lie, either. When she asks if I love her, I tell her.

So does Eddie.

We're called over one Friday evening and she has a surprise for us.

"Beta, guess what? You get to play with others now. The colonel has decided to play only with Alpha."

It is always "play" or "playmates." The colonel is never mentioned by name. We are *never* allowed to use his name with her. Her rule.

In fact, she doesn't use *our* names unless we're somewhere it'd be noticed, like that day at the doctor's office. Even then she uses fake names for us.

Otherwise, we are always Alpha and beta.

Except for the past several months, she has Eddie refer to me as "sir."

I have to check myself one day at chow when I almost call

Eddie beta in front of Kenney and Gohber.

It's weird living this dual life. Literally, we have two extremes. We have the Army and life on base, and we have Elsa.

Except the colonel straddles those lines.

"Why, Mistress?" Eddie asks, and I feel sorry for him. I know from talking to him that he doesn't have family. That's why he enlisted—he'd grown up in foster care. Rejection is something he's painfully all too familiar with. Elsa and I are really the only relationships he's ever had.

I sadly realize that, despite the circumstances, being rejected by the colonel is still another form of rejection he takes personally.

"Well, he hasn't played with you in a couple of months. I told him if he's not going to play with the pet, he needs to share." She rubs his head. "Don't worry. I've lined up other playmates for you, my sweet beta." She flashes him that smile we'd do nearly anything for.

He smiles back, but something tightens in my stomach. I don't like the feel of this, or the reptilian gleam in her eyes.

Then she turns to me. "You, however, are busy tomorrow." She hands me a hotel room key card and a sticky note with the name of a local hotel, its address, and a room number. "Be there at eight in the morning." She pats my cheek. "You don't need to take anything with you."

Fear congeals in my gut, and for the first time, I consider saying no.

Maybe it's my hesitation, but she cocks her head at me. "Is there a problem, Alpha? May I remind you this is a very *special* situation. That man controls your future. You and beta *both*."

Her gaze challenges me. She's hit my other hidden weak spot that I didn't even realize had developed. I don't want to disappoint my family, that's a given. But I'm also feeling protective. And, somewhere along the line, I've come to think of Eddie as *mine*. I have his six, he has mine.

I don't want to be the cause of the colonel coming down on Eddie.

I want to protect him.

"No problem, Mistress," I quietly say. I can't meet Eddie's gaze.

Eddie, however, is to report to Elsa's tomorrow. She doesn't detail their "plans" but I suspect if the colonel doesn't want Eddie anymore, she's going to put him back in circulation with her other "friends."

* * *

The colonel definitely has a sadistic streak in him I hadn't experienced much of before. Not like he can spank me in his office. I'm tied up, beaten, used as much as he can get it up— which, I believe is due in no small part to the colonel's little helper blue pills—and then left there with orders to stay in the room for an hour before I leave to return to base.

He doesn't make me come, but the second time he fucks me, on my back with my ankles over his shoulders, he makes me jerk myself off and call him Daddy while I beg for permission to come. Apparently, he likes that so much that I'm ordered to refer to him as Daddy for the rest of the day. And any time he sees me getting hard, he makes me jerk off and beg Daddy for permission before I'm allowed to come.

What am I going to do? Say no?

No, Colonel, I'm not going to call you Daddy while you fuck and beat me.

Yeeeaaah.

#notstupid

What's worse?

Part of me really likes it, even as I understand how utterly fucked up this is. That confuses me and makes me think Elsa must be right about us after all, that we *are* naturally wired to enjoy this.

Aren't we?

* * *

Eddie isn't back yet when I return to base Saturday evening. I grab a shower and lie in bed, staring at the ceiling and wondering why this doesn't feel *good* anymore.

Wondering when it stopped feeling *good*.

The next morning, Eddie's unusually quiet during PT and won't meet my gaze when I try to get him to look at me. Kenney asks what's wrong with him, and he claims he's working on a headache, but he's lying.

I *know* it.

We're supposed to be at Elsa's at noon, but when we're finally on the bus and I ask him what's wrong, he still won't look at me.

"I'm fine," he quietly says.

Because there are other people on the bus, I can't corner him and demand he talk to me. This fucking feels *wrong*, though.

I was under the impression we were going to spend the day with Elsa going out with her, but apparently that plan changed. We're ordered to strip and don hoods, and Eddie is blindfolded.

She takes my hand and leads me to the far side of the loft, away from the bedroom where she's left Eddie. With music playing, he won't hear what she's saying when she drops her voice.

And she speaks to me in German.

"You, my special boy, get to help today. I am going to run errands. When someone knocks, you let them in, put what they give you in this envelope, and supervise. They must wear condoms when they fuck him. Men are not allowed to use you, but if they ask you to do something to beta, you will obey."

She hands me an envelope and also a leather jock and I dumbly stare at them for a moment. "Mistress?"

"Wear that when you answer the door. Hoods stay on, beta

stays blindfolded. Don't worry." She smiles, rubbing my head. "*Only* speak German while I'm gone. I'll be back in a few hours." I finally realize yeah, she's all dressed up.

Like, *date* dressed up.

Normally, I'd never balk. "Mistress, beta doesn't speak German."

Her grin widens. "I know. You have my orders, Alpha."

"Yes, Mistress," I quietly say.

She grabs my chin and pulls me in for a long, sweet kiss that melts me and hardens my cock. "You may freely use beta," she adds, reaching down and stroking my cock. "If he's a good boy, you may reward him at your discretion." She giggles. "Preferably while he's being fucked. Men love feeling that. Makes them feel important."

She grabs her purse. "First playmates will be here shortly. You know the other rules—no pictures, no names, all of that." Her smile fades. "Do *not* disappoint me, Alpha. I will be checking in with my friends. If you do well today, I will reward you next weekend."

I realize she hasn't even asked me how yesterday went.

And then…she's gone.

Eddie is still kneeling in *Allegiance* on the bedroom floor. I put the jock on and go to him. At least he knows the kneeling commands in German.

I take his arm and coax him up onto the bed. I feel sorry for him, because I know damn well if I break her rule about speaking German, she'll find out.

Hell, she'd probably ask Eddie and he'd tell her the truth. Not to snitch on me, but because we've been trained to tell her the truth.

We're rewarded for it.

So I do all I can do and sit there next to him, with my arm around him and his head on my shoulder while I rub his head through the hood and whisper what a good boy he is in German, using the same tone Elsa does when she says it to him in English.

I hope he understands.

Because after the first playmates arrive and pass over a wad of bills I don't even count before putting them in the envelope, I stay there with Eddie, supervising, helping when ordered, and I'm repeating that phrase to him even when he's crying in pain or groaning in pleasure. I make him come several times, and the only time I come is when one of the playmates orders me to fuck Eddie's mouth while he's fucking Eddie's ass.

While I do, I whisper to Eddie repeatedly what a good boy he's being and stroke his head.

I also whisper how sorry I am.

* * *

Over the next several weeks, I spend two more Saturdays with the colonel at the hotel while Eddie goes over to Elsa's. That's in addition to the once or twice a week I'm summoned to the colonel's office. Also, on two Sundays, I'm left to supervise Eddie's play, as well as a couple of evenings a week.

I never count the money. I wasn't ordered to, and she never asks me about it later, but I feel dark resentment building inside me. I don't tell Eddie about the money. I feel like since I didn't before, it makes me...complicit, in a way. I don't know *how* to tell him about it at this point.

I also don't like how...withdrawn Eddie acts after these "play sessions."

But when we have Elsa all to ourselves, she's even more cuddly and loving, and I watch Eddie carefully and see how he smiles and looks happy when with her.

I find I'm distancing myself from Elsa a little when we're with her, wanting Eddie to be her focus. He won't talk about what happens when I'm not there, and I know what happens when I am.

I can connect the dots. He's earned the attention from her.

I also teach him a few German phrases so I can have more communication with him and feel less guilty when I supervise.

I suppose I should have expected it that Saturday morning when we arrive at Elsa's and are told not to strip. Then she hands me a key card—it's always the same hotel—and a note with a room number.

She also hands me a bag, which contains condoms, lube, our hoods, one blindfold, one leather jock…

And an envelope.

She smiles at us. "My *very* good boys," she sweetly says. "This is a test." She looks at me. "Alpha, you are in charge today. I expect you to take care of beta, the way you have been. The same rules. Understand?"

No.

That's what I *want* to say, but I nod. "Yes, Mistress."

Maybe she sees something in my gaze, I don't know. She walks over to Eddie, talks to him, rubs his head, until he's nuzzling against her and begging to do anything to make her happy and please her.

I recognize that look she gives me—*So there.*

I can look back and see that the nasty jolt in my guts over that was the first contraction of Sarge's birth. The bastard extraordinaire's birth.

She comes to me and catches my chin in her hand. "I'm counting on you, Alpha. I will come for you both late this afternoon."

Eddie's watching me now, and I don't know why he looks desperate. I wish I could talk to him. I'm not sure if he's desperate for me to say yes, or for me to take the lead and say no.

"Alpha?" she asks.

I finally nod. "Yes, Mistress."

CHAPTER TWENTY-FOUR

Eddie and I are in the process of working toward E-5. We get a month-long respite when Elsa has to travel for a work conference and goes on holiday to visit family.

I'm officially in charge of Eddie, but it's just the two of us hanging out on base, or doing mundane things in our free time with Kenny and Gohber.

I make sure we spend private time together every day, and I realize there are times I don't feel like coming, but I always make him come.

Sweet and gentle doesn't work for him, though. He needs to feel used, "forced" to do it.

And so I do that for him.

I'm not sure how to feel about the fact that doing that almost always makes me horny as a result, so even if I start our time together not in the mood, I'm frequently in the mood after he's come and I end up using him anyway.

Which sometimes gets him hard again—and I let him come again.

Elsa would probably say I'm spoiling him, but it makes me feel better to do it.

When Elsa returns and we're summoned that Friday evening, she looks tan and refreshed, and there's a new, naked pet in her loft when we arrive. He's a German kid, nineteen, skinny twig, and despite his nervous expression, his cock is hard. We haven't even stripped yet, because she had us wait to do that.

"Pets, meet beta." Elsa looks at Eddie. "You are now 'gamma'." She reaches over and pets Eddie's head, smiling.

"No."

I don't realize I've said it until I see Elsa frown and the panic that splashes across Eddie's face.

"*What* did you say to me?" she asks.

I think about it for a second. "I want to talk about this, Elsa."

It's the first time I've used her name like this in…

Well, I can't remember. That's how long.

Rage fills her expression. "We do *not* talk. *I* tell *you* what happens. Since you've never defied me before, I'll give you another—"

"*No*. This is the *three* of us. *That's* what you said."

"I never said that!"

Eddie doesn't speak, his wide-eyed horror saying it all.

"All the times you talked about future plans with us?" I remind her, a frigid cold trying to settle in my gut. "All the things we've done for you? What we *had* done for you—that was all talked about like you wanted to spend the rest of your life with us."

Hell, I'd gone so far as to seriously research living here full-time, going to college here. I'd actually visited one of the nearby universities.

I'm guessing the kid's English isn't that great, because he looks confused as hell.

She's livid. "How *dare* you defy me! After everything I've done for you! You should be *grateful* I'm giving you another pet to play with!"

"Everything you've done for me? You mean whoring us out? When do *we* get some of that money, huh, Elsa? It's *our* fucking asses on the line. Especially Eddie's. How much is the colonel paying you for every—"

Her slap across my cheek silences me.

"*Worship!*" she screams at me. "Now!"

I rub my cheek, a cold, hard wall falling into place as I stare down at her. "Fuck you. We can talk about this like adults, but if you ever strike me again in anger, we're *done.*"

Eddie gasps.

Fury contorts her features. When she reaches up to slap me again, I block her arm.

I have *never* defied her before. *Ever.* I've never tried to block a hit, or refused an order.

"Get out!" she yells. "Now! Don't you *dare* contact me again, either! You and I are finished!"

My gaze meets Eddie's and I pause when I see the tears in his eyes. I want to hold him, comfort him.

Ask him to come with me.

Tell him we don't fucking need her.

I also don't want to get him in trouble with her.

And I know that while neither Eddie nor I have acknowledged that, yeah, what we have is a *relationship* with each other, we also know for various reasons that being "gay" probably isn't a viable option. Not with him wanting to stay in the military and with my family. If I tried to introduce him as anything other than a friend, I would catch a ration of shit and probably be cut off from them.

Before I walk out, though, I lean in, grab him by the head, and fucking *kiss* him. "You're a *good* boy," I whisper with my forehead pressed against his. "My door's *always* open to you."

"Get out!" she screams.

Then I leave, slamming the door behind me.

Well, *that* could've gone better.

I wander around on foot for a while, debating whether or not to toss my burner cell. But Eddie texts me on it, too, so I opt to hold on to it.

I wonder if this means my friendship with Eddie is over.

I hope not, because I realize that, somewhere in the middle of all this, I love the guy. I feel...responsible for him.

I'm worried about him and what will happen to him now without me around.

But he's an adult. He can make his own choices, I suppose. I'm not going to beg him to leave her, because I'm no pity fuck.

I make my way back to base and sit up in bed, reading, my door cracked open and hoping Eddie will come talk to me when he returns.

He doesn't. In fact, I know he's somehow managed to sneak in without me hearing when I see a light on under his door when I make a trip to the bathroom.

Okay, then.

* * *

Monday morning, I'm summoned to the colonel's office. Eddie didn't join us for PT or chow, and he wasn't in his room when I went looking for him to talk.

He won't respond to my texts, either.

I stand at attention, even after the colonel locks the door behind me.

From the stony mask he wears, I know I'm in trouble.

"*Worship.*"

I remain standing at attention and keep my voice down. "Sir, I don't understand, sir."

I don't move.

Not a fucking muscle.

He stands in front of me, his gaze narrowed. "Is that the way it's going to be? I heard there was an...issue."

That's one fucking word for it, I suppose. "Sir, I don't understand, sir."

I'm just hoping this doesn't get back to my dad. Fortunately, the colonel desperately needs secrecy even more than I do.

He finally walks around behind his desk and sits. "Last chance," he quietly says. "We can talk about this. *Allegiance.*"

"Sir, I don't understand, sir."

I'm sweating fucking bullets, though. Because I've never bucked an order.

Ever.

Especially not from a fucking colonel.

He leans back in his chair and slowly nods. "All right, then. Dismissed."

I nearly run out of there, because by the time I get outside, I'm puking up my breakfast into a garbage can.

* * *

Eddie rejoins me and Kenney and Gohber for PT and chow Tuesday morning. While he pretends everything's okay, I sense an unease in him that wasn't there before. He assures me he's fine, but when I wait in my room at lunch time, just in case, he doesn't show.

Over the next two weeks, I think okay, maybe things will shake out. I've discovered jerking off isn't very satisfactory anymore. It's not as bad when I remember stuff I did to Eddie, but any time I think about the other faceless, nameless "playmates," or being on the receiving end of things, it kills my boner.

I have more time to spend with Kenney and Gohber, but miss having Eddie around all the time. I sense a growing sadness in Eddie's gaze when it sometimes lingers on me a little too long from across the table during chow. I notice he always stays right behind me in PT, where he can watch me but I can't look back at him.

I keep the burner cell, just in case, but don't really expect to hear anything. He has my regular number, too.

My immediate anger has been replaced by grief, and I mourn

what I thought we had with her, what we did that I enjoyed. I mourn the dream I had built up in my head, no matter how impossible it probably was from the start.

I mourn what I gave up for Elsa while thinking she actually fucking loved me. Then I shove to the back of my mind the fact that I gave up one of *my* dreams for her, and I was so easily cast aside.

Because if I spend too much time thinking about *that* aspect of all *this*?

I'll swing back into rage, and probably do something stupid like hunt her down and kill her.

I feel…stupid.

Elsa finally texts me the next Saturday morning, and I hate the elation and hope that mixes with the dread and anger.

Are you ready to come back yet, pet?

Not Alpha, but pet.

Bottom of the ladder, I suppose.
I reply.

Did you get rid of the other guy, Elsa? I don't mind playmates, but for pets it's just me and Eddie.

She doesn't reply.

It's midnight when I hear a soft tap on my door, and I get up to answer.

It's Eddie, and he looks like shit. He's been crying.

I pull him in and close the door behind him. Then I get him over to my bed, where we sit. He curls up with his head in my lap and cries while I stroke his head and call him my good boy over and over. He leaves about an hour later, without ever telling me what happened. All we did is sit there while he cried, sniffled, and I held him and told him he was my good boy.

That I love him.

I apologized for leaving him behind, and told him if he wanted to leave her, that I'd take care of him.

That I would never leave him behind again if he would just leave *her*.

That we could figure something out for *us*.

Because now I'm fucking lonely as hell and realize I'm willing to risk trying to make something for *us*.

If he'll just leave *her*.

If he'll just choose *me*.

I don't see him Sunday. Kenney, Gohber, and I go to town to see a movie and have some beers. I listen as the guys rate women walking by, but I'm unable to get the sound of Eddie sobbing out of my head.

Another memory I'll never be able to erase.

He taps on my door at ten thirty that night, and I hold him, let him cry, tell him he's my good boy.

Tell him I love him.

I don't ask him what's happening with Elsa.

I don't want to know.

It'll make me angry.

Angr*ier*.

The best thing I can do is simply *be* here for him and hope he decides to choose me, in the end.

* * *

Not every night, but what I'm sure is every night he's spent time with Elsa, I get a tap on the door and he cries. I hold him, rub his head, ask nothing of him. Anger is also tinged with guilt, that I left him behind.

Except I can't force him to leave her.

I'm summoned to the colonel's office on a Wednesday morning, the first time since that day I turned him down, and I nearly puke on my way there.

I run into Eddie on his way out of the building, and he looks horrible, but won't meet my gaze as he ducks around me and scurries off.

I struggle against the urge to run after him and find out if he's okay, barely suppressing my rage over whatever things Elsa is orchestrating being done to him, and holding back my grief over what we've lost.

I stand at attention while the colonel closes and locks his office door. He moves to stand in front of me.

"I don't often give second chances," he softly says. "We can have an…arrangement separate from *her*. It'll be good for your career, and your pocket."

I don't break attention. I think about the money, wonder how good it is, and for the briefest of moments I *am* tempted.

But then the sound of Eddie crying in my arms in the dark fills my brain.

I keep my voice down but do not break attention. "Sir, I'm sorry. I don't understand the question, sir."

He stares at me. "Five thousand a month, cash, and you're…*exclusive* with me. It's what I was paying her. I don't know how much she gave you of that. I hate the new guy, and that friend of yours…" He waves his hand.

Fuckballs.

Rage takes over again, and this time, I meet his gaze. "Sir, I wasn't given one red cent, *sir.*"

He smiles. "Then I guess you'll be happy to accept that offer, huh?"

"Sir, with all due respect, sir, no."

His smile fades. "No?"

"Sir, no, sir." I opt to lie. "Working on my E-5 now, sir. Need to focus on that." Which is an utter bullshit excuse, but since he knows Dad and who my brothers are, I'm hoping that buys me some space and time. I mean, I *am* working on my E-5, but that's likely where I'll end my career. If I bust my ass, I can apply next month.

He's not done trying yet. "If you accept my offer, your career is no longer a worry for you. Eventually, I'd transfer you to my personal staff, so I'd have easier access. You'd have it easy all the way around. Private quarters. Fringe benefits, including traveling with me on official business. It'll be a good life, a pay bump. Better than you can get now. Cushy. No combat. That'll make your mom happy, I'm sure. It'll *definitely* help your career."

Could I live with myself, though, if Eddie, Kenney, and Gohber get deployed and I'm stuck in an air-conditioned office here?

Could I live with myself if I look at casualty reports and see their names?

Could I live with myself, or the memories of dropping my pants and bending over his desk, the sound of his breath in my ear as he fucks me, while knowing maybe one or more of my friends died in a desert somewhere?

I decide no, I can't.

"Sir, with all due respect, I'm sorry, sir."

He stares at me for a long time. "So am I, kid. I thought this would be a perfect solution for both of us."

I also hope he dismisses me soon, or I'm going to be hurling all over him and his office.

He slowly shakes his head. "All right, then. Dismissed."

I leave. This time, I manage to not hurl until I'm several buildings down from HQ.

* * *

I don't tell Eddie about the colonel's offer. Over the next two weeks, Eddie still visits me several nights a week, and guilt is settling deep inside me. I don't do anything sexual with him, just hold him, tell him what a good boy he is, tell him I love him, and rub his head.

I suspect he's not telling Elsa about these visits.

I also try not to imagine what she's doing to him or putting him through without me there to soothe him.

Also, the more I think back on those "play sessions," I can see how much she used me against Eddie, in some ways. Left to go do whatever and put me in charge. Or let men—and a few women, but mostly men—use him as little more than a cum-dump and a doormat.

How she frequently withheld praise from him until after the fact, but never really soothed him.

That job always fell to me, both during and after, because I took the time to teach him German to be able to connect with him.

Two weeks to the day I rejected the colonel, I'm shocked and confused when my commander approaches me and pulls me aside to tell me I've been promoted to E-5.

#thatsnothowthisworks

I'm stunned, confused. I rejected him—*why* is he promoting me early?

He shakes my hand. "Apparently, the colonel likes you. Speaks very highly of you." He smiles, but there's no hidden knowledge behind it. "Maybe your dad put a bug in his ear. Anyway, you have the points, but you get it early. Colonel pushed it through personally and got it approved. Good thing it happened now, too." He turns to go.

A chill washes through my soul. "Sir? Good thing, *why*?"

He glances around before answering. "Keep this under your hat, but looks like we're being deployed in-country in three weeks. FOB Oswald. Afghanistan. Orders should be cut tomorrow." He laughs and smacks my shoulder. "Welcome to leadership, kid." I stand there, stunned, as I watch him walk away.

Motherfucker.

CHAPTER TWENTY-FIVE

Now

I'd opted to drive to TIA and leave my car in long-term parking. It's awaiting me upon my return a little before noon that morning, and I climb behind the wheel with a weary sigh. I didn't sleep well on the flight back, and I'm exhausted.

I text Susa's personal phone that I'm back in Florida, to please hold texts, and to pass that to Owen. That I'll call tonight once I've had some sleep.

In reality, my first stop after my return to Tampa is Benchley's house. I'd already texted him my arrival time before boarding my flight in Germany. I text him that I am en route before I leave TIA, and he's alone when I arrive.

We retire to his office, where he locks us in. I'm sure Michelle is used to this behavior after forty-plus years of marriage to the man, but it still unsettles me considering what I just went through and all the old memories surrounding it.

Memories which are now slamming into me and demanding my attention.

"Handled?" he asks after he sits behind his desk.

I arch an eyebrow at him. "Is what handled?"

His gaze narrows as he studies me for a long moment. Then he shakes his head and chuckles. "You should have been my son."

"You'll have to settle for son-in-law, despite how you and Michelle wish she'd married Owen. By the way, he told me, back then, about you offering him money for dirt on me. He told me as soon as we were alone." I slump back in my chair. "There was a time you would've killed to have this kind of dirt on me."

Benchley smiles. "That was before I found out what a bastard you are. And how good you'd be for SusieJo's political career."

"She hates when you call her that."

His smile widens. "I know."

Bastards know each other when they meet.

Despite being alone in the house, he glances around me again to make sure the office door is closed and locked before he opens a desk drawer. He withdraws a bottle of Macallan and two water glasses, pouring us each two fingers.

He hands one over. "You tell Michelle about this bottle and I'll neuter you myself." But he's smirking as he sits back and swirls his own glass.

I hold mine up in a toast. "I saw nothing."

He holds his up. "Neither did I." He arches an eyebrow at me. "And I'd better not see anything else in the future. I only gave you that freebie as a courtesy. Anything else crops up, you're on your own."

"You won't see anything else." I stare at him. "And this never gets mentioned to *anyone*. Not to Susa, not to Owen. Just like your little 'incident' will continue to remain private between us."

He shrugs. "I don't know what you're talking about. You stopped by to say hello to your father-in-law."

We clink glasses before I throw the liquor back and let it linger on my tongue for a long moment before swallowing. It's smooth, and almost seems a shame not to sip it, but I don't have the time today. "Let's ratfuck David Kelley. You said you've got some stuff on him."

The tip of his head more than the expression he wears belies his confusion. "Why him?"

"His son is the strongest opponent the Dems have against Susa in the primary. No one else they've got in their field can touch her numbers."

"Not much of an opponent, even if he wins his primary. I'm not sure he's worth spending the energy or trouble on."

"He is. He's got the look. We make it appear like David Kelley covered something up for his son, tie the missing girl from his high school class to him through some deep background sources, and get that shit-pot simmering nicely. Even if nothing else comes from that, it'll shadow his entire campaign. It'll always be a sub-lede in every profile done on him. Including if he tries again in four years. Let's do that work *now* and make sure he's out of the way. She'll slaughter anyone else who wins their primary."

Benchley sits back in his chair again and smiles. "You're pure evil Carter." He motions at me in a sort of salute with his glass. "I love it. Glad you're on Susa's side."

I salute with my glass. "I take care of *mine*," I softly say. "Whenever you need to wonder what my motivations are for anything I do, just remember that fact about me."

* * *

I wearily pull into the garage at the Brandon house and let the door roll down behind me before I drag myself out of the car and grab my suitcase.

After a shower and setting an alarm on my phone, I face-plant into a bed I miss far too much to think about right now.

If I didn't know how much Susa wants to be governor, I'd pull her out of the race, sell Owen's house, and the townhouses, and just...

Be a family.

This is my dream. Our sons, any other children we might have, my two pets happy and healthy.

We could all retire, if we wanted to. Susa's smartly managed our money all these years, and we're set.

When I fall asleep, the nightmares start almost immediately, about the day in the desert. I'd started that morning before dawn with Eddie. We bunked together in a tiny room in those shitty, temporary housing units there that were little better than plywood boxes.

But we could start most mornings before we got dressed with him naked on his knees and stroking himself as he blew me. Then I'd spend a moment standing there, rubbing his head as he held my softening cock in his mouth, and I'd tell him what a good boy he was for me. Always in German, the phrases he now knew well, because I found out hardly anyone in our unit spoke it.

Less chance of someone catching on.

It was risky and stupid but we did it. The harder I did it, the more he liked it.

And the more *I* liked it.

We would sometimes sneak in daytime play, too, but that wasn't very often.

Nothing like a blowjob under a clear, desert night sky, though.

When we came under fire, I immediately dropped into a different state of mind—clear, calm, shoving my panic to the side when I saw Eddie go down first, shot in the leg.

The car always rolls up slower in my nightmares than it did in real life. In my nightmares, I'm not able to throw myself over them in time, and all three of them die.

In my nightmares, I'm uninjured and left screaming over Eddie, who asks me why I left him behind before he dies.

I awaken in a cold sweat, the sheets soaked. I sit up and realize I'm trembling, shaking.

As bad as this nightmare is, it's preferable to the other ones, the majority of ones that usually hit me.

The ones where I'm still with Elsa.

* * *

I have a swim, take a shower, shave, and get some food in me in plenty of time to call Owen on FaceTime, where he's alone in his bedroom at the mansion.

I smile at him. "How's my boy?"

"Good, Sir. Miss you."

"Miss you, too, boy." I was going to drive up in the morning, but I know I won't sleep tonight, and another idea hits me.

I keep it to myself.

"How was your trip, Sir?"

"Uneventful, fortunately."

"Will your friend be okay, Sir?"

Eddie stops by the hotel before I fly out and we have a drink in the bar downstairs.

I don't dare risk asking him up to my room. Fortunately, he doesn't suggest it, either.

Before I put him in a cab, I give him a long, strong hug, standing in the middle of the sidewalk in front of the hotel. He smells so familiar, and yet different now.

It's been so damn long.

I still hurt.

I know he does, too, but this is something I cannot fix for either of us, unfortunately. Not any more than I just did. This ache will always hurt and will never heal.

It'll never be enough, but it has to do, because it's all I *can* do.

I kiss the top of his head and whisper to him in German the old words, what a good boy he is, and how much I love and miss him, and how sorry I am that I left him.

And I tell him one last thing. "I took care of her for you. I told her for you. I told her about us, and that you are mine."

I rub the top of his head as his ragged, hitching breath warms my shoulder, the side of my neck, and I pretend I don't hear him sniffle.

"Thank you, sir," he whispers. "Love you, too." I feel his lips press against the side of my throat, and then he's gone, into the cab, leaving.

I stand there with my hands in my pockets and watch his cab take him back to his life.

I blink and focus on Owen's green gaze watching me from my phone.

I sigh. "I hope so. He was better when I left."

"Is he one of the three, Sir?"

I know what he means, but I realize now it has more than one meaning. "Yeah," I say. "He's one of the three."

After I end the call with him, I pull up Skype on my laptop and talk with Susa and the boys. Dray and Gregory are over, too, playing with them while trying to work on re-election stuff with Susa.

"I'll be home tomorrow," I promise, knowing I made the right choice after all, even though it still hurts with that wound now raw and exposed.

Susa's beautiful smile helps. "Love you, Sir."

I smile. "Love you, too, pet."

* * *

It's just after midnight when I park at the mansion and security lets me in. This is not uncommon. They know I was away on business, we have a state to run, and I'm the governor's fucking chief of staff.

They don't question why I arrive at noon or midnight.

They don't *fucking* question *me*, period.

Susa and I have standing unlimited access to the governor.

Owen startles a little when I slide into bed with him after stripping, then he quickly snuggles against me.

"Mmm. Is it morning already?"

I kiss him, inhale, breathe in my boy's scent, and my aching soul settles a little. "No, middle of the night. Go back to sleep."

He rolls over to face me and presses his face against the base of my throat. "Missed you, Sir."

I hold him tightly and swear to myself I will never let him go. "Missed you, too, boy. Love you."

"Love you, too, Sir."

CHAPTER TWENTY-SIX

We make it through the primary. Now it's four weeks before the general election. I'm in Owen's office, going over details with him about the last few campaign appearances he'll make on Susa's behalf, when Julia's voice comes over the intercom.

"Governor Taylor, Senator Samuels is here and wants to know if she can have a few minutes of your time."

Our gazes meet and I know the confused frown he wears matches mine. "Senator *ShaeLynn* Samuels?" he asks.

"Yes, sir."

"Did she say what she wants?"

"To speak with you, sir."

This means the senator is probably standing right there, looming over Julia. Owen's AA does pretty good pushing back against state-level lawmakers and garden-variety assholes.

United States Senator ShaeLynn Samuels, however, is intimidating even to someone like me who's survived active combat and lived with Senator Benchley Evans as his father-in-law for over two decades.

Owen lifts an eyebrow, waiting on me.

I love this. *All* of this.

Our silent communication, the rapport.

The fact that he's governor of one of the most highly prized swing states, and yet he still looks to me for permission.

It still hardens my cock.

Which I have to adjust in my slacks as I nod and round his desk to take my seat in one of the chairs there. She's going to have to physically throw me out if she wants to talk to him alone.

"Go ahead and send her in," he says.

"Yes, sir."

He stands and doesn't even bother rolling down his sleeves. The office door opens, and Julia ushers the senator in before leaving and closing the door behind her.

I remember my manners and stand, giving the senator back every ounce of intimidation and then some that she tries to shove down my throat.

I consider it personal growth that there isn't even a hint of wanting to drop to my knees in front of her rippling through my soul the way it used to in front of Susa in the early days.

"Senator Samuels," Owen says as they shake hands. "This is an unexpected—"

Interruption, distraction, imposition—

"—pleasure."

That's my boy, always tactful.

I shake with her and then retake my seat, silently letting her know that I'm not going anywhere.

She glances in my direction before apparently deciding it's not worth trying to get me to leave. She takes the other seat while Owen returns to his.

"I apologize for dropping in like this, Governor Taylor, but I'm leaving for DC this evening and wanted to do this in person."

I'm immediately wary and on-guard. *Do this in person* is political-speak for *I don't want any kind of paper or video trail that can come back later to haunt me or bite me in the ass.*

Owen leans back in his chair and laces his fingers behind his head, looking deceptively casual. He doesn't always do well with women like the senator. Too close of a reminder of his mom.

Too close of a reminder to Susa. He sometimes struggles not to drop into his default mode.

Another reason I wanted to stay here with him. Both his witness and his strength.

"Do what, Senator?" he asks.

Another glance my way. "What I'm about to tell you is confidential. I would appreciate discretion."

"Anything you want to say to me, you can say in front of Carter," he tells her.

"I'm forming an exploratory committee," she says. "Well, let me correct myself. That's not exactly fully accurate. I *am* running for POTUS. Just haven't officially declared yet."

Fuck.

Me.

Yeah, I can see her doing that, too. Probably winning. Seems like all the rumors I've been hearing lately are correct.

I take a slow, deep breath and force myself not to react.

"Congratulations," Owen says. "But what does that have to do with your visit today?"

"I wanted to know if you want on the ticket. Give you right of first refusal, so to speak."

Owen scowls. "Me?" My boy is adorably clueless sometimes, and I can still see hints of the college kid who was terrified of his own shadow.

"Yes, you. You're a long-shot who won by a landslide. Twice. Not counting your other offices." She glances my way again before focusing on Owen. "You obviously know your ground game. You're popular. It looks like Ms. Evans is going to win her race. Veep like you would grab a large demographic from a wide variety of areas. Midwest, fiscal conservatives, progressive environmentalists, moderates—and more than a goodly chunk of Democrats. We could do big things." She smiles. "And eight years later, I'd back your run, of course."

"Senator, I'm flattered, truly I am. And you can count on my public support for your campaign. Even stumping for you. Except, for starters, I'm an Independent, not a Democrat. Secondly, once I leave office, I'm *done*. I've achieved all I set out to accomplish. I have no higher aspirations than to go back to practicing law, and being a full-time godfather to Pete and Tom."

Dammit. My boy doesn't often make me cry, but when he hits exactly the right weak spot in me, it threatens to unman me in front of this woman.

She tips her head and studies him. "You don't even want to run for the Senate? I figured in two years you'd be asking for my support. I've heard rumors you were going to run."

He shakes his head. "You've heard wrongly, or just wishful thinking from some people. Besides, my personal life has taken enough of a hit over the past eight-plus years. I'm ready to be out of the spotlight, and so is my partner."

I silently groan.

I *really* wish he hadn't said that. I mean, I get *why*, because Samuels is single and reportedly a man-eater, and Owen's trying to nip any potential shit in the bud now.

She scowls. "I didn't realize you had a...partner."

"I do. And they didn't ask to be in the spotlight. So I've literally moved Heaven and Hell to keep them out of the spotlight."

"She's a very lucky woman. Or he's a lucky fellow?"

Owen laughs. "Nice try, Senator, but no. I won't divulge even that much. I made a promise to them that I intend to keep."

Now she focuses on me, even though her comments are for Owen. "I haven't heard any rumors about you being attached."

"That's because Carter is the best there is at his job. He keeps our ship running smoothly and leak-free."

Her gaze narrows just a hair, and I sense the calculations spinning through her mind at warp speed. "*You* want a job?" she asks. "I'm going to need comms, and a campaign manager. Either one could be yours. Could mean chief of staff once we're in, or press secretary. Your choice."

It's...intriguing. I won't lie that, for just a second, I could see myself standing in the Oval Office and running through the morning briefing with her as POTUS.

But without taking my focus off her, I can see Owen in my peripheral vision. My boy will say yes to whatever I ask of him, no matter at what cost to himself.

He's proven that time and again.

I've asked enough of him for one lifetime, and we still have—most likely—eight more years to go.

At least.

Because once we're done in Tallahassee, I'm sure Susa's going to go gunning for this woman's job.

No matter my own aspirations, my first priority has always been Owen.

Always.

Promises to keep.

And there's my answer, right there. "That's very flattering, Senator, but I'm afraid I must decline. If my wife wins her election, which I have no reason to believe she won't, then I'm going to have my hands full being a full-time dad, and with my own job. I miss practicing law."

I toss in a little bit of radar chaff to deflect potential problems. "One of the deals we made when we started this was that Owen got to borrow Susa for eight years, and then I'd get to borrow him during the next eight to help me out while Susa's busy with her job."

She's still fixated on me. "And his *partner* is okay with this?"

I nod. "They are."

Boy, are they.

I didn't even have to lie.

She sighs, relaxing, and I realize we're off the hook. She's probably not going to try again. "Well, that *is* disappointing. I was really hoping to come out of this little tête-à-tête with a running mate *and* a campaign manager."

"Sorry to disappoint you, Senator," Owen says. "We're not your guys."

"Although," I add, to throw her a bone, "I would be happy to discuss potential staffing decisions with you, and point you in a few helpful directions. I'm not sure a Florida running mate would be the best decision for you, anyway."

She settles back in her chair, reappraising me. "Why not?"

"Well, exactly what you said—demographics. You'd be better off with someone from the Midwest, a moderate candidate who can reach a wider audience. Flyover state-friendly."

"Hmm. I don't suppose your father-in-law would be willing to sit down with me to talk shop, would he?"

"I can call him and ask, but he doesn't travel much anymore because of his health."

"That's fine. I'll be back in Tallahassee on Monday morning, and can be in Tampa on Monday evening. I would consider it a personal favor if you could talk to him. I can clear my schedule for any time between next Monday and Friday to talk to him."

I nod. "I'll do that."

She stands, and so do Owen and I. "Thank you very much for your time today, Governor Taylor. Mr. Wilson." She shakes hands with me and Owen rounds his desk to shake with her, as well as to go open the door for her.

My boy remembers his lessons well.

There's a Secret Service agent standing just outside Owen's office door, and he turns when Owen opens it. Guy's good, but I don't miss how his gaze quickly sweeps Owen, then me, before a hard, thick wall descends.

Well, then.

Guy's hot. Even with his suit—or maybe because of it—I can tell from the way his stance shifts just a little that he's dying to adjust things in his slacks. We apparently rev his motor.

Fair enough. He can eat his heart out, but that's *all* he can do.

And he can rest easy that neither I nor Owen will be his competition for the senator's affections or attention.

Because if the rumors I've heard whispered are correct, this is very likely Special Agent Christopher Bruunt, head of the senator's security detail.

And, most likely, a guy she's been fucking.

Getting wrapped up in *that* personal disaster waiting to happen isn't anywhere on my bucket list, thank you very much. I'm perfectly happy with the two pets I have.

Even if I wasn't, there's already a previous claim on my soul.

I nod to Bruunt and he nods in reply, falling into step behind the senator as they leave, and speaking into his mic to someone about bringing the car around.

I glance around the office just to make sure everything's okay, then speak with Julia.

"Hold the governor's calls, please, unless it's Mrs. Evans or Draymond."

"Yes, sir."

I close the door and quietly snap the lock shut, watching Owen as I do.

At the sound, Owen freezes for a second before he turns, his gaze on me.

Always on me.

Damn, now *I* need to adjust myself.

I do just that as I grin and shake my head, walking over to pull him into my arms. "My boy's popular."

"Not with her security."

I snort. "You noticed that, huh?"

"Yep. Kind of obvious. To me, anyway."

"I've trained you well."

"Yes you have, Sir." Pride fills me at the playful smirk he gives me.

I lay a kiss on him, reminding him of all the sweet, loving things I can't wait to do to him once we can sleep in on weekends anytime we want. I'm ready for a break.

I want to take Owen and the boys on vacation.

Susa's dying to take over this office and get to work.

Me?

I'm ready to stand back and let my wife be the gloriously beautiful political beast she was raised and longs to be.

She doesn't need me hovering over her. In this way, she actually prefers I'm *not* hovering. She doesn't need me in the same ways Owen needs me, and I'm fine with that.

We have a very small window of time left before the boys start school. I want to make memories with them before then, Owen and I. They'll always have Mommy, and they know that.

Owen *needs* this time with them. Especially since we have to be careful how we spend it.

His very heart and soul need it.

I can't deny it to him. Hell, I can't deny my boy anything. I never have been able to deny my boy anything, even if he doesn't realize it. I might torture him for our mutual amusement from time to time, but, in the end, whatever he asks of me, I try to move the universe to make it happen, by whatever means I have to.

He wanted unconditional love, to feel wanted—done.

He wanted children—done.

He wanted to be governor—done.

He wanted Susa—done.

He wanted to be able to truly live serving someone who could appreciate all facets of who he is—done, and doing.

He wants the rest of his life to be as peaceful as possible, able to go on and enjoy himself, taking satisfaction that he worked hard and made good changes, helped people—in progress.

I lean against his desk, my hands dropping to his ass to pull his body tightly against mine.

Yep, he's hard, too, but unfortunately we don't have time for me to fuck him over his desk today.

Maybe tomorrow.

Or even tonight. We'll see.

He stares down into my eyes, his smile fading. "You really don't want to work on a national campaign like that?"

"No."

Clouds fill his sweet green eyes. "I...I mean, if you wanted to—"

I *kiss* him. Not just a peck or a brush of lips. I usually try not to *kiss* him like this at work, because we both end up with pink in our cheeks from stubble rubbing, our lips red and swollen. Only when I feel his entire body trying to sink into mine do I finally end the *kiss*.

I cup his face in my hands. "Owen," I gently say, wanting him to know how serious I am, "I love *you*. Do I enjoy the game of politics? Sure. But what I'm going to enjoy even more is sitting at the breakfast table with you and reading the morning paper, or kicking back on the couch with you and the boys and watching movies. Or taking a school day off and after we drop the boys off, taking you home, and we fuck each other over every piece of furniture we own."

He sweetly smiles, but I'm not done.

"I follow *you*," I say, trying not to get choked up. "If you told me you wanted to run for the Senate, or the House, or for POTUS, then yeah, we'd be doing it. We're dads now. I'm with you that I can't wait to be a full-time dad. You know as well as I do that we don't *have* to go back to work, if we don't want to. We can sell your house and quit pretending."

"What about Susa? The campaign?"

I shrug. "We wait to sell the house until after she's re-elected. Doesn't matter, because you have the townhouse, and we technically will be living in Tallahassee. If anyone asks, we say you didn't like having to do the upkeep of a home, and you stay in one of our spare bedrooms when you need to be in Tampa. You're the former governor at that point. No one will care."

In my mind is a photo-shoot from a couple of weeks ago. I haven't shown him the proofs yet, but they're heartbreakingly adorable. Some formal shots, of course, but a few of me and Susa in the background, with Owen rolling around on the grass at the mansion with Tom and Pete, his sleeves rolled up and tie off, all three of them laughing.

They've also sent me the proof of the article that will accompany it, and the headline is *He's Florida's Most Eligible and Adorable Godfather.*

I'm sure that will make Owen a little uncomfortable, the eligible part, but that's on me. I asked the writer to drop subtle hints that Owen's single, despite what we told the senator. I also told the writer why, that Owen *does* have a partner—and again I didn't hint one way or the other regarding gender—and intimated that they could lose their sensitive job in a very specialized sector if public scrutiny is turned their way at this time.

Technically, none of that is a lie.

In return, I promised the writer an exclusive with Susa and I ahead of the election, a candid sit-down and photos, the whole nine yards, as well as another after the election, win or lose.

They were happy to agree to those terms.

It's not like this is a Pulitzer kind of article, either. This isn't deep background for Woodward and Bernstein. This is little more than a PR puff piece, and both the writer and I know it. It's designed to sell issues on the newsstand, to catch the eyes of people standing in line with their Publix chicken dinners on their way home from work. Period.

But having an exclusive with Susa and I would help focus extra eyeballs on their cover, and they know it. They're not stupid.

Hands wash hands.

It also means Owen will grumble in private about all the renewed love letters he'll start receiving.

They'll ease up. They always flood in after one of these kinds of articles, and ease up after several weeks.

Besides, in three months, he gets to change jobs and do what he really wants to do—

Be a full-time dad.

It'll be so good having my boy back.

CHAPTER TWENTY-SEVEN

Election Night

We are, not-so-coincidentally, occupying the same set of suites we have on all of Owen's election nights. We're also surrounded by many of the same people who were here for us on most of Owen's campaigns.

Owen is too focused on taking care of Tommy and Petey to feel nervous tonight, thankfully. It also helps that it's not his head on the block. He can actually enjoy tonight, because either way, his job ends in January, and the next chapter of his life starts.

Being a full-time dad, even if no one knows that but the three of us.

Well, and Dray and Gregory and Ethan.

Susa stands in front of the TV in the suite's living room and stares at WFLA's early election results rolling in when most of the state's polls close at seven. I watch her from the side, and she's focused, intent, a stoked boiler close to exploding. Without thinking about it, she starts nervously chewing on her right thumbnail.

At this point I know there's nothing more I can do. Unlike Owen, she doesn't need me dropping her into pet mode to cope with the stress. She thrives on this adrenaline spike.

God help us if she loses.

God help everyone else if she wins.

Benchley walks over to me and nudges my shoulder, then silently points toward Susa with his glass. A glass I hope contains iced tea and not bourbon, or Michelle will take it out on *me* for him drinking.

"She's fine," I say after glancing around to make sure no one's close enough to hear.

He leans in. "Contingency plan if she loses?"

"Not really, no."

That's a lie. Of course I have one, but it's none of *his* fucking business, Susa's father or not.

How I run *my* family and take care of *my* spouses is none of *his* business, even if he thinks it is.

Benchley stares at me for a long moment with the blue eyes he gave his daughter. "Take care of my baby, Carter," he hoarsely whispers. "Don't let her burn out, please. Don't let her become *me*."

My irritation at him evaporates. I had completely misread him. To be fair, Benchley has never directly expressed this kind of vulnerable emotion to me, not even during those raw, desperate days when we didn't know if she was alive or not. Days when we suspected she was already dead, even though we prayed and hoped and refused to give up.

I pat his shoulder and gently squeeze. "I'll *always* take care of her. You have my word."

Ethan, Dray, Gregory, and a few others who rightfully count themselves part of Susa's trusted inner circle, have gathered around her now in front of the TV. Dray drapes an arm over her shoulders and one over Ethan's. On Ethan's other side, Gregory slips his arm around Ethan's waist.

It reminds me that the three of us—myself, Susa, and Owen—aren't the only ones in this room with secrets to protect.

That this is one of the few safe places there are in our world right now.

The cycle repeats.

It also reminds me how grateful I am to be alive, that I didn't die in the desert that day, and to have found people who will fight almost as hard for my wife as Owen and I will.

It reminds me how grateful I am that Susa survived the plane crash and being shipwrecked. It would have crushed me to lose her, but it would have destroyed Owen in ways I likely couldn't have helped him heal.

Ever.

I might have lost him, too.

Not now, though. He's a father, has other reasons to live besides myself and Susa. He's a damned good father, too. I know he's looking forward to moving back home with me and the boys.

It also eases, in some small ways, my regrets about someone who's not here and never can be. Someone who has to remain in my past, and I have to remain in his.

If I hadn't made certain choices, none of us would be here tonight. I might not have my sons.

Susa might not be alive.

Owen might be miserable and unable to escape his mother for a life of his own where he discovered joy and made his dreams come true.

We've all had dreams come true. I suppose the price I pay for my part of that will forever remain entwined with memories of the sound of Eddie's sobs in a dark room, and the nightmares I might never completely rid myself of.

Susa will be happy having the governor's mansion mostly to herself, because she'll be too busy to even notice those times when we're not with her. We'll make sure we have frequent photo ops so the general public doesn't realize what's going on. Besides, having our townhouse so close to the mansion, and the boys being so young, means that no insiders will gossip too much about us wanting to keep them in the only home they've ever known, away from the harsh political spotlight.

Susa's sons will *not* grow up the way she did, and that's by *her* choice, not mine, not Owen's.

She wants the family business to die with *her*.

They'll be in middle school at the end of two terms, if she's reelected.

They'll barely know her.

Hell, I'll be pushing sixty by then.

I'm going to have my hands full making her take family time, and don't think I don't know that. She did, however, promise me that she would take off four to six years after her second term, before running for the Senate. By then, the boys will be close to heading to college.

Like I could really tell her no.

If she does decide to do that, to run for the Senate, then I'll be her campaign manager and Owen her chief of staff, which is only fair. It'll give us a chance to not need to make excuses being around each other all the time on the campaign trail, or why Owen spends time alone with her, or travels with her. Once she's elected, I'll handle comms, while Owen can be COS.

If he wants to.

If not, once she's elected, the two of us will focus on supporting her on the home front and staying out of her way.

All this was for her benefit, because Owen *damn* sure didn't want it. Not really. He wanted it because *she* wanted it for us. There's an irony there, too, that she's the cut-throat politician, and Owen's happy teaching the boys how to make dolmades and moussaka from scratch, in between helping them learn their *ABC*s and how to swim.

The loving childhood he didn't have, with doting parents he was denied.

And then there's me, the pivot between the two. Owen wants her to be happy, and so do I. We make her happy by supporting her. I want to make Owen happy. Making them happy makes me happy.

Lather, rinse, repeat.

"*Fuck*, yeah!" Dray yells, high-fiving Susa, Ethan, and Gregory as more results roll in.

I loudly clear my throat, and he turns, realizing what he said as he catches sight of the boys with Owen. "Whoops." He grins. "Sorry, Dad."

But I glance over to where Owen and the boys are curled up together on the couch. He's not wearing his jacket, and he's loosened his tie. He's got the boys in his lap, holding his iPad as they play some sort of educational game together that's probably teaching them numbers, or Esperanto, or kid physics, or...something.

Owen spends every spare minute he has—and a few that he doesn't—doing everything he can with the boys. Sometimes I wonder if I should tell him to tone it back a little, until I realize he's being a good dad.

I can't bear to deny a second of that to him.

Owen's counting down the days until he can kick back and enjoy life again. I've already told him he's to take the next six months off, and I've cleared his calendar as much as possible.

On the other hand, Susa's counting down the minutes until she knows her future for certain.

A future she desperately wants, and I'm feeling...ambivalent about.

As her husband, I want her to be happy, even if all I wish is for the three of us to be able to relax and enjoy life out of the spotlight, enjoy this time in the boys' childhoods.

Be a family, where we don't have to worry about people popping out of doors with cameras, or spying on us if we want to walk down the street and browse through shops.

I want to be able to lean over and kiss my wife…and my husband.

And I want them to be able to kiss each other in public, with or without me there.

I want to return to our house in Brandon, be able to sell one of the townhouses in Tallahassee, and cherry-pick the work we do. Let Owen handle environmental cases when he wants to. Maybe I'll do a little campaign consulting. Susa can write her book or throw her opinion in where she wants to as a TV network's political expert.

The love in Owen's eyes when he watches us can't be measured. The joy that's filled his life since we've become parents can't be bought or sold.

In many ways, absolutely, he's *finally* getting the childhood he was denied, even as he's a dad.

Downstairs, there's a stage awaiting us, win or lose. There is a room full of people who started assembling there hours ago, and who are probably starting to get pretty damn loud now that the polls have closed and exit polling numbers are swinging heavily our way in even greater numbers than Owen enjoyed.

There are a couple of FHP officers and several Hillsborough County deputies on duty in the hallway outside the suite. Whether they're going to be guarding one or two governors by the end of the evening remains to be seen.

I have my suspicions it'll be two.

Tomorrow, I already have a full morning slate of interviews booked for Susa, just in case. Some want her win or lose, some contingent upon her winning tonight. That fucking Kevin Markos wants first crack at her, regardless. I decided to tell Dray to book him first for a sit-down and get him out of the way. Any hits Markos scores on her, she can swing back during the later interviews and make him look like an ass. Either way, tomorrow morning's going to be busy.

Except I promised Owen we'd sleep in. Cook breakfast with the boys. Make scrambled eggs and French toast. This suite has a little mini kitchen, and I went shopping.

If Susa wins, Dray is perfectly capable of walking her through her schedule tomorrow. I have to stop holding his hand at some point.

I have to stop holding *her* hand, not that she's needed me to do that.

I needed to do it.

If she loses, she's not going to want me hovering over her anyway. Another way in which my two pets are different. I'd be stupid—and a poor husband to both of them—if I didn't recognize that and give them the space they need when they need it.

Susa can simultaneously exist in a world where she'll both take a loss as a personal rejection of her, or perhaps see it as a series of missteps on our part in the campaign—and beat herself up regardless of the reason, within our control or not.

To her, nothing less than a win is acceptable.

Unfortunately, that's one thing I haven't been able to train out of my sweet pet.

Fortunately, it's that very stubborn spirit that kept her alive and brought her home to us.

I'm sure, as long as there's breath in her lungs, it'll keep bringing her home to all of us.

* * *

As the evening wears on I know, win or lose, I'm going to have to totally go bastard extraordinaire mode on Owen to get him back in his jacket and downstairs to put in an appearance. Since Owen's the incumbent, and Susa's his lieutenant, his attendance isn't optional, unfortunately for him. But Tommy's already dozed off in his arms, and Petey doesn't look far behind.

My boy would rather chew off his own arm than wake either of them when they're asleep.

Except they're our children, and they'll be expected to be seen on stage with us. The photo ops alone are worth it.

Yes, I feel like a shit for thinking that way, but don't think Susa hasn't already thought that ten times more than I have.

Both the thought itself, and feeling like a shit for thinking it in the first place.

What can I say? We're complicated people.

I decide I'll carry Petey and let Owen carry Tommy. I can already see that Petey looks so much like Owen, and having him in Owen's arms might make people ask questions.

We just need to make it through the next four years and her reelection campaign, as long as Susa wins tonight, to avoid people making that comparison.

After that, it won't matter, even if she wants to run for Senate. There will be enough time out of the spotlight for us that we can have peace.

Plus, with Owen and me carrying the boys, Susa can walk out waving, free to shake hands along the front of the stage, and it won't require an awkward hand-off of kids on stage. We've already trained the press that he's "Uncle Owen," not just our best friend but also the boys' godfather. The pictures taken of the boys sitting with him in his office, behind the governor's desk, are treasured keepsakes I will always tear up a little over.

Susa's decided not to go back on the pill, preferring to let nature take its course. I made a deal with her—two years. If after two years she doesn't get pregnant again and isn't in menopause, she'll go back on the pill, or Owen will get a vasectomy. I don't want to risk her health with a late pregnancy after she's already been through so much.

We have more Heaven than I ever imagined. It's plenty enough.

Finally, we have answers, and phones start ringing. Resigned, I mentally begin to prepare myself.

As I stand here tonight and watch my pets, I can't help but smile. I'm going to enjoy sleeping in tomorrow. I also decide fuck it, Owen can leave his jacket off.

He's not the new governor, so why does it matter? Let him enjoy this evening. It'll make him happy.

I, however, have to put mine back on. As the candidate's husband, I ironically no longer have the leeway I did simply being the governor's chief of staff.

In fact, as I stand in front of a mirror and fix my collar, straighten my tie, Susa walks up behind me and wraps her arms around my waist. She's smiling at me in the mirror.

From the day Owen and I met, we had a rapport, a way of silently communicating entire conversations just with our expressions.

It took me and Susa a little longer to reach that point, but we did.

We're having one right now. She glances over toward the sofa, to Owen and the boys, then back to me, with one eyebrow arched.

Can they stay up here, Sir?

Owen's...*done*. He's tired, he's done, but I don't want to do this without him.

Because he loves us, he'll follow us wherever we ask him to go.

All he wants is to be with us, be a family with us. While I appreciate and love her for wanting Owen to have that break now, he needs to make an appearance downstairs.

I lift my eyebrows at her and give her a smirk that's not quite *that* smirk.

Our boy really should *come downstairs with us.*

She glances over at them, sees that the boys are yawning, too, and tries again, a hint of pouty lip.

But they're so cute and tired. Please, Sir?

I pull out the sorta-stern look, and she breaks first, snickering against the back of my shoulder.

"I had to try, Sir," she whispers in my ear from behind. "They look so comfy."

I keep my voice down. "I know." I finish fucking with my tie and reach for my jacket. "But we can send them up early." I turn to her. "Make sure he's at *our* table for the ball."

She smiles. "Yeah?"

"Yeah. On my other side from you. All of us, or none of us. No one left behind. I don't give a shit if people ask about it."

She kisses me. "Thank you, Sir," she whispers.

"For what?"

"For everything. This. Him." She smiles. "You. For no one left behind."

I sigh as I think about the one I did leave behind, and wish there was more I could do for him. Except I know I need to accept that...no.

He will remain a broken promise I can't go back and...*fix*.

"Eight years, pet. Then your ass belongs to us again, for a while."

She smirks. "My ass *always* belongs to you, Sir."

THE END

The Governor Trilogy series continues in *Yes, Governor* (Book 4) and *Pet* (Book 5), which is Eddie's story.

ABOUT THE AUTHOR

Author Lesli Richardson, who is better-known by her more prolific wild-child Tymber Dalton pen name, lives in the Tampa Bay region of Florida with her husband (aka "The World's Best Husband™") and too many pets. She writes a wide variety of heat levels and genres, from mainstream sci-fi all the way to scorching ménage.

The USA Today Bestselling Author (as Tymber), two-time EPIC award winner, and part-time Viking shield-maiden in training loves to shoot skeet and play D&D with her friends. She's also the bestselling author of over two hundred books and counting, including *The Reluctant Dom*, *The Great Turning*, *Cross Country Chaos*, the Bleacke Shifters series, The Great Turning series, the Suncoast Society series, the Love Slave for Two series, the Triple Trouble series, the Coffeeshop Coven series, the Good Will Ghost Hunting series, the Drunk Monkeys series, and many others.

She lives in her own little world, but it's okay—they all know her there.

She loves to hear from readers! Please feel free to drop by her website and sign up for her newsletter to keep abreast of the latest news, snarkage, and releases.

Honest reviews are always welcomed. They help with a book's visibility and can boost its placement on book retailer sites. Even a few lines about what you felt reading the book will help. Thank you so much, it's greatly appreciated!

Visit my website to sign up for my newsletter, find out what's coming soon, and more!

http://www.tymberdalton.com

Made in the USA
Columbia, SC
15 October 2021

46934666R00137